Books by John Triptych

Wrath of the Old Gods series (in chronological order)
The Glooming
Pagan Apocalypse
Canticum Tenebris
The Fomorians
A World Darkly
Eye of Balor
Mortuorum Luctum

Expatriate Underworld series
The Opener
The Loader

Dying World series
Lands of Dust
City of Delusions
The Maker of Entropy

Ace of Space series
The Piranha Solution

The Piranha Solution

Ace of Space Book 1

John Triptych

For Luigi.

Author's note:

Dear reader, I would like to thank you for purchasing this book. As a self-published author, I incur all the costs of producing this novel so your feedback means a lot to me. If you wouldn't mind, could you please take a few minutes and post a review of this online and let others know what you think of it?

As I'm sure you're aware, the more reviews I get, the better my future sales would be and therefore my financial incentive to produce more books for your enjoyment increases. I am very happy to read any comments and questions and I am willing to respond to you personally as quickly as I can. My email is jtriptych@gmail.com if you wish to contact me directly. Again, thank you and I hope you enjoy reading this book as much as I enjoyed writing it!

Please join my exclusive mailing list! You will get the latest news on my upcoming works and special discounts. Subscription is FREE and you get lots of FREE books! Just copy and paste this link to your browser: http://eepurl.com/bK-xGn

I would like to thank the following:

Zachary Gallegos, planetary scientist, for graciously allowing me to use the term Mesopotamia based on his paper for a proposed landing site in Hellas Basin, Mars.

Winchell Chung and his Atomic Rockets website for providing me with detailed information on getting the science right.

And for the beta readers who gave a lot of their time in order to read my manuscript, and helping me out with fixing the science to make it a little bit more plausible: Michel Lamontagne, Jarno Kokko, Michael Cooper, and Phillip Gaynor.

As for me, I am tormented with an everlasting itch for things remote. I love to sail forbidden seas, and land on barbarous coasts.

— Herman Melville, Moby-Dick; or, The Whale

But first whom shall we send
In search of this new world, whom shall we find
Sufficient? Who shall tempt, with wand'ring feet
The dark unbottomed infinite abyss
And through the palpable obscure find out
His uncouth way, or spread his aery flight
Upborne with indefatigable wings
Over the vast abrupt, ere he arrive
The happy isle?

— John Milton, Paradise Lost

Chapter 1

Rover-14 continued its bumpy course along the outflow channel, while a bluish sunset cast the last rays of light over the Red Planet's murky horizon. Formed over three billion years ago, the frigid, dusty riverbed of Ares Vallis seemed to look exactly like it was when the Martian waters receded, its remnants frozen underneath the lower levels of the ground. Within the last twenty years, the smooth surface of the surrounding terrain had been steadily disturbed by numerous vehicle tracks. The rust-colored regolith was ground up, revealing bits of crushed, green-grey sand underneath. Across the sky, the dust and gases of the planet's thin atmosphere scattered the fading light with less refraction than on Earth, filtering out the other hues and giving the waning shine a blue halo. A long period of twilight was to be expected, since the sun's rays on the other side of Mars would be scattered around the night edge of the world by the ubiquitous, high-altitude dust in the atmosphere.

Geoff Menard frowned while gripping the rover's steering wheel. He was coming up at the end of his two-year tour, and he couldn't wait to leave. He had once been eager when he signed up for the job, but now a growing sense of lethargy and boredom permeated his very soul. The first few months in the colony was an eye-opening experience of new sights and pure wonderment. He was one of the few who actually set foot on the Red Planet, and that was now a member of an exclusive group of human beings to set foot on another world. But as the days turned to weeks, and then into months, the sheer monotony of doing the same tasks, eating the same boring food, and the same routine had ground down his interest in all things Martian. It started out as little things. First it was the lack of meat in his diet. While fish was somewhat plentiful due to the aquaculture department's highly successful fish farms, Menard really missed the juicy, flavorful taste of a rare steak. There had been rumors that the higher ups in the company had private shipments of Grade-A USDA Prime sirloin and ribeye sent directly over to them, since they always ate in their private dining rooms. Even rumors of Kobe beef from Japan had been bandied about by the other engineering crews, though there had been an official memo coming from the colony director, which denied such incidents ever happened.

Then it was the things he saw on TV that would depress him. Menard could still remember the smell of home, and its recollections would come to him at the most inopportune times. From the whiff of pine trees, to the earthy smell of the waters by the lake house in northern California that he shared with his wife, it all started to irritate him. Breathing in stale, ionized air that would sometimes stink of sweat and piss from the ones he worked with was steadily making it all unbearable. Even the processed cheese that was produced in the colony was lousy compared to the organic stuff he bought at the farmer's market back on Earth. It was all crap now, and he counted down the days as if he was a soldier stuck in a war zone, waiting to be airlifted out.

The sleeping young man sitting beside him began to stir. Menard gave a quick glance at him before returning his gaze past the front windshield of the rover. When the maintenance alert came through the network, Menard had initially wanted to wait until dawn before proceeding over to the southern transportation corridor, but his assigned partner Katsumi Fujino had insisted that they go out right away, even if it meant that they would arrive at the waypoint sometime during the evening. There were no strict protocols when it came to working at night, but it was an unwritten rule of the other maintenance crews that it should only be done during emergencies, since the solar cells of the rovers would not be able to recharge without sunlight, and if something unexpected was to arise, then it would make everything worse. Nevertheless, Katsumi had insisted that they go out, since there had not been any contact at all with the robots in the southern waypoints for the past two days. Not wanting to be put on report for failing his assigned duties at the eve of his departure, Menard reluctantly powered up the rover and off they went.

The planetary rover they were riding in had the official designation of MMWV, or Martian Multipurpose Wheeled Vehicle. Manufactured by Flux Motors, everyone called them Mwevs for short. The vehicle issued to Menard and Katsumi was one of the older models that was produced on Earth, and sent over during the original construction of Eridu Colony, almost two decades ago. Even though this particular rover had been upgraded with new, high-performance solid state lithium-sulfur batteries, and a more advanced GPS navigational system, Menard still grumbled that they were working with old, outdated equipment. Heck, even the remote, artificial-intelligence robots that had been assigned to them had more advanced vehicles than they had. What made it even worse were Menard's superstitions, for there never was a Rover-13 assigned to the colony, and he naturally considered the Mwev they were riding in as the thirteenth one since it was the one that came after Rover-12.

A slight beeping noise started coming from the heads-up display on the Mwev dashboard. Menard had already activated the vehicle lights, and the red sand and countless rocks around them now had a bluish-grey hue. The sound indicated that they were coming up at the waypoint. In the past few months, the numerous maintenance crews of ACE Corp were laying out navigational waypoints along designated landmarks towards the new colony boundary they were planning to erect in Mar's Chryse Planitia region, as well as a landmark system that would allow vehicles to navigate back to Eridu Colony at the southeast. Menard, Katsumi and four others had been assigned to a pre-building outpost near Batos Crater, just north of the easternmost outflow of Ares Vallis. They had the task of supervising the digger and assembly robots which would do most of the heavy work for infrastructure construction.

Katsumi blinked and sat up. "Good evening," he said. Like all the Japanese he worked with, Katsumi was always exceedingly polite, and was reluctant to show his innermost feelings to his partner, even though they had been working closely together for almost six months now. ACE Corp's Japanese contingent was the experts when it came to robotics, and many of them were regularly assigned to maintain and repair any malfunctioning AI unit. All that Menard knew about the young man was that he was a recent graduate from Tokyo University, and was single. Menard figured he was probably still a virgin too.

Menard pursed his lips while continuing to stare straight ahead. "Did you have a good rest, Katsumi?"

"Yes, thank you," Katsumi said as he leaned forward and started running his small fingers on the touch screen display on his side of the dashboard. Since the Mwev could depressurize the main cabin into a less pressurized, pure-oxygen atmosphere, all the instrument panels and interfaces had non-friction surfaces, lest a single spark ignite and create a catastrophic fire inside the airtight vehicle. It was standard procedure to keep all personal gear in the huge glove compartments and storage bins, so as to lessen the chance of bad habits forming even when the Mwev was fully pressurized.

"We're coming up on the waypoint just about now," Menard said. Although standard operating procedure had mandated that he use the Mwev's self-driving AI, he preferred to use the manual controls since the lidar range finder of this vehicle was on the blink. The AI suite for the self-driving system also drove very slowly, and it would have taken them all night to reach the waypoint if he engaged it.

Something was on the surface of the dried riverbed just ahead of them. Menard put on the brakes just as soon as the object came into view. Both men stared out into the illuminated night in shocked silence. It was one of their assembly bots. The bipedal, vaguely human-like machine was lying sideways on the ground missing one of its legs. For a long minute neither of them said anything.

Menard gritted his teeth and silently cursed. He had thought that perhaps there was a problem with the com-link on the robots, and all they needed to do was to restart the software remotely once they got within rage for a manual override. But with a stricken robot lying on the ground in front of them, they would need to do some extra vehicular activity, or EVA. The Mwev had a rear cabin that served as both an airlock and extra storage, and its sides had the crab suits they could climb into and detach from the vehicle. Menard turned his head and looked at the younger man. "Can you get linked up to it?"

Katsumi was typing in commands on the dashboard to give out to the robot, but he kept getting an unsatisfactory response. His English delivery was both halting and rapid-fire whenever he was under stress. "I'm sorry, but… the modem interface seems to be turned off."

Menard gave him a quizzical look. "What? That's an RUR Industries heavy lifter bot out there, from what I know there's no way you could turn off its modem. Even if it's damaged, you should still be able to access its basic input-output system since that thing is shock and tamper proof, right?"

Katsumi shook his head slowly. "I am sorry, but no response even from BIOS."

Menard sighed. Robots on Mars had multiple redundancy systems. This wasn't supposed to happen. "Jesus. That's the first time I ever heard of this. Are you sure?"

Katsumi placed both hands on his lap and tilted his head down. "Yes, I am sure."

"Great, let me call it in first," Menard said as he brought up the com-link on his HUD. "Rover Fourteen to Batos Outpost, come in, over."

At first there was nothing but static. Menard frowned as he checked and ran a diagnostics on the communications system. When the readouts turned out okay he repeated the same message again. For a few minutes there was nothing but an empty silence on the other line, then some strange electronic noises nearly blew out the speakers in the vehicle. Both men instinctively placed their hands over their ears as the shrill cacophony continued for a few seconds.

Just as Menard was about to mute the volume, a distant, droning voice could be heard, despite the constant crackling sounds in the background. There was no video feed, only audio. "Batos Outpost reading you, over."

Menard squinted. It sounded like Ron Simms, the base camp commander, but the voice seemed oddly misplaced somehow. "Ron? Is that you, over?"

"Yes, over," the voice answered.

Menard put his other concerns at the back of his mind

and focused on the immediate problem. "We've got a situation here. We found one of the heavy lifter bots lying by the gully. It looks like it's damaged and it's not responding remotely. Request EVA for a closer look, over?"

"Yes, go ahead," Ron said. "Contact me again when task completed, over."

Menard sat back and drew a deep breath. That was the first time Ron had ever been so brusque and to the point. Normally the outpost commander would be very talkative, even regaling them with a corny song over the com-link. Ron's voice seemed weird as well, as if he had a sore throat or something.

Katsumi unstrapped his seatbelt. Robots were his specialty, so it was only natural that he be the one to go out there. "I shall go EVA."

Menard checked the status of the Herp-Tech hard shelled "crab" suits that were embedded along the sides of the airlock. With both rigid upper and lower torsos connected to the helmet, the suits resembled eggs with limbs attached to them. Both life support packs and suit batteries were at full charge. "Do you need me to depressurize the cabin first?"

"No, that is not necessary," Katsumi said as he moved his chair back and got into a crouching position while making his way to the rear cabin. "I shall use the crab suit, not my skinsuit."

Menard was thankful for that. The hard-shelled crab suits had high pressure atmospheres inside the suit, which meant that they would not need to depressurize into a pure oxygen atmosphere and spend ninety minutes of pre-breathing exercises, in order to prevent decompression sickness before either of them exited the vehicle. The problem with the crab suits was that they were bulky, and their hand sockets did not have the full range of precise feel or movement, unlike the flexible skinsuits. An operator in the crab suit couldn't move his head or bend his torso. Both types of suits had their strengths and weaknesses, but the last thing Menard wanted to do right now was to spend a couple of hours doing isometric exercises while depressurizing.

Katsumi made it into the rear cabin. After sealing the hatch behind him, the young man carefully entered through the open rear panel of the crab suit, making sure that there were no loose items lying around inside, lest they would create a hazard once he wore the gear. The moment he got his head up and into the helmet, the internal sensors of the suit activated. After verbally inputting the password, the open access way behind him was instantly closed as the backpack, which contained the life support systems of the suit was automatically attached to his back, completely sealing him in an airtight environment. The faceplate of the crab suit was equipped with smartglass, and the optical readouts indicated how much oxygen and power he had, along with numerous visual enhancements that could be activated by voice command. Katsumi tested the semi-rigid but flexible arm and leg joints, then ran an internal pressure diagnostic. Everything seemed fine.

Menard punched up the com-link for the suit interface. "Katsumi, can you hear me?"

"Loud and clear," Katsumi said. "Detaching suit from airlock … now."

There was a green lighted indicator on the HUD of the Mwev, and Menard activated a virtual map on the dashboard, which showed where Katsumi was relative to the vehicle and the stricken robot up ahead of him. "Okay, I have you on the map," Menard said before shifting in his seat and checking the side mirrors of the vehicle. "And I can see you visually. All clear."

"Roger that," Katsumi said as he jumped down onto the ground by the side of the vehicle. Gravity on Mars was only thirty-eight percent that of Earth's, so a slow walk on Earth would equal to a fast run on Mars. Katsumi felt unimpeded with the weight of the crab suit, and was thankful for the lower gravity, otherwise he would have been a little tired by now. Fully turning his entire body, Katsumi used his stubby gloves to reach up for the robotic tool kit and detached it from the sides of the Mwev. With the tools in hand, he began to make his way towards the downed robot.

Menard watched silently as Katsumi trotted over to where the bot was and saw him get into a kneeling position. He had hoped the young guy could somehow repair the bot quickly so they could get back to the task of finding out what happened to the other robots assigned to the transport corridor. Menard had a feeling that it would take days to sort everything out, and was pondering whether to call in for additional help, but just before they left the outpost, Ron had told him that they were already behind schedule, and if the work wasn't finished soon then they would all say goodbye to their company bonuses. That was the hardest news to take. Menard's straying thoughts were jerked back to reality when he heard Katsumi cry out. Menard quickly pushed the reply button. "Katsumi, what happened?"

Katsumi had his back turned towards him as the young man knelt by the downed robot. "I ... I cannot find the robot's CPU. It is missing!"

Since they could see each other's faces with the smartglass interface, Menard had a confused look. "What do you mean it's missing?"

Katsumi's narrow eyes had opened wide. "It looks like something tore out the processing core. Whatever did this, must have used some heavy machinery. There is massive damage on the robot's body."

"Hang on," Menard said as he switched viewpoints and linked up the vehicle HUD with the cameras on Katsumi's suit. The dashboard's video feed showed the front part of the robot, which had been facing away from him when viewed from the vehicle's windshield. Menard gasped as he could see that the front part of the robot had been completely gutted. The entire chest plate had been ripped out. The central control box which contained the robotic AI was missing, along with the solar battery which had given it life. All that remained was a metal skeleton of torn wiring, inoperative joints and lifeless actuators.

Katsumi was silent for a whole minute before he said something again. "What could have done this?"

Menard just sat there, stupefied. This was a problem never experienced by all previous crews on the planet, and it was something that they were completely unprepared for. Then a loud beep suddenly jolted him back into reality. He started running through the vehicle dashboard commands, wondering what it was. A screen popped up in his display, indicating that the vehicle AI had detected something fast that was approaching them. His palms started to sweat. There weren't supposed to be any other vehicles out here.

Katsumi stood up. This was something that he had never trained for. "What is going on?"

Menard's chin started to tremble with fright. He considered himself a religious man, and he did pray a couple of Our Fathers and a Hail Mary when he was first lifted off into space. There were times when he was asleep in his bunk and he would hear strange noises coming from the outside, but he never told anyone just how scared he was, lest they make fun of him. He was the kind of guy who believed in ghosts and monsters, and being mostly alone in a largely unexplored world spooked him out a lot. It took Menard a few seconds to think about it, but in the end he knew he just couldn't believe it. "Get back here, hurry!"

Katsumi didn't need to be told twice. The young man quickly ran over to the side of the vehicle, turned his back on it, and activated the ancillary lifts to bring the rear of his crab suit in line with the airlock. The platform lifted him up slowly as he grabbed the handholds along the sides of the small elevator. The moment Menard saw that his partner was already being lifted up into the vehicle, he wasted no time and he instantly gunned the accelerator. The Mwev lurched forward, before Menard angled the steering away from the downed robot, and the vehicle began a bumpy drive along the ancient gully.

Sweat began to pour down Menard's forehead as he pushed the accelerator up to maximum speed. The rover could accelerate up to a maximum 120 kilometers per hour, but it wasn't recommended due to the chaotic terrain all around them. The Mwev's six wheels were small compared to its body, and the entire vehicle tended to be top heavy. Driving protocols had forbidden everyone to traverse steep-angled cliff sides, but he needed to get away from whatever it was that was coming straight for them. They were rapidly moving south along the narrow part of the channel, and the sloping walls around them were too steep to drive up to. The HUD readouts were explaining that there wasn't enough battery power for them to make it to the predicted destination of Eridu Colony, and popped up an alert, telling the driver to turn around and decelerate. Menard ignored the flashing warnings on the dashboard and concentrated at the desolate landscape ahead, pushing the Mwev onwards as he drove through wisps of grey dust, occasionally making a sharp turn to avoid crashing into the walls of the gully.

Katsumi grimaced as he kept trying to position the back of the crab suit to attach it to the airlock, but the constant bumps and sudden turns kept him off balance. When the rover drove over a slight protruding rock at the bottom of the gully, Katsumi was nearly thrown from the side of the Mwev and only hung on by the skin of his teeth. Just as he was able to position himself back into the side of the airlock, another sudden turn nearly threw him off again, and he ended up hanging on with just one hand, as the stubby fingers of the crab suit had made it doubly hard to hold on. "Please," he said through the com-link. "Give me a chance to attach!"

Menard scowled as he looked at the virtual map and noticed that the object behind them had also accelerated. It seemed to be moving along the ground, and yet it could somehow keep up while the gap was slowly narrowing. There was a rearview camera at the back of the Mwev, but it had been caked with dust, so all it gave was a hazed-filled look at something huge behind them. The channel ahead was beginning to slant to the right, which meant that the massive Aram Crater was located just to the south, with a second, twisting channel that led into it from the Ares Vallis gully. At the vehicle's current speed, Menard knew it would be next to impossible for him to safely make the ninety-degree turns that were needed to drive into the crater without slowing down, so he had to make a choice. He could continue on the present course at maximum speed until he reached the end of Ares Vallis, where the channel would gradually rise up until it melded with the high terrain, though the vehicle would have to eventually slow down due to the elevation. Menard decided to continue along the channel and they would take their chances on higher ground. If they could just get past the incline on the southern outflow delta, he could drive the vehicle up to the stable flatlands of Meridiani Planum to the west.

Katsumi had decided to do something risky. From the smartglass display on his suit visor, he could tell when the vehicle needed to make its turn at high speed. All he had to do was to lift himself up and push backwards, hoping that the sudden bump would throw him up and attach his backpack into the airlock niche in one swoop. Bracing himself, he kept his eyes peeled on the map and calculated the timing at the last second. When the bump finally came, he let go of the handholds along the sides of the lift while he pushed up with his legs. The sudden bump brought the top edge of the airlock's alcove in line with his backpack and the magnetic seal accepted it, but the lower part of his life support pack was still stuck partly outside, and he ended up being partially wedged on the airlock, unable to remove the backpack, yet still attached to the vehicle. Katsumi frantically waved his arms and legs out in the night air. He was like a little bug that had been placed on its back-wriggling, helpless, and scared out of his wits. "Help me!"

It was all too much for Menard. His colleague's screams for help, coupled with the fear of that thing behind him had finally made him lose his self-control. Menard ignored the collision and speed warnings on his dashboard. Instead he kept his eyes focused on the rearview camera feed, which showed their pursuer was only meters away from the rear of the Mwev. Glancing at the hazy imagery in the rear camera view, he noticed that it looked like something out of the darkest part of his nightmares. For a brief instance all he could think about was how that thing could even come into being, and his mind tuned out everything else.

There was a small hill in the middle of the channel delta, which divided the gully into two separate trenches. Menard wasn't keeping attention, and the rover drove into the side of it at close to maximum speed. He sensed the collision a split second before it happened, as the terrain made a sudden incline. Menard turned the wheel, but it was too late. Rover-14's right front wheel hit an outcropped boulder at the edge of the incline and the whole vehicle suddenly tilted to its left side. There was a loud crash, before everything faded to black.

When Menard woke up, his face was surrounded by air bags, which had deployed the moment the Mwev landed on its side and had come to a sudden stop. The lights in the cabin were still on, as well as numerous alarms that were beeping. Unbuckling his seatbelt, Menard pushed his arm past the air bags and used the dashboard to get them deflated. The vehicle was lying on its left side and everything was titled down. Catching his breath, Menard suddenly remembered his colleague. He punched up Katsumi's vitals, and was bombarded by the flat lined readouts in regards to his partner's heart rate. Katsumi was dead, crushed to death when the rover turned over to the side and pinned him underneath while he was still in his suit.

A shadow loomed over the windshield. Menard looked up and screamed. The doubled layered glass was smashed in, and the thing that had caught up to them made a grab for him.

Chapter 2

She ran her tongue along the upper part of her red, luscious lips, and he knew she wanted it. All around them was the rolling surf, but the private beach was off-limits to anyone but the two of them. She ran her hand down to his boxer shorts and gave a little pinch, and he was instantly excited. He could feel the Pacific sun's heat on his back, and it seemed like it was twelve noon. The cool sea breeze just wasn't enough to expel the waves of heat all around him. She had already taken off the top of her bikini, and he could see the tan lines that resembled pale triangles over her breasts. The pressure on his throat felt tighter, and he sensed that he would soon climax in a matter of seconds.

"I'm here for you, handsome," she said, while sliding down her hand until it reached his crotch. She slid off his shorts and began touching him down there. The tightness in his throat was now evident, and he was starting to black out. *Oh yeah, not too long now*, he thought.

In less than a second, the heat cascading over his body had stopped, and the pressure on his throat was loosened.

Even the once soothing voice became more machine-like. "I'm sorry, Stil, but Drone-Seven just picked up something."

The scene around him suddenly stopped, and was replaced by a blank white field. The girl who had been with him was gone, along with the cliff sided beach, the warm sand and the roaring sounds of the California surf. "Goddamn it," he said. "Couldn't you have waited for just a few more seconds, I was nearly there!"

The flat, droning voice was trying to be apologetic, but it came off as more like an alarm clock. "I am sorry, Stil, but you did ask me to interrupt you the moment the video link came through."

Stilicho Jones grimaced as he took off the virtual helmet and threw it on the bed beside him. It was early afternoon in San Diego, and his break time was over. Using both hands, he unstrapped the asphyxiator from his neck and placed it on his desk. Before getting up on his feet, he slipped out of the sex harness and left it on the divan, its dangling uplink cables still attached to the desktop computer near the other side of the room. He needed to add new commands to Maia so that she would prioritize his private time ahead of any other task that was needed to be done from now on. Working for the man left him with so little free time, he had to make do with what he had.

Walking over to the drone station in the middle of the room, he sat down on a high backed chair and looked at the multiple 3D monitors on top of the desk. "Okay, Maia, which one am I looking at?"

The third monitor began to blink and he shifted his eyes over to it. The scene showed a glass house in Point Loma, surrounded by concrete dividers nearly eight meters tall. Maia had deactivated the anti-drone field and several of her units were hovering just outside of the abode. The smartglass walls of the house itself had been opaque, but it was clear that Maia's drones were able to hack through the security systems, and the inside of the building now looked transparent when using the infrared scanner. The interior showed one heat signature, that of an adult male. It looked like he was brewing some coffee.

Stilicho ran his hand along the top of his head to straighten his dark hair. "Okay, who am I looking at?"

"Frank Campos, ex-employee of ACE Corp," Maia said. "One of his uplinks was unsecured, so I was able to sneak inside and take a look at his files. It seems that he was able to download a number of projects into his personal server before he left the company's employment."

Stilicho took a deep breath. "What projects did he copy?"

"He's got schematics for the reactor," Maia said. "Errol will be pissed off if it gets out on the open market."

Stilicho stretched out his arms. "Other than the charge of corporate espionage and violating his non-disclosure agreement, what else can we nail him on?"

A number of images began to float around in the monitor at the far right of the desk, while a video started up in the one next to it. His AI assistant was thorough, and that's what he liked about her. "Take a look at those," Maia said softly.

Stilicho's eyebrows shot up. "Oh wow, can you get me a cup of coffee, please?"

"With pleasure."

Stilicho got out of the Flux S227 sedan before engaging the autopark beside the street. Point Loma was a seaside community, and one of the more exclusive areas of San Diego. The gate to the Campos house was closed, but he knew it wasn't going to stop him. As soon as he strode over to the sensor, the main gate instantly unlocked and opened inwards, revealing an old, internal combustion sports car parked in the incline of the driveway. Stilicho gave a pouty look as he passed by the car and walked up to the front door. He had thought about scratching the paintjob on the old Ferrari, but he figured Mr. Campos would be better off selling it when he knew what was about to happen to him. The front door quickly opened the moment he got to within a meter of it, and Stilicho briskly walked inside.

The living room was immaculately clean. White marbled flooring, Doric columns and a massive stone staircase led to the upper landing. Ivory leather sofas and a huge Persian carpet occupied the center of the room. An antique grand piano lay at the far side of the place, with a rectangular swimming pool out in the back garden area. At the opposite side was a stainless steel kitchen, with a free-standing 3D food printer and a mini-bar with black marbled top. Stilicho rolled his eyes. The idiot had smartglass walls, yet the interior was furnished more classically, and the whole thing felt like an architectural chimera.

A shout from above made him look up. Standing at the top landing was Frank Campos, wearing only his bathrobe. "Hey, what are you doing in my house?"

Stilicho made a wide smile. "Good afternoon, I'm Stilicho Jones, from ACE Corp."

Campos started walking down over to him, there was barely suppressed rage in his eyes. His fists were balled up. "I don't care who you are, how in the hell did you get in here?"

Stilicho pointed at a 3D monitor embedded in the wall near the sofa set. "Let's talk about something more important, shall we?"

"Why you—"

Campos's rant was quickly interrupted when the monitor suddenly activated. Virtual files containing numerous three-dimensional models and once secret email memos were instantly on display. Campos's eyes remained glued to the screen while he just stood there in silence.

Stilicho crossed his arms. Campos's psychological profile indicated he wasn't the violent type, so there was no need for physicality this time. "You were a trusted systems manager for ACE, and this is how you repay the company that gave you this silly-looking, but expensive house?"

Campos slowly turned to face him. "H-how did … you?"

Stilicho pointed at a black-painted drone that was hovering just above the garden. "Let's just say this wasn't the only thing I uncovered. If your ex-wife found about those naughty pics and vids you took of your little girl during her sleepovers here, let's just say she wouldn't be too happy about it, yeah?"

Campos's face turned pale. "I-I don't know what … you're talking about."

Stilicho chuckled. "Ah, come on, don't insult my intelligence, dude. You may have the money to bribe the cops taking you away, but can you take the loss of your reputation when all this goes public on the internet? Think of the never ending-lawsuits that are going to be filed against you, not just from your wife, but from ACE and the company that was supposed to employ you after you sell these plans you've stolen from us. You're gonna lose this ridiculous house and your antique car, that's for sure."

"Please," Campos said softly. "Don't do this."

Stilicho smirked. That was quick. Most of the others he dealt with would usually go into denial first, then they would resort to threats and even physical attacks before attempting to bargain with him. It was like the classic Kubler-Ross model on death and dying, the five stages of grief: denial, anger, bargaining, depression and finally acceptance. Only this time, Campos went right to stage three from the get-go. "So you want to make a deal, then?"

Campos made a slow nod. His eyes were blanked out in shock. "Yes. I-I'll wipe everything clean. I won't hand the files over to the new company I'm working for."

Stilicho looked at him solemnly. "Urizen Holdings, right? How do I know you didn't hand these files over to them already?"

Campos shook his head rapidly. "No, no, I-I just told them what I've got. We were supposed to make the final deal tomorrow. Urizen doesn't have anything yet, I swear."

Stilicho wanted to grin, but he suppressed it. He already knew that Campos hadn't given them the files yet, none of the traces on his uploads contained the files, so on that end he was telling the truth. "Assuming that I even believe you, do you honestly think we can just leave you alone after what you've done?"

Campos looked down onto the shiny floor. "What do you want?"

"You will need to pay a monetary restitution to ACE Corp," Stilicho said. "I am aware that we gave you a separation pay bonus, so we'll get all of it back, and I've also activated a penalty clause."

Campos sighed. "Okay. I'll destroy the files too."

"Already being done as we speak," Stilicho said. "My drones are wiping the files clean, and I'll be taking the physical hard drives. But I am holding on to a copy of your private stuff, just in case you renege on your promises of going straight."

Campos got on his knees. "Please, couldn't you just wipe it all? You don't need anything on me- you can trust me, please!"

Stilicho shook his head. "Sorry, but that's how it's going to play. Once your files are wiped and your drives physically replaced, my AI will be uploading something to your new personal house server, so you can use those files and hand them over to Urizen."

Campos got up to one knee. He had a confused look on his face. "Y-you want me to go through with the deal I made with your competition?"

Stilicho gave him a wink. "Oh yeah, you'll proceed as planned. Only this time we'll be feeding you the info to give over to them."

Campos thought about it for a minute. "So you mean, I'll be planting false information?"

"In a way, yes," Stilicho said. "It's not exactly false, just research that leads to a dead end. And it will take them months to figure out that it's useless. That should give us enough of a head start to mass produce our reactors, thereby beating them to market."

"B-but what if they find out? They'll kick my ass!"

"They might, but that's the risks of the game," Stilicho said. "Oh, by the way, you won't make any money out of it. You need to approve ACE Financial as partner to your bank account. The moment they pay you for the files, we'll take the money out of your hands too."

Campos's eyes opened wide. "What?"

Stilicho shrugged. "Sorry, but I did tell you that there's a price to pay for this. Sure beats losing everything, right?"

Campos was now a broken man. "Okay."

"Tell me," Stilicho said. "Who designed this mishmash of a house? It's totally stupid."

"It was my father's house before the big quake that leveled Los Angeles- I got it after he died," Campos said. "The walls came down, but parts of the foundation were still intact, so I kept those and had new smartglass walls installed over the rest."

Stilicho pushed his lower lip out. "I see. I guess it sort of makes sense- in a weird, silly kind of way."

Campos had a dejected look on his face. "Are you going to take anything else from me?"

Stilicho looked into his eyes. "Just one other thing."

"What?"

Stilicho grinned as he shifted the gears on the antique Ferrari while accelerating down the road. His Flux sedan was on autodrive and following at a fair distance behind him. The electric cars everyone drove nowadays just didn't have the feel and power of the old internal combustion engines, and Stilicho loved to experience the growl and the rhythmic vibrations of the motor as he pressed on the gas pedal. It felt like he was a teenager again. The drive along the newly rebuilt roads of San Diego seemed like old times, and the wind whipping his neck felt very much like the cyber sexcapade that had been interrupted just hours before.

A short, compact woman with long dark hair came out from the driver's side of the sedan, before the car began to autopark itself along a deserted street in Manhattan's Harlem district. Pulling up the collar of her raincoat to partially shield her head from the evening rain, she dashed across the street and came upon a police barricade. She flashed her ID, and the two NYPD police officers gestured at her to go on ahead. The woman nodded as she sprinted over to the mobile command post, a heavy police truck parked beside the building. After lightly tapping on the side door, she was quickly let inside.

Opening the door for her, FBI Special Agent Kordell Jackson grinned and held out his hand. "It's good to see you again, Darian."

Darian Arante shook his hand. "How are you, Kordell? It's been, what … six years now?"

Kordell nodded as a burly police lieutenant stood up from his chair and strode over to them. "Yeah, about that," he said as he gestured over to the cop. "This is Lieutenant Marrone of the Emergency Services Unit. Marrone, allow me to introduce to you NASA Special Agent Darian Arante."

Marrone pursed his lips while shaking her hand. "NASA Special Agent? Like what the FBI's got?"

Darian nodded. "Yes, Lieutenant. With NASA's new mandate, we now have a law enforcement arm that handles incidents up in space and in the other planets."

Marrone made a low whistle. "Well, I'll be damned. I suppose you've been trained and all that?"

"Darian went through FBI training in Quantico, that's how I met her," Kordell said. "We were in the same batch, but she got transferred over to NASA as soon as she graduated."

"I also underwent full Astronaut training in Houston," Darian said, before shifting her gaze to Kordell. "I'm guessing this isn't a social call."

Marrone crossed his arms. "Nope. We got a hostage situation here. Some loon has threatened to kill two halfway house caretakers." He pointed over to the 3D monitors lined up along the interior of the command post. A virtual map indicated that two police drones were hovering by the sides of the four story brick building. A team of ESU troopers had made it to the second floor and deployed several scout bots to get a clearer picture of what was happening. There were three infrared heat signatures in a room just above them. Two figures were lying on the floor, huddled together, while a third was walking back and forth, at times stooping over the cowering pair, waving what looked to be a pistol in the air.

"The suspect is a transient by the name of Robert Tsuda," Kordell said. "Prior records indicate arrests for vagrancy, disturbing the peace while under the influence of drugs, but nothing really violent until now. Seems he was undergoing mental health treatment as a resident of the halfway house, then he just went berserk."

"Our hostage negotiation team is in touch with him," Marrone said. "He's been making demands to go back to Mars, or so he says. He demanded to speak with whoever was in charge of sending people back to the Red Planet, so we contacted the FBI and they sent Kordell over."

"And then I sent for you," Kordell said to her. "Since NASA did tell me that you were the closest special agent they have in the area."

Darian pursed her lips. "Tsuda … that name sounds familiar to me."

"Checking his background it seems he was a former member of Mars First," Kordell said. "Does that ring a bell?"

Darian's eyebrows shot up. "Oh my god. Now I remember! He was Silas Balsamic's personal assistant. I interviewed him a few years back."

Marrone scratched his chin. "I'm not familiar with all this. Could you two bring me up to speed?"

"Mars First was a private, non-profit group that

advocated humans set up a permanent, colony on Mars at any cost," Darian said. "They were actually more like a cult. Their leader, Silas Balsamic, was most probably a sociopath. They were able to get funding and set up a one-way trip and colony base on the Red Planet, but within a few years it all went to hell. In the end, a number of them died and they ran out of money. The US government had to fund their evacuation and there was a huge outcry. In response, a new space treaty was signed by almost every member of the UN, and it put into place many regulations that restricted future settlements on Mars."

"I read a few articles on the news, but that was a long time ago," Marrone said. "Something about a cover up?"

"Yeah," Kordell said. "Reports came in that some of the Mars First members didn't die because of accidents on the Red Planet, but were murdered. Others claimed incidents of torture, cannibalism and rape. There was an investigation, but nothing came of it due to lack of evidence."

"Robert Tsuda was rumored to have very high influence in the Mars First Colony," Darian said. "He was considered to be a fanatically loyal lieutenant to Silas Balsamic. Like his master, there were plenty of allegations by former members of the cult, but no charges were ever brought up."

One of the technicians manning the drone console looked over in their direction. "Lieutenant, he wants to talk again. He's demanding to speak with someone in charge of rockets, he says."

Marrone gestured at Darian to take a seat beside the drone controller. "Could you talk to him? My men are just outside the door, ready to make a breach. I would like this to be resolved peacefully, but if he starts shooting, we're going in."

Darian nodded and sat down on the chair. The drone technician handed her a smartglass visor and headset, which she placed on her head. The police had been able to deploy a tracked robot inside of the room and it had a com-link that allowed her to communicate directly with Tsuda. "Okay, I'm all set," she said.

The drone controller tapped her on the shoulder. "We've got audiovisual on him, but he's only got audio on you."

"Got it," Darian said before tapping the speak button on the console. "Mr. Tsuda, my name is Special Agent Darian Arante of NASA. You said you wanted to speak to a Federal representative on space launches. What can I do for you?"

Tsuda was wearing a bathrobe over his jeans and t-shirt. His hair was disheveled, and he would periodically turn to look closely into the lenses of the robot, bringing his constantly shifting eyes into a close-up. His voice had a nervous tick to it. "Y-you are with NASA?"

Kordell leaned over and whispered in Darian's other ear. "He's been taking antipsychotic medication, but we don't have a confirmation on dosage."

Darian nodded in acknowledgement before returning her concentration on the screen. "Yes Mr. Tsuda, I am the official representative of NASA. What is it that you want?"

Tsuda waved the pistol back and forth, then he scratched his grizzled chin with the tip of the barrel. "You gotta help me, I need to go back."

Darian leaned forward. "Go back where, sir?"

Tsuda's eyes fluttered back and forth. "To Mars, I need to go back to Mars."

"Why do you need to go back to Mars?"

"He told me I should," Tsuda said, his voice lowering by a few octaves. "At first I said it would be hard, you know, I've gotten old and I'm not in shape anymore, but he insisted. Then I told him there was no way I could do it because I didn't have the money, but he kept telling me to do it anyway. Then I told him that the government would never allow me to go back, then he said okay, forget it. Then the silence came … then I started missing his voice. Then I knew, I knew he was back there. I was his second in command. Don't you see? He always trusted me! I have to go there to meet him!"

Darian scowled as she tried to discern his body language. "Who is telling you to go back to Mars, Robert?"

Tsuda rolled his eyes as he waved his arms in the air. "Who else? Silas! Silas told me to go! He's there right now! Don't you see, I have to join him over there, he needs me!"

"How did Silas communicate with you, Robert?"

"I was watching TV, then I just heard his voice," Tsuda said. "Every time I went online, I got messages from him. He's there, I'm telling you, he's there! I need to go right now, the synodic transfer orbits will happen in a few days, I need you to put me on a flight right away."

Darian placed her thumbs underneath her chin. Synodic transfer orbits to Mars came in once every two years, and presented an optimum way to get to the Red Planet. Since both planets would be properly aligned, and any spacecraft using the orbital maneuver would get there much sooner than at any other time of the year. *So it was clear that he knew the timing was right, which seemed to indicate that he was still somewhat sane*, she thought. "Robert," she said. "Silas returned to Earth, with you. Don't you remember? He can't be at Mars. You both came back together."

Tsuda started to get agitated. "I'm telling you, he … is … there! He must have found a way to get back there. Why else would he tell me to go? You've got to believe me!"

Darian's voice was calm. She needed to deescalate the situation. "I believe you, Robert. I can arrange for you to get on the next flight. But I need you to do me a favor, okay? I need you to release the hostages. Can you do that for me?"

Tsuda growled. "No! They're staying with me! I want you to book three passengers on the next launch. They have to go with me, I can't take the risk of you breaking your promise to me!"

"Robert, I promise you that you will get on that flight, but you have to do something for me," Darian said. "It's called reciprocity. I do you a favor, and now you have to return a favor to me, can we agree on that?"

"I-I don't trust you," Tsuda said as he pointed the gun at the two cowering old women lying on the floor. "I need these two. They're my insurance."

"Insurance for what, Robert?" Darian said.

"Silas told me not to trust you people," Tsuda said, his voice breaking. "He told me … god how I miss him!"

"Robert, I can assure you that everything is okay," Darian said. "Just stay calm. What I need for you to do is to just let one of them go, okay? Just one, and I can bring a car over that will take you all the way to the launch site."

Tsuda's whole body started to shake. "I can feel him inside of me," he said. "He's telling me that … you're all lying to me."

Marrone started to key in commands to his ESU troopers using his own headset. He leaned over to Darian's side. "He's going unstable, calm him down or my men go in now," he whispered.

"Robert, take it easy, we can work this out," Darian said.

Tsuda's eyes had a glazed, faraway look at them. Then he suddenly turned his attention over at the hostages on the floor. "He told me … he told me that you're all scum!" Leveling the pistol, he fired a shot into the side of the wall. The two women on the ground instantly began to scream.

Marrone grimaced as he spoke into his headset. "Damn it! Go, go, go!"

Darian stood up. "Wait!"

The robot fired a tear gas canister at point blank range, narrowly missing Tsuda. He staggered backwards in shock for a brief second before aiming his gun at the hostages once more, but the billowing smoke was rapidly filling the room and he couldn't get a clear bead on them. He was able to fire one wild shot that missed, before the ESU team breached the door. Tsuda turned and aimed the weapon at them. The lead ESU trooper fired a short burst from his submachinegun that hit him squarely in the chest and he went down. The hostages continued their coughing and screaming until they were brought out.

Darian stood in Robert Tsuda's tiny room in the halfway house. A team of forensics experts were going through his possessions, but they were just doing cursory checks since he was already dead, and the case was closed. Darian couldn't help but think that it would have been better if he was taken alive, but the lives of the two hostages were at stake so the police couldn't take the chance.

Kordell walked into the room. "Pity it turned it out this way, I thought you were about to convince him to give up one of the hostages, then he just went totally nuts all of a sudden."

Darian sighed. "Yeah, I thought we were making progress."

"You want to go for a cup of coffee or something?" he said.

Darian shrugged. "Sure, why not."

As they both started walking down the stairs, Kordell could see that the rain had stopped. A few more hours and the sun would be over the horizon. "Darian," he said. "When you mentioned his boss, that Silas guy, why did you insist that he wouldn't be on Mars?"

Darian stepped down onto the base of the stairs. "Because Silas Balsamic is dead. A few years after being back on Earth, he went nuts, just like Robert Tsuda did tonight. He killed himself almost a decade ago."

Chapter 3

Stilicho caught the last transcontinental flight that evening. The new supersonic passenger jets resembled the old needlelike Concordes, only they were much larger. It had taken a few decades for the public to get used to flying in an electric plane that maneuvered using gimbals instead of rudders. With electric turbofans that gave these aircraft a speed in excess of Mach-3, he made it to Florida's aptly named Space Coast in less than forty-five minutes. ACE Corp's automated limousine service picked him up at the arrivals terminal and quickly whisked him away towards the Kennedy Space Center, which had now been opened up for commercial use after NASA began phasing out its own launch operations over thirty years before.

After getting out of the passenger side door, he noticed that there were a large number of cars still in the parking lot fronting the ACE Corp headquarters building. Stilicho suddenly remembered that his boss was doing a press conference, but it had been delayed due to some last minute work they were doing on the reactor in Texas. Stilicho surmised that the proposed new breakthrough that his boss was going to present to the world had experienced some sort of technical glitch, and he was probably doing his best to dampen any disappointment.

He passed through the main glass doors and strode over to the receptionist kiosk. A strikingly beautiful girl in her mid-thirties noticed him and smiled. She wore a red and black blouse, and her sandy blond hair was perfectly coiffed. Stilicho gave her a big smile as he walked over. "Hello, Natalie, you look as gorgeous as ever. Your husband is one lucky man. If I were him, I would work two jobs, just so that you wouldn't be wasting your hot looks sitting down here in this dreary, godforsaken place."

Natalie giggled. She pointed over to the auditorium down the main hall. "He's still finishing up the conference. You can wait in his office if you want to."

"Nah, I think I'll go see what kind of bullchip he's spewing out right now," Stilicho said as he winked at her and then walked towards the amphitheatre.

After going through the double doors, Stilicho turned and sat down by the aisle, at the last row of padded seats in the auditorium. The chief executive officer of ACE Corp was sitting in the center of the stage, and there was a gargantuan sized smartglass monitor screen behind him. The front row was fully occupied by numerous media crews and reporters, their holovid cameras recording every second of the conference. Two foot-long drones with quad rotors hovered just below the ceiling, providing a live, overhead view of the proceedings. The rest of the moderately packed theater were watching the whole event using their smartglasses, cycling through different camera angles, at the same time they were sorting through online news articles with their other eye, before deciding on where to focus their attention. Not wanting to be left out, Stilicho pulled out his own pair from beneath his shirt pocket and put them on.

Unlike everyone else, Errol Flux used a monocle for his smartglass, like a goggle over his left eye. Still only in his mid-forties, Errol was born to a Swedish father and a Canadian mother, spending most of his early childhood vagabonding across Europe. His family eventually immigrated to the United States and became naturalized citizens while Errol was still in college, graduating with honors in applied physics at Stanford University in California. While still doing graduate studies in applied science at the Massachusetts Institute of Technology, Errol quit in order to join with a group of friends to start up one of the first quantum computing companies, which was later absorbed into his personal holding company, Flux Corporation. After becoming a millionaire overnight, Errol soon invested his entire fortune into another startup company that manufactured electric vehicles, eventually naming it Flux Motors, after himself. As his personal fortune grew, he eventually created his own space transport and colonization firm, calling it Advanced Conceptual Endeavors, or ACE for short. In a scant twenty years, ACE Corp became the leading firm in the entire industry. But Errol wasn't finished. Now he was planning an even bigger goal: to find a new fuel source to power a new breed of ships-ones that could venture out even farther and explore the nearest stars in the galaxy.

Errol adjusted his monocle slightly, making sure the adhesive around the rim would not come loose. "Like I said before in a previous conference, the advent of quantum computing was a major game changer for humanity. Before that, computers used binary encoding with just two digits: zeros and ones. But the almost limitless potential for quantum processors made everything else possible. Quantum computing is analog and we use quantum bits, or qubits, which are not limited to two states, unlike the old binary computers. Since qubits can exist in superposition, it allows them to work on millions of calculations all at once, which was impossible to do with binary processors. This has enabled today's computers to be infinitely faster, and has opened up whole new branches of applied research in all things. The carbon composite materials that our automated factories produce are many times stronger than the old stuff. We can now build more efficient batteries for our electric vehicles, which enabled the widespread use of supersonic planes, and the replacement of internal combustion engines that once polluted our highways. And all this is just the tip of the iceberg."

Stilicho sat back. Every press conference with Errol always ended this way, for he would go from one subject to another. Everything seemed intertwined, and in a sense it was.

"Which brings us back to the fusion reactor we are building in Texas," Errol said after a brief pause to take a drink from the water bottle on the table beside him. "Our advanced computer modeling indicates that we are on the verge of a breakthrough in the magnetized fields to keep the plasma in play. Then our new, powerful electrical generators will fire the microwaves into it and raise its temperature past one hundred million degrees and keep a sustained reaction. This was made possible by more powerful magnets, efficient batteries and more robust building materiel, all of which was made possible due to quantum computing. I predict that this can happen any day now, and I will update you all once this has been confirmed. Now, are there any questions?"

Here we go, Stilicho thought. *The moment he asks for questions, the media starts veering off into different things. I wonder just how much damage control I need to do after this.*

A middle-aged man with a thick beard raised his hand. "Del Warner, America National News Network. Could you please comment on the rumors about your takeover of RUR Industries, namely that you were one of the last person to see Karl Rossum alive, before he went missing?"

"Karl Rossum was a good friend," Errol said. "We knew each other well since we started Flux Corporation together, and he agreed to sell his own company's shares to me, which happened to be the majority. The RUR board of directors voted to approve the sale of the company to ACE Corp, so I don't really see what you're getting at here, Del."

Another reporter was about to ask a question, but Warner interrupted him. "But that doesn't answer my question, sir. Do you have any comments about Mr. Rossum's disappearance? Especially since there is visual evidence of you meeting with him just days before he was never seen again. Rossum was considered to be the genius who invented a highly advanced, self-aware artificial intelligence suite for his robots, correct?"

Errol raised his hand to indicate it was his turn to speak. "First of all, that is a misnomer. The current AI suites that we have are not really a true AI. Quantum processing cores have made computer and robotic assistants more lifelike because they can process information faster, and quite a few of the latest ones even passed the Turing test, but let me be clear: AI central processing units nowadays can perform millions of calculations at once, which enables them to process a most likely reaction from a list of responses that have been programmed into them, and they simply react based on outside stimuli. Think of it as an animal with instincts. Instinct is simply a set of pre-programmed responses that an animal will make when it encounters something in its environment- it will run away, fight, eat or mate with its kind. Today's robots do the same thing, but instead of just a dozen responses like what animals have, we have programmed millions of potential responses, and the AI will simply make a best guess based on environmental factors and calculate that along with the consequences of its actions. So it all comes down to what type, and the number of responses you place into the software and the predicted repercussions of its choice. A human being can think abstractly, but a robot can't do that, not yet. As for the second query, I have spoken to the police and his family about it, and as you can see I have been cleared of any suspicion in his unfortunate disappearance. I will continue to cooperate with the authorities until he is found."

Stilicho gritted his teeth. So it seemed that the media were spinning conspiracy theories about his boss as being the one behind Karl Rossum's disappearance now? Just so that ACE Corp could take over the company? Ridiculous.

Warner was completely focused on that one issue, and he pressed on. "So you're saying that Rossum's agreement to sell the shares in his personal corporation over to you, and his subsequent disappearance right after that happened, is merely coincidence?"

"The police seem to think so," Errol said, "while the conspiracy theorists on the net say otherwise. I think I would prefer to believe the authorities than a bunch of kooks. Next question."

A man in the second row raised his hand. "Gene Stuyvesant, Reuters. From the financial reports of the last stockholder's meeting for ACE Corp, it says that the fusion project has cost the company hundreds of billions of dollars in research expenses alone, which is why overall profits are down and this could bankrupt the company. Why should we even develop a fusion reactor? Since you've stated that one of your corporate goals is to benefit mankind, why commit all that money into something that no one has yet been able to succeed in building? Shouldn't you be more focused in helping other countries to develop more sustainable resource consumption here on Earth?"

"Good question, at least we're finally back on subject, for once," Errol said. "The reason why ACE is committed to developing fusion power is precisely because of the very problems you have just put out. We need to develop a new source of fuel that is environmentally safe and efficient enough to lower costs to the point we don't have to worry about it. As I've mentioned, once we get a sustained reaction in the test reactor, this will change everything. We can open up the rest of the Solar System for expansion and even nearby stars such as Alpha Centauri will finally be within reach."

Another man in the front row raised his hand. "Robert Tan, All Asia News. Could I ask, why would your company push for further expansion in the Solar System when the current colonies are barely surviving? On Mars for example, there are only two functioning colonies left, one is ACE Corp's, and the other Chinese. The Russians and Mars First already abandoned their colonies, evacuating all their personnel back to Earth years ago. My point is even if you could develop fusion power, what guarantees could you make that will enable permanent colonies in the other planets?"

"Fusion power will change the dynamic in so many different ways," Errol said. "Even though we use nuclear fission reactors in the two existing colonies on Mars to augment our solar batteries, we still have to mine for radioactive minerals and process them before we can add them into the reactors- that takes a lot of energy on its own. The Chinese in Ba-Dian Colony have to expend a tremendous amount of energy just to extract water from hydrated minerals, and that is one of the reasons why their colony is expanding so slowly. With the advent of fusion, it will completely eliminate all our power needs, and allow the personnel we have on Mars to move on to the next phase, which is to terraform the planet to give it a breathable atmosphere and bring back the oceans that were once on its surface."

A woman with silvery gray hair raised her hand. "Eileen Babra, Reuters. Can you comment on recent reports on the net that claim there's a problem in the new Mars colony region of Chryse Planitia that your company is building? Specifically the reports that state the internet coming from that area has gone haywire, and the viruses being uploaded from the link in that region is wrecking havoc on the net backbone here on Earth?"

Errol raised his eyebrows. "Well, that's news to me. My IT department hasn't said anything about that at all. I guess we'll look into it. It's just probably a glitch, or some hacker here in Earth is bouncing malicious software from Earth to Mars and back again."

A younger reporter raised his hand. "Hector Camacho, Intervox. Can you comment about the rumor of delays on your Cloud City Colony project on Venus? There have been reports that state the lining material on the balloons that keep the colony afloat will not last against the corrosive atmosphere for very long. Any truth to that?"

Errol smiled as he stood up from the chair. "None at all. Cloud City is proceeding as scheduled, and you will get a live update once we deploy the first of the blimp probes later this month. I'm sorry, but now I have to get going. Goodnight, everybody."

Chapter 4

Stilicho entered the CEO's office less than ten minutes later. The door to the bathroom was open and he could see Errol washing his face. Stilicho walked over to a chair that faced the desk and sat down on it. It was close to midnight and he was dead tired. He was expecting that Errol would just postpone their meeting until the morning, but it seemed that something was on his boss's mind. Stilicho hated these kinds of meetings, for it usually meant that something was bugging his boss, and it indicated that Stilicho would have to solve the problem as quickly as possible, and at any cost.

Errol walked out of the bathroom, a small hand towel draped over his shoulder. "Stil, how was San Diego?"

"Everything went well," Stilicho said. "Campos has been neutralized, and his copies of the reactor magnet design have been switched for a fake one. He's already authorized the finance department to take the money back from his account. All's well that ends well."

Errol sat down with a sigh on a high-backed chair behind his desk. "Good job. We've got another problem though."

Stilicho crossed his arms. "I figured as much. Campos was small fry, and I could have just emailed you the report. But you wanted to see me in person, why is that?"

Errol's answer was a single word. "Mars."

Stilicho gave him a quizzical look. "Okay, what about it?"

"I'll put it to you plain and simple," Errol said. "We've lost contact with the entire construction team in the Chryse Planitia region."

Stilicho's eyes narrowed. "The new colony site you were building?"

Errol nodded slowly. "Yeah."

Stilicho was feeling sleepy. He was now starting to regret having those bourbon shots on the transcontinental flight. His mind wasn't working at peak capacity and his response came a little late. "You mean … those rumors about viruses being sent from that area on Mars is … true?"

"We did get malware from the outpost uplink at the building site, and my technicians shut down the node a few hours ago," Errol said. "But I think the problem's bigger than that."

Stilicho pursed his lips. "So it's not just a prank from the outpost crew then?"

"Simms is a pretty good team leader, no way would he allow any of his men to do that juvenile nonsense," Errol said. "Before the virus stream happened, we'd already lost contact with the outpost for a whole week. We then sent in a search and rescue team as soon as the outpost failed to check in at the last scheduled update."

Stilicho was intrigued now. A sudden spurt of adrenaline

put his mind back in focus. "So what did the rescue team find?"

"That's the problem," Errol said. "The rescue team failed to check in as well."

Stilicho's eyes opened wide. This never happened before. Everyone was always accounted for in Mars. "What?"

"Yeah," Errol said. "No response for over a week. Then came the virus stream, which uploaded onto the satellites, which then sent the packets to Earth's internet. We're still assessing if there was any lasting damage, but so far the relay network is still operating at near peak capacity. There was something strange about the virus too."

"What do you mean?"

"Normally when we deal with viruses, it's usually a denial of service attack, which disrupts the network by overloading it with remote requests from software bots," Errol said. "But this one seems to be a worm of some sort. It only made a few selective attacks before shutting itself down."

"What kind of attacks?"

"It went after specific entries in the database of numerous public archives and private servers," Errol said. "My IT team is working with system administrators from other corporations and the Library of Congress, for it seems a number of government records were tampered with. We haven't narrowed down the exact entries that have been corrupted or altered, but we will, in time."

Stilicho smirked. "Well, IT isn't exactly my specialty. I'm more into dirty tricks like blackmail and counter corporate espionage. I suppose you want me to lean on someone in the government or with another company to track down the hacker then?"

Errol shook his head. "No, I need you to go to Mars."

Stilicho was stunned. "What? Is this a joke?"

Errol stared straight into his eyes to indicate he wasn't fooling around. "I'm serious, Stil. This is big. I need eyes on the ground down there, and I trust you more than anyone."

Stilicho started to stammer. "I- that's an insane idea! I'm … no Martian, I love the Earth!"

"You're the man for this job," Errol said. "You've been off-planet before, right?"

The shock nearly made Stilicho stand up, but his knees buckled. "I … no! The most I've ever done was to take a couple of suborbital tours, and that's it. I'll be totally out of my depth there. If it's that important then shouldn't you be the one going?"

"I would go myself if I could," Errol said. "But the fusion reactor project is at a critical stage, and the technical problems with Cloud City are also acute right now. I just can't go, so I'm sending the next best thing- you."

Stilicho's chin trembled. "Now wait just a minute here, I'm totally unqualified for this! I deal with people on Earth, not with robots on some other planet."

"We'll get you up to speed," Errol said. "Though it will be a crash course since the synodic transfer orbit is coming up."

Stilicho didn't have a clue as to what he was talking about, so he quickly activated the smartglass he was wearing and cycled through the online encyclopedia. The synodic transfer orbit was a maneuver that spacecraft used to transfer from one circular orbit to another. The transfer period came only when Earth would be closest to Mars. It also said that these synodic periods only happened once every two years, when the needed orbits for both planets coincided. "So when is this transfer orbit going to happen?"

"Three days from now," Errol said. "Our colonial planners call it the start of the Mars tourist season. We'll get you on a transporter with the first driveship we'll send out, that way you'll beat the crowds."

Stilicho leaned forward. "Three days? Are you freaking kidding me?"

"We normally run a two-month training and orientation program for our tourists, and a six-month program for our colony personnel before they launch," Errol said. "In your case, we can wing it."

Stilicho finally stood up. "This is insane! I won't go!"

"Sit down, Stil," Errol said calmly. "You've been by my side ever since I plucked you out of college. I knew then that you were special. You're not that old, you're in generally good shape, you're smart, and you can think on your feet. Those are the qualities I was looking for when I handed you the job of corporate troubleshooter. Think of this as being nothing more than another assignment. I know your talents, and I'm sure you're more than up for this."

Stilicho sat back down. He had a dejected look on his face. "Please don't do this, Errol. You must have someone more qualified than me for this. I don't know a damn thing about Mars, or the colonial operations ACE has over there."

Errol smiled. "Like I said, we'll get you up to speed, so quit worrying."

"But, three days? You can get me qualified to go up there in three days?"

"It's my company, which means that I can circumvent a few things, so don't worry about the clearances and all that, I'll take care of it," Errol said. "You remember Dave Conklin, our training director, right?"

"Yeah," Stilicho said softly. "Former NASA astronaut who joined up with ACE … like, a long time ago."

"Exactly," Errol said. "I told him to run you personally through an accelerated program to get you in shape for the launch which goes up in forty-eight hours. You'll be considered as VIP and you'll have the transporter mostly to yourself. Our ships are designed to carry two hundred passengers, so you'll have plenty of room."

The thought of being stuck in a confined space while in microgravity for days filled him with dread. Stilicho's eyes looked down on the floor. He knew he didn't have a choice. All of his stock options, and his pension fund would be held hostage if he didn't. "How long will it take to get to Mars?"

"The delta-v of our driveships is normally sixteen kilometers per second," Errol said. "With the trans-Mars injection from low Earth orbit, that provides an extra six kilometers per second, for a total of twenty-two. You'll be in the orbit of Mars at around thirty-two days after launch, give a day or two."

Stilicho exhaled slowly. He would be stuck on a spaceship for a little over a month. A part of him was interested, but it was a very tiny part. The rest of him felt like it would be a death march. "Is there any other way to do this?"

"You'll be heading to Mars using the fastest way possible," Errol said. "Once the transporter launches from Earth, you'll link up with the driveship. The driveship will then get the transporter to Mars orbit, then you'll detach and go in for a landing right into Eridu Colony. While on the ground, the transporter will undergo ISRU refueling and will wait for you until you solve the problem, then it's back up to orbit and link with the driveship for the journey back to Earth. The driveships we use have got NERVA propulsion, so they provide the fastest way of going there. In fact, they're so fast that they normally go way beyond the standard injection velocity, so the ships end up doing a braking maneuver just to slow down before they even get there."

Stilicho's smartglass display was on voice-activated learning mode, and it indicated that NERVA was an acronym for Nuclear Engine for Rocket Vehicle Application. The concept had been developed and tested successfully by NASA in the 1960's, but was ultimately canceled a decade later due to budget cuts. Essentially a nuclear reactor injected with propellant for thrust, NERVA engines had very good and prolonged delta-v acceleration, but current treaties restricted their use in planetary atmospheres due to possible radioactive fallout, so only the driveships that traveled in between space were equipped with them. The transporter ships that he would be a passenger in still used the old-fashioned hydrogen and liquid oxygen chemical rockets. These were good enough to get the ship to low Earth orbit, before they needed to be attached to the more economical NERVA driveships to ferry them the rest of the way. ISRU was an acronym for in situ resource utilization, which was the process of manufacturing fuels at the landing site itself, and the transporter would replenish its fuel tanks using locally produced elements while on Mars. Everything seemed so neat, so well thought-out, but the whole thing still bothered him. "Once I get to Mars, then what?" he asked.

"Edgar Roth is the colony director for Eridu, and I've already talked to him," Errol said. "He will be at your disposal. You've met Ed before, right?"

Stilicho nodded. "Yeah, a few years back. I actually interned for him when I was still wet behind the ears as I started here."

"Good, good," Errol said. "You will have full authority to run the investigation. Just make sure you don't get in the way of the projects they're running in Mars, unless it conflicts with the issue that you're solving. In that case, you could talk to me and we could then work it out with Ed."

"So we'll stay in contact then?"

"Of course," Errol said. "Mars isn't some out of the way place where you have to send a telegram in order to talk to me. Net latency has a twenty minute delay, but other than that whatever you can access here on Earth is accessible on Mars too. I know today's generation wants instantaneous access to communications and information at their fingertips, so you'll have to learn to be patient. Twenty minutes isn't all that long."

Stilicho was feeling lightheaded. His mind was slowly accepting the fact that he was going, and he needed to know a lot of things in order to get the job done. Since he was already sitting down with his boss, he might as well ask him everything now. "What do you think is the problem out there?"

Errol shrugged. "It's hard to say. The outpost had a six man crew, and they were always working in pairs, like having a dive buddy when doing Scuba diving, so no one was ever left alone. A catastrophic failure of the outpost habitat is a possibility, but they would have had some time to put on emergency life support gear, unless they were all somehow unaware or unconscious when it happened. One of the men doubled as a medic, and any sort of emergency would have always been reported and on the net within minutes."

Stilicho rubbed his grizzled chin. He needed a shave. "Were there any reported problems before contact was lost?"

Errol activated his monocle. "It says here that they lost contact with some of their robots that were assigned to mark the transportation corridor to the south. A team of two men was dispatched to find the bots. That was the last entry."

"So if there was a failure of the habitat, then only four of the six would have been affected," Stilicho said. "What happened to the other two?"

"No contact with them either. The GPS locator of their rover was detected in Ares Vallis, before we had to shut down the node in that area due to the virus attacks," Errol said. "Ed sent the rescue team over to the last reported location of the rover first was since they were closer, then the colony lost contact with the rescue team as well. This happened two days ago."

"So whatever could have affected the outpost might have affected the rover crew as well?"

Errol sighed. "I have no idea. Once the link with the rescue team was lost, Ed and me agreed to restrict all EVA and vehicle travel to within Hellas Planitia- no expeditions outside of the basin. Most of the staff in the colony isn't aware of what's going on, so it's best you and Ed keep this information to yourselves for the time being. I don't want a panic to start."

Stilicho thought about it for a minute. "Do you think it might be some sort of microorganism that they caught?"

Errol smiled a little. This was what he liked about Stilicho, his troubleshooter was always good at thinking outside of the box. A virus was something he had not considered. "That is a damn good guess, Stil. When I talked to Ed the subject never came up, but nevertheless I think we need to initiate new protocols just in case there was some sort of biological contamination. We sure as hell can't ignore the possibility of that occurring."

"Broaching on that subject, wasn't there a news report about the living things we've encountered on Mars?"

"You know from learning at school that we ultimately did find some life still living on Mars," Errol said. "But they were just simple bacteria that could survive the radiation and the extreme cold temperatures of the planet. Most of them were found beneath the topsoil or underneath rocks. We've never found anything remotely larger than a microbe."

"Or maybe it's a dormant virus that mutated after coming into contact with a human being?" Stilicho said.

"We've deployed crews in the Chryse Planitia region for years and never encountered anything that proved to be dangerous," Errol said. "All outposts also follow strict procedures to prevent contamination. Any water extracted locally has to go through a heat and filtration system that would kill any bacteria still living in it. If any of the crew used skinsuits for EVA, they would have to go through mandatory quarantine before they were allowed into the main section of the outpost habitat."

"Well, if Martian bacteria can survive radiation on its surface coupled with extreme cold, don't you think they might survive the purification system we've set up?"

"The purification system has been tested time and time again," Errol said. "Strict use of the health protocols has ensured that nothing like this has happened yet."

"Well, maybe there was a breakdown of some sort that enabled an alien virus," Stilicho said. "Or it could be something else. Perhaps the Chinese did it."

Errol snorted. "The Chinese? Why in the hell would they do that? They mostly keep to themselves ever since they set up that colony of theirs in Gale Crater. I see no reason for them to try and kidnap our people, much less intercept a search and rescue team."

"Who knows? Maybe they all went nuts or something," Stilicho said. "Have you heard from them?"

"Yeah, they send out a constant stream of nationalistic bullcrap and how they are doing so great and all that," Errol said. "But the latest reports I've been getting is that they are operating at a loss, and their taxpayers are grumbling about the money they are pouring into the place."

"Well, they are communists and all that so it's not a surprise is it?"

"The Chinese are communists in name only," Errol said. "I would describe their system as closer to fascism, since their government controls many corporations to serve the national interests. They love to point out that Ba-Dian Colony is a privately run enterprise by the Xintian Corporation, but we all know that the government controls that firm and heavily subsidizes it. But still, I think it would be highly unlikely that they would be behind this."

"You never know," Stilicho said. "Maybe some Chinese in their colony went rogue and are now taking hostages."

Errol chuckled. "You've watched too many movies."

"The other possibility is maybe some sort of Martian lifeform that we've never encountered before suddenly came out of hiding and is now killing our crews," Stilicho said.

Errol rolled his eyes. "As I've said, you watched too many movies."

"Maybe it's the Russians," Stilicho said. "The new colony you're setting up in Chryse Planitia is awfully close to their old colony isn't it?"

"Don't be ridiculous," Errol said. "Their old colony in Valles Marineris is almost two thousand kilometers away to the southwest. Anyway, there are no Russians left on Mars except a small academic exchange team in Eridu, and they're all accounted for."

"Maybe they landed back there without us knowing about it," Stilicho said. "After all, they did lay claim to that whole region and some others. Even though they don't have a colony now, they are still telling everyone that you need to ask them for permission before you go to that area, right?"

"The Russians can make claims all they want, but the fact is that they have no official presence on Mars anymore," Errol said. "They can't stop our people or the Chinese from going over their old colony base and stripping it clean. Then again it's been years, so I doubt that any of their facilities would still be operational. They pretty much took everything that wasn't bolted down back with them when they evacuated, or they just wrecked it, like what they did with their rovers. I still have the inventory manifest from that operation on my desk around here somewhere."

"Okay, so the possibilities as to what happened are either man-made or some sort of environmental factor that we haven't been aware of," Stilicho said. "Since members of the outpost team were in two separate locations and so was the rescue team, then it's gotta be people or a monster, there is no other logical explanation. I'm betting it's the Chinese, they're the only other colonists on Mars."

"Ed and I came to that conclusion as well," Errol said. "We've made some high level inquiries with the Chinese, but they are denying that they have any personnel in the Chryse Planitia region- nor did they encounter any of our crew, so unless you find proof of something, I can't exactly accuse them out in public now can I?"

Stilicho rubbed his palms together. All he could do was

speculate. He would need to go out to the region in question to get more information. "Were any of the outpost personnel or the rescue team equipped with any weapons, or anything like it?"

"Outpost crew have no weapons, but they could improvise with the tools at their disposal," Errol said. "The rescue team had two security officers with them, and they would be equipped with handguns for emergency use."

"If it were humans that did this, then I would need to carry a gun for self protection," Stilicho said. "How equipped is the colony we have for military weapons and personnel?"

"The UN has pretty much implemented the Antarctic treaty for Mars and everybody signed it," Errol said. "Just like Antarctica, military activity is prohibited on Mars, but it's kind of vague when it comes to weapons other than a clear ban on nukes except for fuel. There's a security team in Eridu that liaisons with the NASA representative that's permanently stationed there. We've got handguns and a few rifles, but nothing major. Our security personnel are not allowed to carry guns unless there's a clear emergency, so they just walk around with stun guns and tear gas. If the Chinese have got military hardware on the planet, there's been no official word on it other than the conspiracy websites that claim that there's a nuclear arsenal out there."

"Okay, well uh, I think I would like to pack some heat when I go over there, if you know what I mean," Stilicho said.

"I'll see that the cargo manifest gets a small shipment of weapons, but we need to clear it with NASA first, so if they say no, then it won't happen," Errol said.

"Can you get clearance for it in two days?"

"It'll be tough, and I will have to let them know about our problem if I do," Errol said.

Stilicho winked at him. "Can't you just sort of like, sneak them in along with the boxes of steaks you'll be storing in the transporter's cargo hold?"

Errol shook his head. "No can do. If NASA finds out about this after the fact, and they almost usually do, then they have the power to revoke our franchise for the colony, and there's no chance in hell I would allow them to do that. We're the only real functioning colony left on Mars, and I'll be damned before I have to be forced to evacuate my people."

"Well I'm going to need a gun, I don't want to be caught with nothing out there when the crap hits the fan," Stilicho said.

Errol looked away and was deep in thought for a bit. Then he swiveled his chair and looked into Stilicho's eyes. "I've got an idea. I'll ring up a manifest for weapons along with a new team rotation for the security staff that will be heading for the colony. I doubt that NASA would find a routine personnel transfer as suspicious. I'll include your name as a security officer so you'll be allowed to carry firearms."

Stilicho grinned. Some good news for once. "Woohoo! This makes me feel a whole lot safer now. I'll need some heavy duty firepower just in case. I think an assault rifle with a laser pointer and a grenade launcher ought to do it."

Errol leaned forward so that Stilicho could see that his boss was serious. "Look, Stil. Tourist season is upon us with the synodic transfer period- and this happens only once every two years. All those visitors bring in much needed cash to mitigate the expenses that the colony is gobbling up. This is why the Russians and Mars First failed- because they tried to make a go of it by themselves. They couldn't see the commercial potential for tourism and the money it brings in to pay for the tremendous expenses. The Chinese are being subsidized by their taxpayers, so we are the only commercial colony that's over there. ACE Corp is in the red right now with all our other ventures, so I need you to solve this problem as quickly as possible before the tourists get down there. Because if you don't, then this could be the end of our Mars venture, and it'll probably be the end of the company too. You got it?"

"I won't let you down," Stilicho said softly.

"You better not, or I'll make sure you never get back to Earth."

"Hey!"

Chapter 5

Emma Rossum gestured at the large room while standing by the doorway. Upstate New York was slowly waking up from the previous winter, and a bit of green could already be seen from the backyard. "That's his workshop. Feel free to look around."

Darian smiled as the two NASA technicians behind her walked into the room and started to power up their computer pads. "Thanks, Mrs. Rossum. I'm so sorry for bothering you on such short notice, but we traced one of the malware worms from Mars making its way over to this location."

Emma betrayed no emotion. "No problem. Would you like a cup of coffee?"

"That would be wonderful, thank you," Darian said.

Emma walked back out towards the kitchen area. "Follow me."

Darian accompanied her back into the central area of the house and stood behind the counter. Emma looked to be in her late fifties, with buxom thighs and arms beneath the simple dress she wore. Her graying hair was cut in layers that seemed to make the strands stand up along the sides of her head. The crow's feet at the side of her eyes were somewhat masked by the thick makeup she wore. Emma placed three spoonfuls of aromatic ground coffee into the espresso machine and activated it. The room was soon filled with the sharp, roasted spice of Blue Mountain and Maragaturra beans.

"I drink mine as an espresso," Emma said while she placed a small cup in front of the machine. "Ever since that trip to Italy, Karl and I vowed to only drink this type of coffee from then on, since we found out that the locals never drink cappuccinos in the afternoon. I can add milk to yours to make a cappuccino or a latte if you'd like."

Darian shook her head slightly. "An espresso is fine. No sugar for me, please."

Emma placed the small, shot-sized cup on the counter. "You're just like my husband. He always liked his coffee black and bitter."

"I wanted to ask you, Mrs. Rossum," Darian said softly. "Even though your husband disappeared from the face of the Earth more than two years ago, you've never filed a missing persons report with the police. Why is that?"

Emma looked away while holding her own cup. "The police were already here to ask me some questions, so let's not bring this up again. I'm cooperating with you now, aren't I?"

"That's not what I asked, ma'am," Darian said. "The only reason why you didn't report him as missing is because you know where he is, don't you?"

Emma looked at her for a full minute before shaking her head. "No, I don't know where he is."

"Aren't you concerned about his well being?"

Emma sighed. "Karl can do whatever he wants. We stopped sleeping together about fifteen years ago, if that's what you're asking."

Darian noticed a set of pictures on a nearby wall. She walked over and stared at them. The first photograph showed the whole family: Emma, Karl and their three children standing together while posing in the backyard of their house. Joseph was their eldest, and he was the one who joined up with Mars First, only to die in the final year of the colony's existence, his body buried somewhere in the Red Planet. Jill was the second, and she was the one who filed the missing person report on her father. The youngest in the picture was a young boy of about seven or so, grinning wildly at the camera.

Emma stood beside Darian and pointed at the young boy in the framed photograph. "That's Joshua. Our youngest."

Darian looked at her. Her smartglass revealed the time stamp on the picture, and it was more than fifteen years ago. "Did the police talk to Joshua about his father's disappearance? I don't recall reading a file about him at all."

Emma exhaled slowly before she responded. "Joshua died a few months after that picture was taken. Highly aggressive form of Leukemia. We tried everything, but there was nothing the doctors could do."

Darian looked down. "I'm sorry."

Emma pointed to another picture on the wall. It showed Karl and Errol making faces at the camera. "After Joshua died, Karl just plunged into work and stopped talking to us. The only time he ever gave anyone any attention after that was with Errol. They were both great friends, and they trusted each other implicitly. So when I had found out that Karl entrusted all of his shares in RUR to Errol in case something ever happened to him, it didn't surprise me. My daughter wanted to fight it in court, but I told her that Errol was a friend of the family, and we would be well taken care of. In the end I was right, Errol came over to visit and made sure we were financially secure."

Darian looked at the picture. "I've never met Errol Flux. I've seen him on TV a lot, and he strikes me as the outgoing type."

"He is," Emma said. "Errol was the visionary, and Karl was the tinker. My husband preferred to just sit in his workshop and work on the hardware and software for the quantum computer he wanted to build. Errol wanted to go out and explore the galaxy. They had opposite personalities, but they got along better than I ever did. Errol allowed him to work from home, and I had to force Karl to eat and take baths many times over the years. If I hadn't, he would have starved to death from just working on his programs. Karl loved working with math and computers, he would tell me that equations would be the key to unlocking the secrets of the universe."

"So they made a formidable team," Darian said while sipping the last of her espresso.

Emma nodded. "Oh yeah. They were better than their competitors. Errol was a risk taker, but he always made calculated gambles when it came to pushing out a product. He knew that even though my husband rarely gave him any updates on what he was working on, they would always hit the deadline of a particular project, often at the last minute. Errol had complete faith in Karl, and he provided the seed funding when my husband wanted to create his own company that produced robots. Karl was never good with people, but Errol was and still is."

"Do you know what the reason could be as to why your husband decided to sell his ownership of RUR Industries to Errol and then disappear? I would think that if he truly liked working on quantum AIs that he would just stick with it." Darian said.

"I think he might have felt guilty about what happened to Joe, my firstborn son," Emma said wistfully.

"Could you give me your take on it?"

"Like I said, after Joshua died my husband started ignoring us," Emma said. "Joe took it hard, and Jilly moved out and never bothered to even invite her father over to her wedding. When Mars First became popular, Joe was one of the first to sign up for it. He had an automated allowance from Karl, and he saved up every penny and donated it to the cause. The only time I ever saw Karl raise any emotion after that was when the news of Joe's death on Mars broke on the news. That's when my husband truly lost it. He was screaming and crying for days. I wanted to call the paramedics because I was afraid he might hurt himself. Then he just stopped and retreated back into his shell again. After that he didn't even bother with his own company anymore, and Errol had to stand in for him during board meetings. Then things got darker. He started working on a project so secret, he would shut everything down the moment I came into the workshop to bring him something to eat."

Darian's eyes narrowed. "Any idea on what the project was about?"

Emma shook her head. "No idea. I used to help him a lot during the early days, but then he started working by himself, with no input even from his own colleagues. He would just deliver the files to them, ready to go, and they would install it into the robots. There would be a few bugs every now and then, but Karl always tinkered with his programs, so patches and fixes were just around the corner. The one time I was able to get a glimpse of his work was when I came into the room, and he was so engrossed with an equation that he didn't notice me for about a minute before he turned the monitor off."

"Do you have any clue as to what kind of equation it was?"

"It looked like a quantum algorithm of some kind," Emma said. "Just looking at the notes in the workshop after he disappeared, it seems like he was working on a self-aware AI suite. When I logged in after he was gone it must have triggered a self-destruct process, since his files started to wipe themselves from all of his servers after that. The name of the file disturbed me."

"What was the name on the file?"

"Joshua," Emma said. "Maybe it's just me but I think he's trying to bring our boy back from the dead. The last thing he told me was that he wanted to create artificial life so that people would never have to die. When Karl built robots that could interact with humans, he didn't even bother to talk to people anymore. My guess is that he wanted to create an AI that could act as a substitute for our youngest child."

One of the technicians walked into the room. "Ma'am, I think you'd better take a look at this."

They both followed him into the workshop. Karl Rossum's studio occupied a full wing of the house, and it had several long tables with all sorts of hardware and computer workstations. Every nook and cranny was filled with spare parts for robots and computers. Darian was reminded of those mad scientist labs in the movies. Boxes of wiring, robotic frames and interface networks were strewn about haphazardly all over the place. A small bed lay near the door. The main computer console stood in the center of the room, and one of the technicians had managed to activate the server. A stream of codes and equations floated around in the 3D monitor screen.

Darian stood beside the second technician while she cycled through the files displayed on her smartglass. "Okay, what are we looking at here?"

The first technician was busy interfacing with the main console. "It looks like the worm did come into the network and corrupted a number of encrypted files. The damned malware is hard to detect because it constantly changes its signature. I don't think those are retrievable now. But then again, since the files were encrypted with a quantum algorithm, we've no clue as to what they contained in the first place."

Emma turned to look at Darian. "So the rumors on the net about a malware worm coming from Mars are true then?"

Darian nodded. "Yes. We've implemented a protocol upload limit on all incoming data from Mars. The worm disrupted a number of important databases, including the FBI's national fingerprint identification system. Plenty of personnel records have been affected. Please keep this information to yourself for the time being."

"I haven't talked to the media in years," Emma said. "They tried to get a comment from me on the recent acquisition of my husband's company by ACE Corp, and I didn't tell them anything. Were my husband's records affected?"

"Yes," Darian said. "His on file fingerprints, pictures, and other means of identification have been wiped clean or corrupted. Even the backups were affected, and we still don't know how. It's as if he's trying to cover his trail."

Emma placed her hands on her hips. "My husband wouldn't have done that. It's not his way to ever disrupt the net just to conceal himself."

"Does your husband have any enemies?"

"No," Emma said. "Not unless you care to count Silas Balsamic- my husband publicly called him out as a scam artist and cult leader, but then again he's been dead a long time."

"Perhaps a friend of Silas, then? Would anyone from Mars

First know anything about your husband on a personal level?"

Emma paused while deep in thought. "There could be one person who might shed some light on this. Her name is Jennifer Till, she was close to Joe. I think she was his girlfriend in the Mars First Colony. My son always talked about her when he sent emails to me from the Red Planet."

Darian ran a check on Jennifer using her smartglass. "Okay, she's in a skilled nursing facility in Maine. I'll go check on her after this."

The technician working on the console threw his hands up. "That's it. The worm shut itself down, but it wiped pretty much everything."

Darian grimaced. Just another dead end. "There's nothing left on his files that indicates what he was up to?"

"All I've got are snippets of corrupted files," the technician said as he sorted through the virtual inventory. "Wait, I've got fragments of an audio only file- it's still accessible. Trace routing says it was downloaded from the Mars relay two years ago. It's mostly corrupted, but I think I can run a small portion of it."

"Play it," Darian said. Karl had gone missing right around at that time.

The audio was scratchy, with plenty of resonating feedback. The voice was faint and the volume would modulate every few seconds. "Dad, it's me ... I know ... we've had our differences. Please help me, I'm still here ... on Mars. Don't tell anyone ... please. Come get me .... You're the only one who can."

Emma's eyes opened wide. The voice was Joe's, her first born son. She started to scream.

The Gorham Advanced Care Facility was located in the southern part of Maine. Partially funded by the government, it housed a number of survivors from the disastrous Mars First Colony. Equipped with pressure chambers and special indoor swimming pools, the structure also contained a unique wing reserved for the Martians, the sickly children born on the Red Planet before their final evacuation more than a decade ago. Months after the public uproar, new laws were put in place strictly prohibiting pregnancies and childbirths on Mars. A number of individuals and corporations had taken these new treaty laws to the courts, but so far the prohibitions were upheld in the UN.

Darian sat by the round plastic table, her palms pressed firmly on its cool surface. The recreational hall had a high ceiling, and one could see the manicured grounds from the glass windows. Within a few minutes, a medical orderly came into view, pushing an old-fashioned manual wheelchair in front of him. The woman who was sitting on it looked pathetic in her loose hospital gown. Jennifer Till wore a bandana over her bald head, her spindly arms were crossed upwards over her sagging chest, and her skeletal legs were hunched to one pedal at the base of the wheelchair. She was barely thirty years old, yet she looked like someone living in the final years of her life. Mars First didn't have a whole lot of money when they started sending their people to the Red Planet, so they took the cheapest, one-way rocket flights to get to Mars, and many of them paid for it with either their health, if not with their lives.

The orderly parked her chair beside the table. His

nametag had the name of Julius on it. "You've got half an hour," he said, just before he turned around and walked over to the far end of the room.

Jennifer gave Darian a toothy smile. Her gums had receded, making her exposed molars look like beaver teeth. "And who might you be? I don't get a lot of visitors, just usually the press, but I don't like 'em, you know. They always gave us a bad rap."

Darian leaned back on the plastic chair that she sat on. "I'm Special Agent Darian Arante from NASA. I just wanted to ask you a few questions."

Jennifer's eyes gleamed with interest. "NASA? Wow, does this mean I can go back to Mars now?"

Darian cycled through her medical records using the smartglass she wore. Jennifer had lied about her age when she joined up with Mars First in order to get to the colony. She was just sixteen when she was launched into a three-month journey across space. Her muscles and bones had atrophied considerably when she returned, making her too weak to move around in Earth's gravity. She also had lung and liver cancer, no doubt caused by the lack of radiation shielding in the substandard colony habitats that Mars First used. Jennifer had been also exposed to cosmic rays during transit, and the transport ship that carried her crashed during the landing phase, damaging her spine. Nevertheless she carried on, becoming the poster child for determination, and her ordeals were broadcast live back to Earth in order to generate donations.

"I wanted to talk to you about Joseph Rossum," Darian

said. "I understand that you two were close during your time on the Red Planet."

Jennifer's right eye had a milky white pupil, there was no doubt it had a cataract. "Joe, he was so pure. He loved me and I loved him. We we're gonna have a child, you know? We were gonna have our own little Martian baby."

Darian bit her lip. Jennifer was in constant pain, so they obviously doped her up. This was going to make her questioning that much harder. "Yes, you clearly loved Joe. Did he treat you well?"

"Joe was the nicest, kindest person I ever met," Jennifer said softly. "Even when I got hurt, he always took care of me. When I was sick in bed he always stayed by my side till I fell asleep."

"That's good to know," Darian said. "Did he ever tell you about his father? Karl Rossum?"

"Oh yeah, he always talked about him," Jennifer said. "Joe only talked about his daddy and Silas. Those were the only things he ever talked about. Joe said he loved his dad, but his daddy didn't love him back."

"Did Joe ever talk about his dad with the others? Did Joe ever talk to Silas about him?"

"Oh yeah," she said. "Silas would talk to him for hours about his dad, and how Joe's daddy never truly loved him, only Silas did. And that was true … Silas loved all of us. Silas said he loved us, and that was why he chose us to live with him on Mars forever. It was such a cool time when we we're there. I wish we could go back there. Yeah."

"Did Silas ever make any sort of threats to Joe's dad?"

"Silas never made threats, he wasn't that kind of person," Jennifer said. "He would just look at you, and you'd know it."

"Know what?"

Jennifer scowled. "He gave you that kind of look, and you could tell that he just wanted to kill you, yeah. Silas was special, because we would do anything for him, you know. If Silas wanted you for the night, then you'd do it. Doesn't matter if you were somebody else's girlfriend or wife, or daughter, you know. If Silas wanted you, he'd have you."

"Did Silas ever say anything about Joe's daddy to the others?"

"Silas always treated Joe well," Jennifer said. "He knew that Joe's daddy was famous and all that, yeah. Only Robert Tsuda hated Joe, because he was jealous of him, I think. Tsuda tried to have Joe pushed out of the airlock, but Silas protected him. Joe was in awe of Silas too, yeah, until the final days."

Darian leaned forward. "What happened in those final days?"

"A few people started going crazy," Jennifer said. "We started running out of food, and Silas would order a few people out of the airlock as a test, you know. He said that if you truly were a Martian, you wouldn't need a suit to go out there. A dozen people did just like that, and we never heard from them again. Of course, we were able to get some meat a few days later, so that was good. Tsuda was a good cook."

"Is that how Joe died?" Darian asked.

Jennifer looked away. "Joe, I dunno what happened to

him in the end. The last few days, there were rumors that the government was coming to get us. To take us back to Earth. We wanted to fight them all, but we didn't have any guns or nothing, just knives and forks. Joe was upset, he didn't want to go back. Silas and Joe would talk privately many times. Then one day Silas came into my room. After he used me, he told me that Joe was dead. He said that Joe killed himself because he didn't want to go back. I started crying and he assured me that Joe was now a true Martian."

Darian ran through the reports on her smartglass. Of the original one hundred and twenty members of Mars First, only sixty-six survivors were brought back to Earth. Testimonies from several witnesses stated that Joe had died of asphyxiation, and was buried near the colony site. Silas had been detained by the FBI the moment he had returned, but was eventually released. "So you never saw Joe's body? Silas never told you how he died?"

"I searched for Joe, but I couldn't find him anywhere in the colony base. Tsuda says he killed Joe, but I didn't believe him, he was always full of crap. Silas told me his body was outside, and we just didn't have enough suits to wear," Jennifer said. "I wanted to go out without a suit like the others, but Silas told me not to, for I was chosen to deliver the message back to Earth, so I obeyed him."

Darian's eyes narrowed. "Message? What message?"

Jennifer looked at her with her one good eye. "We stopped calling him Silas when we were on Mars. He had a secret name that only people like us knew about, and we never told it to the cops either, we kept that bit for ourselves, yeah. But since you know Joe, I'm gonna tell you. Silas's real name is Ares, the god. That's what he was called on Mars. He would stand in front of everyone, and we would all bow our heads and pray to him, yeah. He was Ares alright. And his message was only for the people who died on Mars, and it gave us hope."

Darian pursed her lips. "So what's the message then?"

Jennifer grinned as she remembered her time on Mars. "It's in the Book of Ares, that was Silas's personal book, and he left it behind on Mars, I think he hid it, that's the last thing he told me before they took us all away. He read a few passages on it, yeah. There was one message on it that he always read to us after our morning prayers, and it was everybody's favorite. It basically said that anyone who died on Mars wasn't truly dead, that they would return to life in a few years' time. And once they came back to life, their voices would be heard once again."

Darian blinked a few times. This was getting weird. "Could Joe have been alive and maybe … left on Mars accidentally?"

She pointed a crooked finger at Darian. "I know why you're here. And I know why you brought up Joe. You heard from him, didn't you? You heard his voice, yeah."

Darian didn't reply. She simply didn't know what to say.

Jennifer's body started shaking. She stared up at the ceiling and folded her spiderlike hands in a gesture of prayer. "Joe, it's me! Take me back to Mars, back to the arms of our loving god Ares. Please, I want to be with you forever! I hate it here. Take me now!"

Darian stood up when she noticed that Jennifer was now convulsing. Julius ran over to them. The orderly tried to calm her down, but Jennifer continued her seizure as her eyes started rolling and she fell forward, right into Julius's arms. Two more orderlies came running towards them. Darian knew her time was up so she turned around and walked away.

By the time she got back in her car at the parking lot, her phone started ringing. The sun was beginning to set over the horizon, and the air was still chilly as the spring season had not yet begun. Darian sat on the driver's seat and put on the earpiece before accepting the call. The smartglasses she wore over her eyes was a universal communications device, able to send messages through the internet and it could also take incoming calls.

It was from her supervisor at NASA, Martin Ballast. "Darian, what in the hell have you been up to? I just got a call from an ACE Corp lawyer threatening to sue us over harassment. He said that you went and visited Karl Rossum's wife, causing her go into hysterics. Paramedics were called, and she's now under observation at the hospital for a nervous breakdown. You were only supposed to do a routine check on her servers to track the worm down."

"Marty, I didn't put her in hysterics, she did that herself when she heard her supposedly dead son's voice over an audio recording that her husband had been keeping from her," Darian said.

"And I just got another message," Martin said. "It says

here that the doctors at a Maine care facility are treating a patient for a seizure, right while you were talking to her? This latest stunt of yours wasn't authorized, Darian. What are you up to?"

"I was talking to the former girlfriend of Karl Rossum's son, she was on Mars with him," Darian said. "It seems that Joseph Rossum's body was never identified when the authorities evacuated the Mars First Colony all those years ago."

Martin made a slight pause. It was clear from his voice that he was holding back his anger. "What does Mars First have to do with all this crap you're giving me, Darian? You were just supposed to follow up on the malware trail and that's it."

"Listen, Marty- remember that hostage situation that happened a few days ago? It's all tied in with the worm that came from the Mars network," Darian said. "I was in negotiations with a former cultist of Mars First who said that Silas Balsamic had spoken to him, and he demanded to be taken back to the Red Planet. Then today we traced the malware worm to Karl Rossum's house, and it wipes out his files except for one that has the voice of his supposedly dead son on it, telling him to go to Mars and find him. I had the technicians trace the audio file and it was definitely from the Red Planet, and it didn't come from ACE Crop's colony, nor did it originate from the Chinese netlink. Now it's clear that no one ever saw Joseph Rossum's body or knows how he died, so maybe he's not dead?"

Martin sighed. "Stop. Hold it right there. Mars First was

evacuated more than fifteen years ago. Both ACE Corp and NASA supervised the repatriation. They searched the base from top to bottom. No one was left behind."

"I understand that," Darian said. "But what if he wanted to make it look like he was dead, but instead hid, perhaps inside a rover or just wore a suit and waited outside until everybody left. From the reports I read, all we did was do a headcount after the search and assumed that anyone who wasn't present was dead, we never bothered to look at the gravesites located just outside."

"That's an insane theory," Martin said. "You're telling me that Karl Rossum's son faked his death so that he could stay behind? The Mars First Colony was gutted. There was no food in there. Their air recycling system was on the blink. Their greenhouse was dead. No way could anyone survive alone in there for fifteen years without resupply."

"I know it sounds wild Marty, but someone sent a message to Karl Rossum from Mars, and it motivated him to sell his shares over to ACE Corp and to disappear," Darian said. "He was reported missing by his daughter, and we would be remiss if we didn't take this theory into consideration. Even if Joseph is dead, we do have an obligation to find his father. Also, there is the malware attack coming from an unknown source on the Red Planet, and the net was just hit by rumors of people disappearing from the colony. Everything points over there."

Her boss let out a deep breath. "So what do you want to do?"

"I need to get to Mars," Darian said softly. "When's the next launch date?"

Chapter 6

Stilicho rolled up his shirtsleeve. The office he was sitting in had pearly white walls, just like in hospitals. He always hated going to the doctor ever since he was a kid, only this time he was indeed in a medical facility, for he happened to be at ACE Corp's astronaut training center. There was a small bandage over his elbow since he had just given up some of his blood.

Dr. Catherine Niven was sitting on the chair opposite to him. She wore thick glasses, and her red hair was neatly clasped in a pony tail. Stilicho figured she had nice breasts, if only they weren't covered up by the white lab smock she wore. "Okay," she said. "It looks like your blood sugar, cholesterol and uric acid levels are all normal. You passed."

Stilicho winked at her. "I really don't wanna go. Is there a way you could fail me, Cat? I'll do anything for you."

Dr. Niven giggled as she pressed a button on her console. "Oh, you."

The door behind them opened, and in stepped David Conklin, ACE Corp's spaceflight director. He was nearly two-meters tall, and his lanky frame tended to sway at times when he walked, giving him an awkward gait. David had thinning hair and a grizzled chin, while his smartglasses were thicker than normal, owing to his short-sightedness. "Howdy, Stil," he said as he whipped out a very big right hand. "It's been awhile since I saw you in person, buddy."

Stilicho stood up and shook his hand. The grip was like cold iron. "How are you, Dave? Yeah, the last time we talked was last year's Christmas party. Everything good?"

"I'm busier than ever due to the tourist season coming up. We'll be sending a whole fleet to Mars, and it's shaping up to be a good one, though not as good as the early days, of course," David said, before turning his attention to Dr. Niven. "So how are his tests, Cat? Did he pass or do I give the bad news to Errol?"

Dr. Niven leaned back on her chair and smiled. "Stilicho is good to go. His blood tests are fine, his cardio is adequate. He has a fatty liver though, but the spaceflight should help since he won't be imbibing any alcohol during the trip."

Stilicho's eyebrows shot up. "No drinks? Oh, come on!"

David chuckled as he took Stilicho by his elbow. "Let's go, time to give you the rundown on what's happening. See you, Cat."

"Take care, boys," Dr. Niven said just before they left her office.

They both started walking along a wide corridor, making their way towards the orientation area. Along the walls stood a number of displays, including scale models of the rockets they were using, as well as life-sized exhibits of the numerous spacesuits that were once used during the early years of spaceflight. The hall was meant to serve as both the museum and an interactive learning display for school kids during their fieldtrips. Wall-mounted monitors would regularly show old newsreels, documentaries and movies detailing man's early years in space.

"Okay, so you want to go out into space," David said as they continued on. "This is a good place to start. First of all, you need to realize that it's quite simply the most dangerous environment known to man. But even then, there's a number of misconceptions that's been caused by too many science fiction movies which didn't get the science part right."

Stilicho shrugged. "Honestly Dave, it wasn't my intention to go to Mars. Errol is sort of like … forcing me to go."

David chuckled again. "I hear ya, buddy. I was kind of shocked when I got an email from him telling me to prep you up for our first launch of the season, which will be in two day's time. I guess I'm just going to have to give you the accelerated version of our training course."

Stilicho rolled his eyes. "Great, so where do we start?"

"Right here," David said as he stopped by a display. It showed a pair of adult diapers. The stitching seemed more robust than what was normally seen in box illustrations along the grocery aisles.

Stilicho pointed at the display. He couldn't believe it. "Is that what I think it is?"

David grinned. "Your eyes aren't deceiving you, buddy. Beneath the clothes you'll be wearing is a diaper. Let me give you a history lesson as to why. Back in the early days of spaceflight over a hundred years ago, an old NASA astronaut named Alan Shepard was sitting in his space capsule, waiting to be the first American to be launched into space, right after Russia's Yuri Gagarin. Now, there were numerous delays and the launch was postponed for a couple of hours. Poor Shepard needed to go to the bathroom but the hatch was already bolted down, and it would have been delayed even further if they allowed him to leave the capsule. So in the end, he pissed in his spacesuit and became the second man in space … and the first with dried urine at the rear of his flight suit, all the way back to Earth. From then it was practical that all astronauts wear a diaper."

"I guess they never talk about this on TV," Stilicho said.

"They don't," David said. "It's one of the less glamorous things about spaceflight, and by no means the only one. So you'll be wearing a diaper just before liftoff. There is a tube you need to attach to your cock, in the early days they just used condoms. The lining material is made from sodium polyacrylate, and can absorb up to three hundred times its weight in water. Each diaper can hold up to two liters in urine and feces before you need a new one. There are vacuum toilets on the transporter too, but it's prudent that you sleep with the diaper on anyway, just in case of emergencies."

Stilicho gave him a blank look. "Nocturnal emissions?"

"Maybe, but if there's a sudden decompression or any other emergency, then it's best you stay suited up and ready to go, just in case," David said, before he walked over to another display. In front of them was what looked like a padded wetsuit and an accompanying helmet. "Which brings us to another issue, the vacuum of space. In the event of a hull breach and loss of internal atmosphere, you have some time to put on your emergency gear, like the suit we have here," he said, pointing to the outfit being displayed. "This is the Andark Block-Two skinsuit, which I'm sure you've already heard about since they've been featured on TV a lot. The suit itself is skin-tight, made from a combination of advanced composite spandex, Nomex and Kevlar, and each suit measurement is tailored directly for its wearer, because there can be no gaps at all in any part of the body."

Stilicho nodded. "So that's why you guys were taking my body measurements earlier this morning."

"Yup," David said. "Our 3D printers are working overtime to get three pairs of your own personal skinsuits ready for fitting tomorrow. Some areas of the suit will have fluid-filled bladders like the armpits, the crotch, the knees and elbows. This is to prevent pressure gaps, because the suit and your body will act as a mechanical counterpressure in case of being exposed in a vacuum. The skinsuit has certain advantages over the hard shelled, full-pressure suits in that it's very light and flexible. It means you can wear it all the time, like a uniform. All you need to survive in a vacuum is to put on the bubble helmet and the life support pack so that you can breathe, just don't forget your gloves and boots too. If there is a puncture on the hard suits, then your entire body will depressurize. With the skinsuit, any punctures are localized, and you can just slap on a patch in the affected area and go on with what you need to do. Your skin might get bruised from the exposure to vacuum, but at least you won't have to worry about the rest of your body."

"So tell me," Stilicho said. "Why are they nicknamed fart suits?"

David started laughing. "Are you a diver?"

"Yeah," Stilicho said. "Advanced open water certified."

"Good, then you know about Boyle's law," David said. "At the event of a sudden decompression and exposure to vacuum, you'll experience a syndrome called high-altitude flatus expulsion. Since the skinsuit is low pressure, there will be a spontaneous passage of rectal gasses the moment you enter a vacuum. When that happens, forget tact and just let it all out, or you'll damage your intestines."

Stilicho scratched the back of his head. "If this skinsuit is so great, why don't we just pressurize it so we don't have to deal with the farting?"

"Putting a soft, flexible suit under high pressure is impractical," David said. "Because it'll blow up like a puffer fish and you'll be unable to move. Only rigid, hard-shelled suits can be fully pressurized. And this brings us to another matter. Since the skinsuits are low pressure, this means you will be breathing pure oxygen. If you remember your diver training, you need to decompress before you switch from high pressure to low pressure. We call it pre-breathing."

"How long do I have to pre-breath before using the skinsuit?"

"Ninety minutes, with light exercise," David said. "Knee

and arm bends while you breathe in pure oxygen. Also, you are not to wear anything on your head that's combustible, because pure oxygen is an extreme fire hazard. The last thing you want is your face on fire and you can't take the helmet off because you're in a vacuum."

Stilicho shook his head. "Wonderful. What if it's an emergency and I don't have time to pre-breathe?"

"You could get decompression sickness," David said. "I would suggest you swallow a mouthful of aspirin before you don the helmet, because your joints will be in pain. Oh, and be sure to slap on an anti-nausea patch on your thigh or arm before you do any EVA, the last thing you want is to get sick and puke while you're wearing a space suit, because you could drown in your own vomit. Packets of pills and the patch are normally attached to the hip pockets of your suit."

"This just keeps getting better and better," Stilicho muttered.

"A few more things," David said. "If there's a puncture in the hull, the entire room won't depressurize immediately, air still has to exit from the hole. The pressure drop will depend entirely on the size of the breach and the room that you're in. To give you an extreme example, let's say the entire side of the room you're in gives way, and you get exposed to hard vacuum in only a few seconds. Now, contrary to what you see in the movies, you won't get sucked off into space- not unless you're right by the hole, or you were hanging onto the part that gives way. Even then, you've got about fifteen to thirty seconds tops before you lose consciousness. As with sudden pressure changes, do not hold your breath while in a vacuum, exhale slowly so that your lungs aren't damaged- it's like when you ascend during an underwater dive. Your first priority would be to get to a cabinet that contains a helmet to go with your skinsuit. Pop the cabinet open and take the helmet, then put it on. Don't worry, all the helmets have universal fit. Each helmet by itself has an internal oxygen cartridge which will give you five minutes of air. So turn it on once you got the helmet sealed over your skinsuit's neck ring. You with me so far?"

Stilicho nodded. "Yeah, go on."

"Good," David said. "The next thing is the life support backpack, and they are usually in the same cabinet that houses the helmets. Remember that when you're in a vacuum there will be plenty of resistance, especially when you use your gloves- it's going to be hard to grasp anything so you've got to work at it. Fortunately, all you have to do is to turn around, stick your back to the pack and put the straps on. Then take the air hose and either plug it at the back of the helmet or at the front, the multiple jacks will work either way- just be sure to turn it on. Got it?"

"So your body doesn't explode when exposed to the vacuum of space?"

David shook his head. "That's a misconception from Hollywood. You will get exposed to cosmic radiation and eventually freeze to death as your body rapidly cools, but you will die from asphyxia long before that happens. The good news is that you should have a complete recovery if you survive, that's under the assumption you were only exposed to vacuum for less than ninety seconds."

Stilicho glanced over at the opposite display featuring the crab suit. "So no need to go into pre-breathe if I use the hard suit?"

"Nope," David said. "The pressure inside of the crab suit is almost equal to the pressure of our habitats on Mars and the transporter ship interior, which is mostly nitrogen and less than thirty percent oxygen."

"In that case," Stilicho said. "Can I have a crab suit put in my stateroom before takeoff?"

David shook his head as he gestured at another display, this time pointing to what looked like a handheld plastic bag. "This is a barf bag, and they come standard issue in all compartments. It has a dual lining, so you can seal it after placing your mouth on it. Please be sure to close it up after use, because you don't want your puke floating around with you."

Stilicho crossed his arms. "Come on, Dave. You really think I'm gonna get sick up there?"

"You could," David said. "Space adaptation syndrome is experienced by half of all space travelers in microgravity. Your body will be confused the moment you get up there and it won't be able to tell up from down. One thing Errol didn't tell you is that SAS is responsible for the deflated market of space tourism. After experiencing all the hardship that comes with going to a place where our bodies aren't adapted to, about half the tourists we've brought up there never want to go back out into space ever again."

Stilicho nodded. "I see. No wonder he's under a lot of pressure to get this season's tourists over there."

"I tell you, Stil," David said. "The colony is hanging on

by a thread. This is why Errol is doubling down on the fusion research. With what we've got right now, Mars is nowhere near self-sufficient, so unless we get a faster drive that won't be dependent on synodic transfer orbits every two years, then we may have to pack up and leave Mars for good. That's the last thing Errol wants to see happening."

"Right," Stilicho said. "I know the stakes."

"Good," David said, pointing to a third display. There was another, thinner bodysuit behind the glass partition. "That is an electrical stimulation suit, or what we call our shock pajamas."

Stilicho raised an eyebrow. "And why are you telling me this?"

"Living in microgravity for extended periods will decalcify your bones and atrophy your muscles," David said. "You need to engage in at least two hours of full body exercise on a daily basis. Full isometric, isotonic and cardio. In addition to that, I would suggest you wear the shock pajamas when you go to sleep. The inner lining of the garment is studded with wiring which will send an electrical current along to your muscles, causing them to contract without you having to do anything. The sensation is like a slight burning and itching at low levels. Of course, if you're a sadomasochist, you can bring it up to maximum."

"You can't be serious."

David smiled. "I have to admit the first few nights won't be comfortable, but you'll get used to it. I'll have a suit scaled to your size waiting for you in your stateroom at the transporter."

Stilicho scowled. "Dave, I'm not wearing it."

"You're gonna have to if you want to keep your muscles," David said as he began to walk to the end of the corridor. "Come on, follow me."

Stilicho accompanied him over to the next wing. A number of displays showed scale models of the rockets and digitized topographical maps of the numerous planets. A huge diagram of the Eridu Colony interior occupied one side of the hall. David walked over to a display featuring a two-foot high model of the multi-purpose interplanetary transporter. The ship resembled a long, smooth white-painted rifle bullet which stood upright on three landing struts.

"This is the workhorse of the ACE Corp fleet of ships," David said. "It consists of two stages. The first stage, which is the lower part- is the heavy lift launch system. The upper stage is the multi-purpose space ship, sometimes called a lander or transporter. The first stage is purely engines and fuel, and is designed to launch the ship into orbit, then the second stage detaches and goes on. Both stages are fully reusable, which is a big factor when it comes to cost. Once detached, the first stage will return to earth and land vertically for refueling. If you want to launch it again, all you have to do is to attach another second stage to it, and that can be done in less than an hour. We use chemical drives for orbital launches: a mixture of hydrogen and liquid oxygen, or H-LOX for short."

Stilicho peered closer at the model. "So the first stage is fully autonomous?"

"Exactly," David said, pointing to the top part of the

model. "Now the second stage carries the crew and passengers. There are other types of space ships like tankers which do not carry any passengers or cargo, and substitutes the free interior with more fuel tanks. Our transporters have in-space refueling capability, but you'll only need one refueling stop for the Mars trip, so that means the transporter will not have to refuel again until it lands on Eridu Colony in the Hellas Basin. The hulls of these ships are made of carbon fiber with advanced polymers made possible through quantum research. The transporters have a four hundred ton payload, while the cargo versions have twice that amount. The one you'll be riding in has a two hundred passenger seating capacity, though yours in particular will have a lot less, for obvious reasons."

"What's the name of the ship I'll be on?"

"The *Duran Duran*," David said.

Stilicho's eyes opened wide. "The what?"

"That was Errol's idea," David said. "You see, pretty much all the Greek and the old astronomer's names have been picked. We've sent out hundreds of probes and ships over the past few decades and all the corporations started running out of names. There's been at least a half dozen *Argos*, *Keplers* and *Magellans* out there and everyone was getting confused, so we needed to come up with names that had yet to be used. We've used up pretty much every name in literature when it came to naming craters, valleys and other stuff on the planets and moons of our system. Errol always had a fondness for late Twentieth Century rock bands, so we started cataloging our ship names that way."

Stilicho sighed. "Well, at least the ship ain't called the *Deee-Lite*."

It was David's turn to be confused. "The what?"

"Never mind, go on."

"Okay," David said. "So, once the transporter is up in high Earth orbit, it'll make a refueling stop at the orbital propellant depot, then rendezvous with the driveship at the Lagrangian point two, just beyond the moon's orbit. A Lagrange point is a location in space in which the combined gravitational forces of two bodies- which could be planets, stars, or moons- and allows an object to maintain a stable position relative to them, so no need for continual adjustments to keep the orbit. We already have a drydock and refueling stop for the driveships out at L-point two, but Errol actually has plans to build a permanent off-world space colony there, but he doesn't have the money for it yet. You'll be missing the Moon entirely, since you don't need to go there for this trip."

"How long will that take to get to the rendezvous?"

"Four to five days at full burn," David said before walking over to another display, this one showing a spaceship that resembled a horizontal broom. "Once there, the transporter will begin automated docking procedures with the driveship." He pointed at the new spaceship's long length. "The *Duran Duran* will attach itself along the spine of the driveship. Once there are sufficient transporters fitted along the length of the driveship, then the real journey begins."

Stilicho narrowed his eyes. "How many other transporters will be coming along with my ship?"

"Three cargo ships will dock along with yours," David said. "They are needed to resupply the colony, as well as bringing the replacement staff for those in the colony that's due to transfer back to Earth. Most of the stuff they're transporting will be for accommodating the tourists who are scheduled to go over the next few days."

"Like what kind of stuff?"

David shrugged. "Oh, the usual hanky-panky tourist stuff. Flavored bath soaps, booze, gourmet frozen food and all that. Our employees in the colony love it when the tourists are gone and they can buy the unused stuff for their personal use at a discounted price. Errol sometimes does giveaways to boost morale in the colony during the off-season times. The tourists are a double-edged sword, they demand attention and disrupt everyday work and research in the colonies, but the supplies they bring over and leave behind are a welcome treat."

Stilicho shifted his attention back to the driveship model. "I'm guessing this is a bigger ship then."

"Oh yeah," David said. "The official designation is the Long Range Interplanetary Transport Vehicle, but we call them driveships for short. Each is three times the length of a transporter. Driveships are limited to outer space and cannot land on planets; they are used strictly for ferrying the ships that do." He pointed to the end of the broom. "They use nuclear thermal rocket engines, or NERVA drives. Attainable core temperature is around three thousand two hundred Kelvin. They can get up to sixteen kilometers per second using atomic hydrogen. Of course, treaties prohibit the use of nuclear powered drives in planetary atmospheres, which is the reason why NERVA drives are only used by driveships and not transporters."

"Let me guess," Stilicho said. "It probably is named *Hoobastank*, or something like it."

"No, the driveship that's taking you to Mars orbit is called the *Wanderer*," David said.

Stilicho was impressed. "Well, that's definitely a better name."

"Right," David said. "Now, once the driveship ferries the four transporters to Mars orbit, it will sit there and await the servicing of its NERVA reactor from Phobos station, which will probably take a few hours, since it's modular and can be separated from the hull. Meanwhile, your ship detaches and heads down to the Martian surface. Mars has a very thin atmosphere so the transporter will be using aerocapture with direct descent. This means the ship will fly sideways for bit- to induce maximum drag- before it uses its gimbals and grid fins to align itself vertically during the final descent. That's usually the danger point, but it has been done successfully for the past few hundred landings without a crash, so the odds are on your side."

"Well that gives me a sense of relief," Stilicho said.

"I'm glad you're so positive," David said as he started to walk towards the next hall. "Follow me."

The adjoining hall was much bigger, for it featured a number of full-sized vehicles and robots on display. Stilicho followed David as they both walked over to where the Martian rovers were parked. The vehicle had six wheels, and the dual glass windshield had a wraparound view from the outside. Two crab suits were sticking out from the sides of the rear airlock.

"It feels like I'm part of a lecture tour rather than undergoing training," Stilicho said.

"That's because we don't have the time for any actual training, which involves VR simulators and full classroom instruction," David said. "I would prefer one of our more trained employees for this trip, but Errol has complete faith in you, so don't let him down."

"So you keep reminding me," Stilicho said.

"It would have been nice if we put you through the heavy grav simulators, as well as a suborbital flight demo, but time is of the essence. Normally our spaceflight candidates also go through intense psychological testing and evaluation, so we're skipping that too," David said. "I have given standing orders for our flight crew to incapacitate you should you ever go psycho up there, knowing you."

"Actually that wouldn't be a bad idea," Stilicho said. "With all this crap you've told me about just how dangerous spaceflight really is, maybe it's better you just dope me up, put those electric pajamas on me, and let me snooze for the rest of the trip. Just don't forget to stick an IV needle in my arm and wake me up when we've landed."

"You're nuts," David said. "An IV drip won't give you the proper amounts of nutrition to keep your muscles from atrophying, and there's the problem of bubbles forming because of the microgravity- even though there's a micron filter in the IV fluid tube, it's still possible that you can get air embolism. If you got any other dumb ideas, it's better to let it all out right now."

"Oops, scratch that one then," Stilicho said.

"I gotta tell you, Stil," David said. "The UN is really screwing us over with that Child Ban Treaty. We're working overtime to have it overturned, but it's tough going, especially with what happened to the Martians."

"That's the nickname that the media people made up towards all the children that were born on Mars, right?"

"Yeah," David said. "A total of twenty-three children born on Mars since we first arrived there. Six of them from Mars First, two that we know of from the China colony, five from the Russians, and ten from our own. They grew up sickly and had to be evacuated. Most of them are now living in specialized care facilities because of stunted growth, weak bones and muscles." He shook his head. "I totally pity the ones from Mars First, they're all buried somewhere out in the Red Planet."

Stilicho looked away. "Maybe we aren't meant to go out there."

"Everyone in ACE Corp believes in what we're doing," David said. "We have to. All the achievements we've done has inspired a new generation of astronauts, scientists and engineers to go out even further. I know it in my heart that if we could just get past this hurdle, and find a way to bring forth healthy babies on Mars, then we can truly go to the next step and make it a permanent settlement out there. That's what I believe in and I'm going to fight for it."

"So no new babies on the Red Planet since the Martians

were evacuated fifteen years ago, eh?"

"None that we know of," David said. "Women in the colony are encouraged to use contraceptives and they're provided free of charge. Anyone who gets pregnant must be transferred out back to Earth on the next available launch, unless they choose to abort it. There's been rumors that the Chinese are secretly raising a new generation of Martians in their colony, but we have no real proof of that."

Stilicho placed his hand on the hood of the rover. "I see. Is this the new vehicles that are currently being driven on Mars?"

"Yup," David said. "These Mwevs are six-wheeled drive vehicles. A huge improvement over the first manned rovers that landed on Mars thirty years ago. Back then, the maximum speed was ten kilometers an hour, but these new babies can go up to one hundred and twenty, though it's not recommended because of the patches of rough terrain in many parts of the planet. If you go close to full speed it'll be like the Dakar Rally with all the bumps and shakes since there's no roads out there." He pointed at the reinforced metallic wheels. "Each wheel can pivot three hundred sixty degrees if necessary. Smartglass on the HUD, along with GPS and a waypoint finder. Lidar and radar, with fully autonomous driving technology built in."

"What's their range?"

"Eight hundred kilometers at full charge," David said. "They have solar cells on the roof, and they re-charge automatically during the day. If night falls and you're low on charge, go to the nearest waypoint- there's usually an automated charge station with it where you can juice up. Or you can spend the night in the rover since they have full life support systems, and wait till the sun comes up to charge your batteries again."

Stilicho nodded. "Personnel capacity?"

"They can fit six comfortably," David said. "Probably double that if you want to crowd it. Though I wouldn't recommend it since you'll be taxing the life support systems. The carbon dioxide scrubbers would need to be serviced every few hours, but it can be done. Twenty day's life-support for around six, and halve that with twelve people. Even with those limitations, you could still travel a fair bit of distance."

"How is the waypoint network?"

"It's far from complete. In fact, you might say there's preliminary waypoints that have been erected and that's it," David said. "There's maybe six in and around Hellas Basin, and maybe less in the Chryse Planitia region."

Stilicho turned and pointed to a full-sized robot. "How many bots do we have on Mars?"

"Hundreds," David said. "The most common are the sweeper bots. Very simple machines whose job is to wipe away the dust that accumulates on the solar panels in the colony. Most of them are fully autonomous. The larger ones are the transport and lifter bots, and they are usually found on the construction sites."

Stilicho took out a small plug drive from his pocket. "I'll be bringing Maia with me. Can she override their command modules?"

David's eyebrows shot up. MAIA was shot for Mobile Artificial Intelligence Assistant. They were the next generation in quantum AI suites, and could be used to hack into systems and provide instantaneous advice for their users. "You've got a Maia? I thought they were only at the prototype stage."

It was Stilicho's turn to give him a wink. "This is a Maia Version-Two, actually. Only Errol and me has one right now. I have to say, she's been invaluable when it comes to handling the problems I'm faced with."

"You'll need the override code to hack into the bots, but I'm sure Errol will give them to you," David said. "But why would you need to hack into the robots anyway? Are you expecting some kind of trouble out there?"

"I'm not sure, to be honest," Stilicho said. "I guess Errol already outlined the problem to you."

"He did," David said. "And I honestly don't know what's going on out there."

"Best to be safe," Stilicho said. "Guns do work on Mars, right?"

"Of course," David said. "Our corporate security teams have them. Firing them outside muffles the sound because of the thin atmosphere, and there's less bullet drop due to the low gravity, which means a greater range. With the low gravity, you can move faster with much less effort. Jumping will be much higher. Throwing someone will be in slow motion and your throw will be longer."

"I've asked Errol to include some weapons for me as well," Stilicho said.

"I've already signed off on the manifest," David said. "I'm also sending a full complement of security personnel with you. As you know, we normally hire former cops and put them through astronaut training. I hope that they'll be enough to deal with any potential problems you'll have out there."

Stilicho exhaled slowly. "I hope so too. If you don't know what the problem is, I'll be damned if I could figure it out. If this gets worse, who do we call?"

"In the event everything goes to hell it would have to be the US Military, I suppose," David said. "The Air Force's Space Command is the only government arm now that still does manned spaceflights, since NASA reoriented itself into a regulatory agency. I don't know what their capabilities are since all their space operations are classified, but I think Errol will go balls-up ballistic if we ever need to ask for their help."

"Well if that should happen then I'll need to find a new job if I ever get back to Earth," Stilicho said.

"If you do get back to Earth you'll get a complimentary, commemorative gold medal, courtesy of ACE Corp that says you went to Mars and back," David said. "We give out a bronze pin to those that complete the space training program, and a silver pin to those that made it to low Earth orbit. Tourists love them."

"Wonderful," Stilicho said. "Do I still get that medal if I die?"

"No," David said, winking. "You just get your name etched on the Mars Memorial in Washington DC, right beside the names of the dead people belonging to Mars First. Who knows, your name might even be placed right beside Silas Balsamic's."

Stilicho frowned. "Don't quit your day job."

Chapter 7

Less than forty-eight hours later, the *Duran Duran* lifted off from the Kennedy Space Center launchpad on Merrit Island. In addition to the crew there were ten passengers, along with extra cargo containers to fill out the interior. During the liftoff phase, all the passengers wore their skinsuits and helmets, before they gathered together at the transporter's escape module, located just below the crew cockpit. There they were strapped down on their accelerator couches and were plugged into an independent oxygen supply system. In the event of a critical emergency during launch, the entire nose of the ship could eject away from the stricken rocket via the use of explosive bolts, and could land back to Earth safely using retro thrusters and a parachute system. The crew was highly experienced and the automated launch protocols were followed to the letter. In the end, it was a successful launch and the passengers were escorted by the cabin crew to their respective staterooms once low Earth orbit was achieved.

Stilicho groaned slightly as he stayed wrapped up in his

bed. The sleeping bag that he was strapped into resembled a giant golf bag, and his head was sticking out in between the zipped up lining. He was nauseous, and it felt like his throat was connected directly to his stomach, ready to expel the last remaining contents still lodged precariously inside of it. Stilicho couldn't tell up from down, and all he could do was to stay still and close his eyes, but it didn't stop the lightheadedness. A used barf bag lay floating just a meter away near his face, and he was too weak to place it along the wall.

The stateroom door opened and a compact, dark-haired woman floated inside. She had a wide smile on her face. "Hello, Mr. Jones. My name is Asha, and I'm your personal spaceflight attendant. Mr. Flux has told me a lot about you and he says to take good care of you. So how are you feeling now?"

Stilicho wheezed. "What do you think? I feel … sick."

Asha kept smiling. She had been trained for situations like this. The attendant took the floating barf sack and placed it in a trash bag she had strapped by the side of her skinsuit. "Yes, you're having a bout of space adaptation syndrome, it's quite a common occurrence."

Stilicho closed his eyes and nodded slightly. "Yeah, SAS. So they tell me. Have you got something … to treat me with?"

"We have motion sickness-medications, but it's better that you work through it naturally," Asha said. "Because the side effects will make you drowsy, or worse. You ought to feel better in a day or two, if not sooner."

Stilicho sighed. "I ... don't think I can keep this up."

Asha giggled. "Sure you can, Mr. Jones. Just rest for now. I will be back later for your dinner. If you're feeling better by then you could actually go over to our restaurant, it's located just below this deck. Just go down through the central accessway, you can't miss it. We have custom-made salads, smoked salmon, fettuccine carbonara and beef burgundy for this dinner course. We usually serve the fresh produce right away in the first few days, so you don't want to miss that. There's cheesecake, fruit, gourmet cheeses, ice cream and hot baked brownies for dessert. If you want to order off the menu with items such as grilled hotdogs or a cheeseburger, we could accommodate you for sure."

Stilicho grimaced. "Please ... don't talk to me about food. It just makes me want to throw up more."

"Very well, sir," Asha said. "Oh, Captain Deladrier received a priority one message and told me to pass the good news on to you. It seems that Mr. Flux has personally directed the driveship from L-point two to head over here- at near low Earth orbit- and rendezvous with us. We should be matching heading and velocities soon. This means that we will be docking with them in the next few hours, and our travel time to Mars will be reduced by at least four days."

"That's the first good news I've heard since we lifted off," Stilicho said, his mood brightening. He pointed at the cabinets around the cabin. "Are any of those things actually real beds?"

"You're lying in your bed right now, Mr. Jones," Asha said.

"This isn't a cabin, it's a closet," Stilicho said. Talking to her was distracting him from his discomfort, so he kept at it. "And I feel like an old jacket just hanging on a peg."

Asha giggled again. "A true spaceship isn't like what you see on TV, Mr. Jones. In this ship, accessways go up and down, like an elevator in a building, not side to side corridors like in a sea-going vessel. That is why your bed is vertically positioned along the wall." She touched the side of one of the cabinets and it opened, revealing a virtual helmet. "We have full net coverage, and our entertainment system contains all the movies, music, literature and TV shows produced by the entire world for the past hundred and fifty years. I would suggest you not use the VR simulator until your bout of sickness has passed."

Stilicho took out a remote control unit that had been velcroed to the wall and activated the TV monitor located at the opposite side of the cabin. He began cycling through a few thousand channels. "Well, maybe this might not be so bad after all. I just need to stay pegged here and watch movies all day and night."

Asha pointed to a rectangular black box at the bottom end of the stateroom. "That is your personal exercise unit. Just plant your feet on the bottom and grip the handles. Bend down and pull yourself up and repeat. It's like doing squats back on Earth. We have more elaborate machines in the gym, which are two levels below your cabin. The security officers are currently hogging all the treadmills and gravity resistance machines, but with your VIP status I can definitely ask them to make room for you. If you want a more social form of exercise, a zero-gravity ball game is scheduled with the crew at the main common area a few hours after breakfast tomorrow, if you'd like to attend."

Stilicho shook his head. "I'm not really in the mood to exercise just yet."

Asha nodded. "Okay, we can wait until you're feeling better. But once you're up to it then you must exercise at least two hours every twenty-four hours. It is imperative that you do this, or you will lose muscle mass."

"Yeah, yeah," Stilicho said. "I've been told of this countless times already."

"I'm sorry for having to insist, but I will be checking on you every few hours," Asha said.

"Okay," Stilicho said. "Can I take off my diaper now?"

"I would suggest you keep it on even if you haven't used it," Asha said. "The toilet is three doors to your left or right once you come out of your room. It uses a vacuum to bring the waste products into its system, so it may be a bit uncomfortable at first. Just read the instructions before you use it."

Stilicho blinked. "So it doesn't use water?"

"That would be impractical with no gravity," Asha said. "The toilet papers are wet wipes, and you can flush them into the toilet after use since they are biodegradable as well."

"Wonderful," Stilicho said. "Since I'll be here for a month and a half, how about taking a bath?"

"Unfortunately we follow strict water rationing rules while in space," Asha said. "We have a special zero-g bathroom in which you can use a sponge bath while wearing your pressurized helmet, so that the loose water molecules don't enter your lungs. Once you are done, you can activate the vacuum seal to draw the floating droplets back to the draining walls. You won't be able to exit until that is done. You can only do this once a week. If you want to take more baths, you can use the liquid wipes."

"No windows to see out in space?"

Asha smirked. "There's an observation deck you can check out, but you won't be seeing much until we begin docking procedures with the driveship. The best time to be there is on our approach to Mars, and you can see the Red Planet in all its glory. You can also switch to channel one on your entertainment system and cycle through the cameras located outside of the ship. You can toggle settings like infrared mode or zoom in using the telescopic mode for a closer look. Those things give a much better view of the outside than a window ever could."

"Okay," Stilicho said. "When I'm feeling better, could I get a congratulatory drink?"

Asha shook her head. "If you mean an alcoholic drink then I'm afraid we don't have any available. Current NASA regulations state that no alcoholic beverages can be consumed during spaceflight. If you want water, fruit juice, coffee or a soda I can get you almost any brand you like. If you want something stronger, I can whip up a mean vanilla milkshake, which I'm sure will satisfy your cravings."

Stilicho bit his lip. It was about as bad as he expected. He was used to staying in luxury hotels while traveling, and this was shaping up to be an unpleasant experience so far. "Okay, I guess I don't have any other questions for now."

"One other thing," Asha said. "In the event of a solar flare, the alarm will sound. That gives you twenty minutes to stop whatever you're doing and head immediately to the escape module- same place where you strapped down during takeoff. It's the most heavily shielded part of the ship. Once the flare is over, you can go back to your activities. Cosmic radiation is a continuous bombardment, but the inner hull is constructed with hydrogenised, high-density plastic which stops most of it."

"Hookay, just another thing to worry about. Hopefully I can still have children after all this is over with."

Asha smiled again as she pointed to a nearby touch console. "I'm available on call. Just push that button. If I can't stop by, then another attendant will be with you shortly." With that, she turned around, opened the door behind her, and left the cabin.

Stilicho looked around. It seemed that the stateroom was completely sealed, and could function as a fully pressurized habitat in case the other compartments lost any atmosphere. The filtered air was dry, and he needed to unpack his small jar of petroleum jelly to coat the inside of his nose, otherwise he would be getting a sore throat soon enough. Another cabinet, just an arm's length away, contained a breathing helmet and life support backpack, ready to be used in case of an explosive decompression. He remembered all the things David Conklin had told him a few days earlier, and hoped that he wouldn't have to experience such an event.

After the second day, Stilicho felt well enough to go out of his cabin and explore the rest of the ship. For security reasons, only the crew was allowed in the cockpit, but he was able to have a meal at the restaurant with Captain Deladrier. Although the establishment had sit-down tables and a nice looking menu, the food that was served to him resembled a TV dinner, with trays velcroed onto the table. Stilicho was taught to use his knife to make an X-shaped incision on the plastic liner that covered the top of the dishes, to minimize runaway food particles in the microgravity environment. The meals were mostly pre-packaged but still somewhat tasty. When he ordered a steak, the meat was already pre-cut, though they managed to make it somewhat tender enough to be enjoyable. For obvious reasons, no crumbly or powdery food textures were ever served in space. Even the salt and pepper condiments were liquefied, and he needed to touch the tip of the squeeze bottle onto the surface of the food to get it to stick. When it came to drinks and soups, sipping through a straw was the way to go about it. There were clamps located near the tips of the straws, and he had to lock it in place in between sips, lest the liquid float out into the compartment. The metal utensils were magnetized, and could be placed onto the metal tables and would stay on it.

The eight security consultants mostly kept to themselves, so Stilicho didn't bother to hang around with them. The only other passenger was a woman, and she seemed a little snobbish when Stilicho gave her a greeting as they floated by each other along the main accessway one day, so he ignored her from then on. Asha was always friendly, and he learned that she was a former flight attendant in the airline industry. Only in her mid-twenties, Asha was ultimately qualified for astronaut training, so she jumped at the chance for a career that rewarded her with increased pay to start a fund for a college degree.

With his stomach finally adjusted to life in space, Stilicho settled back in his cabin after taking his first weekly bath. It had been several days since the transporter docked with the driveship, and the latter had engaged its powerful NERVA engines for the journey to the Red Planet. He had finally adjusted to the constant freefalling sensation, and Stilicho was starting to feel better about the whole thing. Now it was time to do a little work. He took out a small plug from the lining of his skinsuit and inserted it into the cabin's local internet port. In less than a second, Maia was online, speaking through the ear jack of his smartglasses.

The neutral, monotone voice was exactly the same as the last time he used it. "Hello, Stil. I must apologize once again for interrupting your auto-asphyxiation session. Please forgive me."

Stilicho shook his head. "Look, forget about that, okay? Just erase that incident from your history files."

"Done," Maia said. "What can I do for you today?"

"First off," Stilicho said. "Change your voice mode. Make it a woman's with a pleasing personality."

The voice changed into something sultry, slow and definitely feminine. "How does this sound, Stil?"

"Too sensuous," Stilicho said. "Ease up on that part."

The tone quickly became more businesslike. "How about now?"

"Better," Stilicho said. "Okay, have there been any updates on the growing Mars rumors on the net?"

"A number of conspiracy sites are saying that the Chinese have secretly declared war on ACE Corp, and they are planning to attack the colony directly. No credible proof of that line of thinking exists. The mainstream media sites are interviewing worried relatives of the advanced construction crew back on Earth, since their personal com-links were silenced after the virus attacks. Errol's only official comment was that there was a temporary communications problem, and an update will be forthcoming in a few weeks time. Company PR is doing its best to deny any conflicts with China and is busy quashing rumors about a Martian plague. In fact the Chinese secretly proposed to send a rescue team over to Chryse Planitia the moment they heard of the problems, but Errol declined the offer. Based on our satellite flybys, the Chinese are hunkering down in their colony until more information comes out," Maia said. The advanced AI architecture enabled it to access and disseminate all the incoming news reports on the net in less than a second.

Stilicho bit his lip. There would be no time for any fun the moment he landed on Mars. His boss needed answers right away. "How many people are on Eridu Colony as of right now?"

"Excluding the twelve that are missing, there are five thousand, one hundred and twenty-six men and women in the colony," Maia said.

"Out of those, how many are security personnel?"

"Twenty-eight at present."

Stilicho rubbed his lips with his finger. He couldn't deploy the entire security department out to the construction site in

Chryse Planitia- it would have to be a small team. Himself, an engineer or two, a medic, and the rest would be security officers. "Can you access the inventory for any armaments in the colony?"

"Yes, Errol has allowed me full access to all corporate databases," Maia said. "There are fifty handguns with an average of sixty rounds each. Twenty semi-automatic rifles with an average ammunition count of ninety rounds each. Forty-eight stun guns and one hundred ninety-eight tear gas defensive sprays are accounted for. The rescue team took two stun guns and two tear gas sprays with them."

"So they didn't take any real guns, then," Stilicho said.

"That is correct."

"Okay," he said. "I'm assuming that the eight consultants that are on this flight will be augmenting the total complement in Eridu Colony. I'll need to assemble a security team to act as bodyguards when I head over to the site, any ideas?"

"There will be pros and cons," Maia said. "The security personnel that are already in Eridu have the experience of being on the planet for a number of years, and so they would have knowledge of EVA operations as well as the terrain. The advantage of the reinforcements that are traveling with you is that they are all ex-military special forces, with extensive combat experience, and they have less muscular atrophy due to having just come from Earth."

Stilicho smiled. "Good old Errol, he figured that if there's gonna be a fight, then hire the best. What's the background of the security officers currently in Eridu? None of them have any military experience?"

"Out of the twenty-eight currently on Mars, there are six," Maia said. "But their average age is forty-four, and none of them served in special forces. The others are ex-law enforcement officers, and none of them have SWAT team experience."

Stilicho nodded. The current compliment of security personnel were geared towards a law enforcement focus; investigating and preventing crime in the colony were their goals. "Okay, so maybe we could use a mix. Bring along an old security guy from the colony with us to have some experience, and the rest will be in the group that's traveling with me. Who's the best candidate to lead the security contingent?"

"Based on my analysis, the best candidate is on this flight. Matthew Trevanian, goes by Matt or Trev," Maia said. "Age forty-one. Former US Navy SEAL, he joined Darkwater LLC after his honorable discharge. According to classified records, he achieved the rank of master sergeant, and was awarded the Silver Star medal for his actions in the Spratlys Conflict. Also underwent training in microgravity combat."

"Darkwater? I'm not familiar with that company."

"A private military company that provided contractors for both corporations and numerous government agencies. They became infamous for a shootout that killed and wounded hundreds of civilians during the Second Belarus War," Maia said. "After the congressional investigation that went nowhere, they later changed their corporate name to Spartan Reactions Limited."

"Oh yeah, now I know who they are," Stilicho said. "I thought only Air Force space troopers were trained in microgravity combat and all that."

"In the past twelve years, US Navy Seals have begun to incorporate space combat training as part of their curriculum as well," Maia said. "It seems that the Navy brass was jealous that the Air Force had a monopoly on all military aerospace operations, so they quickly implemented a program that would enable their own personnel to be deployed in these operations too. The Army and the Marines are also trying to start up their own program, but the Air Force is predictably fighting them tooth and nail in order to be the only branch of the military to have that capability."

"Typical government types, they so love their monopolies," Stilicho said. "I'm assuming this Trevanian guy is also the team leader of this group?"

"Yes he is," Maia said. "The others have high respect for him, so that's why he would be my candidate to lead your security contingent."

"Okay, I'll go with your assessment," Stilicho said. "What about the frigid chick that's on this flight with me, what's her story?"

"She is NASA Special Agent Darian Arante," Maia said. "Age thirty-two. Has been with the agency for ten years since her graduation from college. Her assessment reports are good, though nothing spectacular. Never married, no current relationship. Based on her psychological profile, it seems that she is completely dedicated to her job."

Stilicho raised an eyebrow. "A NASA special agent?

What's she doing here? Did Errol tell NASA what had happened?"

"I can find no records of Errol making a report of the recent problems to his NASA liaison," Maia said. "Miss Arante uses a government virtual private network when sending out her emails, so I am not sure as to what her intentions are. The only correspondence I can access from ACE Corp is a demand from NASA that she be included on this flight, and that suitable accommodations be reserved for her when she gets to the Martian surface."

"Can you hack into it?"

"I could," Maia said. "But please be aware that if I do, it would be considered a federal offense, Stil."

"Do it anyway," Stilicho said. The stakes were too high for him not to know. "Send an email to Errol too, ask him if he knows anything about it."

Maia paused for a minute. "One moment … email sent. Password cracked. It seems she used a very basic code to access her account. Her net search history is not encrypted so it makes for a very interesting set of subjects that she is accessing."

"Well, now that you have everything, please enlighten me," Stilicho said.

"A lot of her web searches and correspondence to her superior concerns my creator, Karl Rossum," Maia said.

"What?"

"As you well know, Karl completed my architecture and algorithm just before he disappeared," Maia said. "Karl turned over my program to Errol as his parting gift, who then modified it and as you can see, I am the final product."

"Right, I already know that part," Stilicho said. "Why is she coming to Mars?"

"Based on the updates to her superior, it seems that she is convinced that Karl Rossum came to Mars soon after his disappearance on Earth," Maia said.

"What? Are you kidding me? Karl Rossum is so well known that everybody would have found out if that had happened," Stilicho said. "It's an insane theory. Why would she think that?"

"She apparently listened to a two-year old audio recording that was found in Karl's workshop," Maia said. "The voice on the recording is that of Karl's son Joseph. Joseph apparently pleaded with his father to come and rescue him."

"This is getting weird," Stilicho said. "Did you say two years ago? Does that date coincide with the previous synodic transfer period?"

"Apparently it does," Maia said. "The transfer orbital period would have given Karl Rossum a perfect opportunity to leave Earth in disguise, and make his way to Mars."

Stilicho shook his head. "Blasted Chinese. Send an email update to Errol, tell him that the Chinese might have smuggled Karl into Mars during the last transfer orbit."

"Update sent," Maia said. "Though I think you are missing the obvious here."

"What do you mean?"

"Errol and Karl are like brothers," Maia said. "They knew and trusted each other for decades when they started up Flux Motors."

Stilicho scowled. It was Errol. He was the one who sneaked Karl over to Mars. "Check the passenger lists of all ACE employees as well as tourists that flew to Mars two years ago. Crosscheck with Karl Rossum's biometrics, as well as anyone who isn't accounted for."

"One moment," Maia said. "One name stands out. Oliver Dodd. The birthdate on his passport is the same birthdate of a child that died in infancy. He was listed as a replacement employee in the communications department of the colony, but present shift logs show that he has never worked there. The picture on his passport is a near biometric match with Karl using facial recognition. I am accessing a vehicle inventory checklist- it seems that one rover was taken in for maintenance and never brought back to full operational capacity. Looking at the rover logs that particular vehicle should still be in the colony hangar bay, but it is not there."

Stilicho frowned and leaned back along the wall of his cabin. So Errol must have gotten him onboard one of the Martian flights as an employee, and given him a rover to search for his son. He stayed silent for nearly ten minutes.

"I've got an email reply for you- from Errol," Maia said. "It's in full video."

Stilicho sighed as he looked up at the wall mounted monitor. "Play it."

Errol's face came to life on the screen. "Hey, buddy. I hope you're enjoying your flight. Yeah, I've got a confession to make. Two years ago, Karl came to see me in private. He looked like hell and I could tell something was bothering him. Karl told me he got a message from his son through the Mars relay, telling him to go to over there and find him. I thought he had gone nuts, and I did everything I could to discourage him from going, but in the end, he was my dear friend. So I set him up with a new identity, and gave him one of the rovers- then I erased his name on the logs because that's what he wanted. In return, he gave me Maia and the keys to his own company. There was no way his son would still be alive, and maybe … maybe he knew it too, but I guess he wanted to find the body just to be sure. So I let him go. He's probably dead out there somewhere. I think he knew that anyway. Well, that's it. I'm sorry I never told you about this, but I figured it was a completely separate issue to the problem we got now. I thought it would be okay until NASA started calling me and demanding I put one of their field agents up on that flight with you. I know this puts another brick up your butt, but if you could do your magic, I'll have a big bonus for you when you come back. As always, if you need anything, feel free to email me again. Take care, Stil. Bye for now."

Stilicho bit his lip. "Jesus H Christ."

Maia lowered its voice to indicate concern. "What will you do now, Stil?"

Stilicho looked at his watch. "Go eat lunch, that's what."

Chapter 8

Darian double-checked the seat restraints to make sure she was strapped tightly to the crash chair. The escape module was constructed to hold two hundred people, but there were only a total of ten of them, so there were plenty of empty seats. The eight security consultants who had been traveling with her for the past month sat near the sealed outer doors, ready to leap into action in case of a malfunction during reentry. The remaining male passenger was sitting at the opposite side of her, as they both chose seats near the central accessway. The module had a circular layout, with their padded crash chairs facing upwards to the ceiling. Darian had been studying the personnel files of the other passengers for some time, and she was somewhat surprised to find Errol Flux's personal envoy to be present in the same ship. She had surmised that the rumors of disruptions along the Mars net relay were true, and it was probably such an acute problem that the head of ACE Corp would send in his most trusted subordinate to fly to Mars, despite having never been to space.

Captain Deladrier's voice was calm. "Attention. We are about to begin entry into the Martian atmosphere. Please stay in your seats and prepare for high-g acceleration."

Darian's smartglass readout in her helmet visor was linked directly with the ship's sensors. It indicated that the *Duran Duran* had already detached from the orbiting driveship over two hours ago and they were about to enter the upper layers of the Marian atmosphere. Although landings like these had become routine over the last twenty years, there was still a tremendous amount of danger when it came to setting down on the Red Planet. During the early days of Martian exploration the Soviets had no less than nine failures to try to get at Mars, before their tenth mission finally succeeded in just getting into orbit, much less land on the surface. The thin atmosphere meant that ships would be entering the Martian atmosphere at hypersonic speed if they didn't have parachutes to slow their descent, and quite a number of unmanned landers in the past ended up as nothing more than bits and pieces on the ground.

"Acceleration. Stand by," Captain Deladrier said over the intercom.

Almost immediately, the room began to shake. At first it seemed to be nothing more than a slight, droning vibration, but Darian knew the worst was yet to come. Less than ten seconds later, the shaking became even more pronounced, and her world began to spin. Darian had undergone high-g training years before, at NASA's new training facilities in Texas. Every astronaut candidate had to strap themselves onto a massive centrifuge that spun them around a circular room, and a quarter of them had dropped out during training because they could not withstand the high-g forces that they were subjected to. The liftoff from Earth had been bad enough, but this time the reddish tinge in her vision meant that there was an excess of blood flow to her eyes and brain. It was an indication of negative g-forces, because the ship was accelerating downwards faster than the rate of natural freefall.

The live updates on her readouts indicated that the transporter now had a speed of Mach-25 as it entered the Martian atmosphere. Older spacecraft used parachutes to slow their descent, but the *Duran Duran* was using an aerobraking maneuver, flying sideways and using its hull to slow its plunge. Darian was now being suspended almost upside down as the room had tilted over to its side, the intense vibrations made it feel like the walls around her would suddenly rip open, and hurl her helplessly outside, into the thin upper atmosphere. The disorientation was total, and Darian actually closed her eyes and clenched her teeth. During astronaut training at NASA, she had been given a boxer's mouthpiece to wear, so that she wouldn't bite her tongue off. Darian actually brought her old mouthpiece with her, and she had placed it over her teeth, just before donning the helmet. With the exposed terror of finality coursing through her body, Darian bit down hard on the mouthpiece, hoping and praying that things would somehow turn alright.

After a long minute of near-panic, the room began to tilt once more, bringing the module back to its original angle.

She could hear the roar of the thrusters underneath her as the ship had gone fully vertical again. Despite a huge sense of relief washing over her senses, Darian knew the danger wasn't over yet; if the engines had fired too late or too soon, there was still a chance they would crash onto the landing pad. If any of the engines gave out, there was a danger of the ship tilting over even if it landed on the pad, with the possibility of dying in a massive fireball the moment the ship broke apart on the ground.

Captain Deladrier's voice was heard once more, like a mother soothing her terrified child. "Landing struts deployed."

The vibrations gradually began to die down as Darian felt the ship land on solid ground. There was still the danger of any of the three landing struts giving way, and it would still topple the ship sideways, but as the seconds ticked by and the angle of the room didn't change, then it was clear that it had been a perfect landing. Only when she heard the engines being shut down did Darian finally open her eyes and let out a muffled sigh of relief.

"Mr. Jones, you can wake up now," a warm, calming voice said.

Stilicho slowly opened his eyes. He was still strapped to the chair while Asha stood over him. "What happened?" he said.

Asha smiled. She had taken her helmet off and her long hair was finally drooping over her shoulders, instead of floating around the back of her head while in space. "You passed out during the Martian atmospheric entry. But that's okay, it's a common occurrence."

Stilicho gulped as he began to unfasten the straps to the chair. His voice was hoarse, and he felt a weight on his chest. Gravity felt like a long lost friend who had returned, and was now giving him a suffocating bear hug. "Okay."

Asha helped him take off the last of the restraints. "We've touched down safely at the International Colony of Hellas Planitia- otherwise known as Eridu. Welcome to Mars."

Stilicho stumbled forward for a bit as the carry bag he had slung over his shoulder made him unbalanced. Four and a half weeks in space gave him a wobbly gait, even in the low Martian gravity. Asha had told him it would take a few days for his body to adjust, and he was cautioned to take things easy for now. His main luggage was being unloaded and delivered to his suite at the hotel, but he had insisted on bringing his carrying bag with him. He could barely feel his legs, but Stilicho knew that he needed to get stronger quickly, since there was plenty of work to be done. Looking at his watch, he could see that Errol had scheduled him to meet with the colony director later that afternoon.

He was now teetering slowly along the transit tunnel that led towards the passport control section. The other passengers had already disembarked ahead of him and Stilicho was alone. TV screens along the walls sent back vivid commercials of life on Mars, and the many amenities that tourists could avail of. Stilicho nearly spat out a glob of saliva in contempt. He felt like a decrepit old man that had just woken up from a thirty-year coma.

A uniformed attendant stood by the side of the

concourse. He was young, tall and lanky, with an ACE Corp baseball cap at the top of his head. "Do you need any help, sir?"

Stilicho shook his head while shuffling past him. "I think I can manage, thanks."

Right after he said those words, Stilicho's knees started to buckle. He fell forward, his hands extending outwards to cushion his fall. The attendant quickly reacted as he grabbed Stilicho's arms to stop him from face-planting onto the ground. "Easy there, Mr. Jones," the attendant said. "I can have them bring over an electric cart for you."

Stilicho sighed as he slumped onto the side of the passageway. "Goddamn it."

In less than a minute, a white-colored golf cart drove into the wide passageway. Sitting behind the wheel was Edgar Roth, the colony director. He stopped a few meters away from Stilicho and got out, extending his hand. "Stil, long time no see, ol' buddy. How long has it been?"

Stilicho willed himself to stand fully upright as he shook the man's hand. "Not sure, six or seven years, maybe?"

Edgar nodded. He wore thick glasses and had a bald spot at the top of his head. He was one of the shorter male senior officers of the company, his forehead barely reaching Stilicho's shoulders. "Well, it's great to see you again. Hop on board!"

The attendant helped Stilicho over to the front seat and placed his bag at the back of the cart. "Take care, sir, your other luggage has been sent to the Barsoom Hotel."

Stilicho nodded. "Thanks."

Edgar got back behind the wheel, turned the cart around, and stepped on the accelerator. "Don't worry about your legs, you'll be back to normal in about a day or two. Spaceflight takes a toll on one's body, and you'll need some time to adjust. Martian gravity is about a third that of Earth's so you'll have an easier time here."

"That's good to know," Stilicho said. "I was supposed to meet you officially later this afternoon, but would you mind if we get started right away?"

"No problem, Stil," Edgar said. "With the situation not getting any better, I've decided to devote my whole day over to you. We need to fix this issue, and as soon as possible. Shall we head to my office?"

"I was hoping we could get something to eat first," Stilicho said. "I'm craving for some real food."

"You bet!" Edgar turned the wheel and the cart made a sharp turn into an adjoining corridor, completely bypassing passport control. A few staff members noticed them, but quickly waved them through an employee access corridor with hardly a protest. Stilicho was supposed to go through a mandatory physical examination right after being cleared through passport control, but being Errol Flux's right hand man did have its privileges.

Within a few minutes they were driving along the main concourse. Eridu Colony was shaped like a Celtic cross- the bottom length held most of the farming units, while the three other lines had a mixture of laboratories, workshops and residential habitats. The ring that encircled the other parts of the colony served as the commercial and administrative hub of the place, while the central axis point led to the nuclear power plant. Stilicho could see that it was mostly uniformed staff making their way along the nearby walkways. The tourists were still several days behind. Errol had given last minute instructions for the incoming fleet to remain in orbit even after they had arrived, just in case of a possible evacuation.

Edgar stopped the cart as they faced the entrance to the Barsoom Hotel. "Do you want to freshen up first?"

Stilicho shook his head. "Nah, let's just grab a bite to eat. How's the hotel restaurant in this one?"

"The other one's better, it's just on the other side though," Edgar said.

"Let's go to that one, then."

Edgar pushed on the accelerator again. "You got it."

Stilicho rubbed his legs. "I can feel my strength returning."

"That's good," Edgar said. "We normally have a fleet of these carts at the arrivals terminal, since quite a number of tourists get wobbly legs the moment they land. Tourists are pretty fickle. About ten percent of them want to go back home the moment they reach low-Earth orbit, so we drop them off at the space station and refund half their money back. By the time they get over here, there's no turning back, so the rest try to stoically endure the rest of their trip. The reason why we get so little repeat tourism is not the colony's fault, it's getting to and from here. The constant stresses of takeoffs and landings takes their toll, and if we include the uncomfortable time spent in microgravity, then you just get a rolling set of circumstances that doesn't work in our favor.

Even the tourists that we bring over have to achieve a certain level of fitness just to go up into at the space in the first place and they can't bring any kids, so it's not the ideal market for everybody."

"Well if it's important for Errol, then you know the colony's survival is at stake," Stilicho said.

Edgar nodded, as he maneuvered around a maintenance crew doing minor repairs on the roadway. He pointed to an adjoining tunnel. "Over there is the corridor leading towards the farming units. We're pretty much self-sufficient when it comes to growing veggies out here. Lettuce, cabbage, soybeans and spinach take up most of the hydroponics area when it comes to the green, leafy variety. Root veggies like potatoes, carrots and onions grow too, but we have to double the amount of time that we spend monitoring them. I've asked Errol if we could just leech out the perchlorates from the Martian soil and grow them with it, but he's afraid of the local bacteria out here. We need to do more tests before proceeding on that end."

Stilicho turned to look at him. "I told Errol that maybe it's some kind of Martian virus that took out the outpost and the rescue team. You're not afraid of that?"

Edgar shook his head. "It's a crap theory. There's been Martian rocks that have landed on Earth over billions of years. Pathogens that are dangerous to humans on Earth have been trying for millions of years to get into our bodies. Martian bacteria are very similar to Earth bacteria and there's even a plausible theory that life in fact, originated on Mars and was transferred to Earth. This planet has no plant or animal life for a possible Martian pathogen to infect. It's like a mango tree getting chicken pox- nothing evolved out here that would be dangerous to us because we haven't been on this planet for very long."

"Or so you say," Stilicho said.

Edgar stopped in front of another hotel. Unlike the previous one they had just come from, this one had a space-age theme. "Welcome to the Rocket Hotel. Their restaurant is like a diner, but they serve a pretty damned good breakfast here."

Stilicho's legs felt better as they strode through the lobby and into the adjoining coffee-shop. Padded red leather booths, along with metal tables and art deco influences greeted them. A waitress wearing a starched teal uniform with a matching cap seated them at a nearby booth with a smile.

Stilicho scanned the menu before looking up at the eager waitress. "Can I get an American breakfast platter with real eggs?"

The nametag on the waitress's uniform said Marie on it. "You sure can," she said. "We got our first batch of eggs this year, courtesy of the very ship you came in with."

"Make that two: eggs over easy for me," Edgar said. "And some fresh-brewed coffee, please."

"I'll take mine sunny side up. And some extra pancakes for me, please," Stilicho said.

"Coming right up," Marie said, before she turned around and headed over to the kitchen.

Stilicho placed his elbows on the table and leaned forward. "Okay, if it isn't a pathogen, do you think the Chinese are behind it?"

Edgar shook his head. "I doubt it. Even though we had a brief conflict in the Pacific a few years back, both sides don't want to start anything out here. Ba-Dian Colony in Gale Crater is too busy trying to sort itself out to start something like this. I'm not buying it."

"But they're the only ones who would have the capability to take out both teams, right? I mean, the Russians are long gone, as Errol told me."

"We have a small Russian contingent of scientists here on an exchange program, and I have no doubt that some of them are FSB agents," Edgar said. "But I just can't conceive of a reason why they would attempt something like this either, it's got to be something else. Just what that something else is, I just don't know."

Stilicho touched the frame of his smartglasses to activate it. "Okay, I'll be sending to you the names on the team that I want. I also requested Errol to give me some rovers. I'll be heading out there myself to find out what's going on."

Edgar tapped the frame of his own smartglasses as the memo appeared in the lenses. "I'm checking the transporter's manifest now. Looks like Errol brought enough parts to assemble two new rovers. Thank god for that."

"How many rovers did the advanced construction team have with them?"

"Two for a standard six-man crew," Edgar said. "The rescue team also had two rovers when they set out for the outpost. So that's four rovers missing and unaccounted for. It's a huge blow to our long-range land transportation capabilities."

"Did you try and get any drones into the area?"

"Every time we try to send an aerial drone into Chryse Planitia, we lose contact with it," Edgar said. "Our satellites encounter some sort of interference when we program them to take pictures of the area, it's as if something doesn't want us to know what's going on out there."

"There's another rover that's missing," Stilicho said as he sent over the unedited, master inventory list that he got from Errol over to Edgar's smartglass. "This one was deliberate."

Edgar's eyes opened wide. "Holy cow. I was never told of this!"

"Neither was I until I was already in transit," Stilicho said. "Seems Errol did a favor for a trusted friend of his, and this complicates matters a whole lot."

The waitress arrived with plates of food. The two men instantly became quiet and waited until she left the side of the table. Stilicho was hungry and he ate with unexpected gusto. After a few minutes, the dirty plates were taken away and all that remained on the table were two cups of brewed coffee, the aromatic steam from the beverage rising slowly between them. Sugar and spices would be coming in the next ship, so they had to make do with artificial sweeteners in the meantime.

"I met Karl only once," Edgar said softly. "At a party over at Errol's house, like twenty odd years ago. Strange guy- mostly kept to himself. I hardly even knew he was there."

"I met him twice," Stilicho said. "Once at a press release, and the other time at a shareholder's conference. Shook his hand when Errol introduced us, but I never got to know him."

Edgar made a low whistle. "To think he was right here all this time gives me the shivers. For him to go out there with no one but Errol knowing … why didn't he ask for help from us?"

Stilicho shrugged. "Beats me. Errol thinks he came out here to die and be with his son."

"I remember those Mars First lunatics," Edgar said. "I was just a young administrator when I first came here, and I had to do the paperwork for their evacuation. They had started with a hundred twenty members in their own colony, and in the end only slightly more than half of them survived."

"You ever met their leader, Silas Balsamic?"

"They were all nuts, but he was the nuttiest one of them all," Edgar said. "He was brought in for processing before they put him on the rocket back to Earth, and he didn't want to go, so they had him in restraints. He was sitting at the same distance from me as you are right now. I was asking him a few questions and he just looked at me as if I was some sort of fly under a microscope. I still get nightmares about it."

"None of them ever mentioned anything about Karl's son?"

Edgar looked up, as if lost in thought. "Yeah, there was a young girl who I think was his wife or girlfriend or something. Forgot her name. She was in hysterics. They ended up having to dope her too, I think."

Stilicho downed the remaining drops of coffee in his cup. "Do you think there's a chance that Karl's son might still be alive?"

Edgar shook his head. "No way. How long has it been? Fifteen years? Even if his son had the entire colony to himself, he would need lots of spare parts to repair the life support, much less grow his food. Things break down all the time, that's the reason why nearly half of Eridu's population are engineers. Our repair and maintenance crews have a full time job just to keep everything in working order here."

"But the reason why Karl decided to come to Mars was because he heard his son's voice on an email sent from here," Stilicho said. "That was two years ago. So who sent the audio file from Mars? Maybe the Chinese lured him out here to kidnap him?"

"Well that's a possibility I guess, even though I don't know why the Chinese would want him," Edgar said. "Please remember we won't be able to do anything about it unless you make all this public."

"That's going to be tricky," Stilicho said. "I'll send an email to Errol and ask him if we could do that."

"The problem with doing it that way is you'll have to make Errol publicly admit that he smuggled someone over here, right underneath NASA's noses," Edgar said. "That will not sit well with the government."

Stilicho frowned. NASA had a tremendous hold over the company since they were the governing body that issued licenses to launch rockets and build bases on other planets. "You're right. Goddammit, what in the hell do we do?

"Here's what I suggest," Edgar said. "Let me send a private inquiry to the Chinese. I'm in regular contact with my counterpart at Ba-Dian Colony, and if I let him know that we are actively searching for Karl, perhaps they might just hand him over to us, assuming he is with them."

"Okay," Stilicho said. "That sounds like a better idea. I'll support you on that suggestion. But we got another big problem to deal with."

Edgar's straightened his back. "Oh, what's that?"

"NASA knows about Karl being sent here," Stilicho said softly.

Edgar grimaced, just before he put his head down. "Crap. We're screwed."

"I think I can still do some damage control over this whole mess," Stilicho said. "Let me think of a solution."

"NASA could come down hard on us, just for that," Edgar said. "And with the missing outpost crew, this whole crapstorm just got even worse."

"Who's the NASA administrator here?"

"Mary Davis," Edgar said. "We get along fine, and she mostly stays out of our way. But who knows how she'll react when she gets a whiff of this."

"Let me worry about NASA," Stilicho said. "You just need to get those rovers assembled so I can take my team out there."

"Okay," Edgar said. "I know you get things done, and Errol wouldn't have sent you out here if he didn't have faith in you."

"Thanks," Stilicho said. "I've got a question for you."

"Shoot."

"Why is this place called Eridu anyway?"

Edgar tapped his fingers on the metal table. "Since we're

located in between two valleys that were once river outflows, the original proposed landing site for this place was nicknamed Mesopotamia, which is Greek for the 'land between two rivers.' Mesopotamia was the area where Earth's first cities were built- the dawn of civilization, so to speak. The people of the area were called the Sumerians, and according to them, their first city was called Eridu. So when the name was proposed, Errol approved it. I think it's a fitting name for the first city on Mars."

"A more fitting name ought to be Purgatory," Stilicho muttered.

Chapter 9

Back in his suite, Stilicho was finally able to take a real shower for the first time in weeks. Eridu Colony had plenty of water, since there were massive glaciers of frozen ice just sitting outside, ready to be extracted and used. After getting a full rubdown at the hotel's massage parlor, he decided to get some exercise by strolling out on the streets for a little while before meeting Edgar again for lunch and a brief tour. The vehicle crews were working round the clock to assemble the new rovers that had been shipped over from the transporter, and Edgar had guaranteed that they would be ready to go by tomorrow morning.

Lunch was fresh salads and stir-fried vegetables, along with stone-grilled tilapia and catfish from the aquaponics area, their crispy skin drizzled with Martian rock salt. They finished it off with some rice pudding that seemed pedestrian compared to the entrees. By early afternoon they decided to drive over to the greenhouses in order to see just how self-sufficient the colony was.

Edgar parked the electric cart near the entrance. "So, how

did you like the taste of our local cuisine here?"

Stilicho rubbed his tongue on the roof of his mouth. "I can still taste the rice pudding we ate."

Edgar chuckled and gave him a playful slap on the back. "Sorry about that, we're still trying to get the desserts to taste right. Vat grown rice has a slightly different consistency and flavor. The lack of natural sugar and milk also plays a part since we have to synthesize our sweeteners and creamers. Perhaps in another few years we'll come up with something better."

Stilicho followed him as they both strode through the entrance. "This is my first, and hopefully last time on the Red Planet."

Edgar snorted. "Hate it already, do you?"

"Ever heard of landlubbers? Well I'm an earthlubber," Stilicho said. "I'm perfectly fine being on Earth and nowhere else."

"You and your prejudices," Edgar said.

After strolling through the reception area, they were met by a tall woman wearing a white lab smock. Dr. Verna Fisher was the farming director, and she knew Stilicho well enough to stride forward and give him a big hug. "Stil! When I heard the news you were coming over I was jumping out of my socks," she said.

Stilicho smiled. "How you doing, Verna?"

Edgar had an amused look on his face. "You two know each other?"

"I've known Stilicho since we went to college together," Verna said. "We both started out as interns at ACE, then he got a promotion!"

"Trust me, if you knew the work I have to do for Errol, you wouldn't be so jealous," Stilicho said.

"Well, I think we both got what we wanted. You got your dream job and I got mine," Verna said.

Stilicho pulled out a large, red-tinted plastic bottle from the bag he was carrying and gave it to her. "I got something else you wanted."

Verna beamed as she held the bottle in her hands. "Oh my god, sriracha sauce! Stil, I love you and I'll never forget this gift!"

Edgar couldn't help but laugh. Spices of all kinds were worth their weight in gold here. The colony psychologists had to deal with cases of staff depression due to the fact that mundane items like peppers and chocolate were in such short supply. Rumors were rampant that someone had stashed away boxes of candy bars and hot sauces, and these stories refused to die down, despite official denials.

"I knew you'd like that," Stilicho said. Looking around, he could see that the massive passageway was built like a subway tunnel, with separate glass greenhouse modules situated along the sides of the underground channel that extended for two kilometers. Soft classical tunes were being piped through the intercom system, for Verna believed music helped to stimulate plant growth.

Verna placed the bottle in a large pocket beneath the folds of her lab smock. "I'd better hide this. If the others find out I've got hot chili sauce right on the first transport, they would kill me."

Stilicho chuckled. "So how's life out here?"

"Can't complain since I'm now the chief agronomist in the colony," Verna said. "I've always wanted to stay on Mars, so I'm living the dream. What do you think of it so far?"

"Well, I had fresh fish for lunch, which was a surprise," Stilicho said. "It's not luxury, but it ain't bad either. So tell me about this place."

Verna pointed at the interior of a nearby greenhouse. The plant bed was situated up high, close to the heat lamps. The massive tanks containing the fish were located just below it. "The aquaponics we've set up is a completely closed system. We've combined the growing of plants, and their waste products are transferred to the bottom tank, where the fish live. The fish feed on the plant material and their poop is filtered back up to the hydroponics section, which fertilizes the plants growing there. I've petitioned Errol to see if we would bring some clams and even prawns over from Earth for a saltwater version, but so far they ended up dead in transit. We'll try again in another couple of years."

"So you're mostly pescetarians, unless it's tourist season," Stilicho said.

Verna nodded. "Assuming we even find a way to safely transport one, a cow needs a lot of grazing land just to be raised properly, so it's just not feasible. We tried transporting chickens a few times, but they all died in transit. Fertilized eggs that are ready to hatch can only be transportable for three weeks at the most, and the ones we tried to bring over didn't seem to develop in microgravity. Fish eggs weren't too much of a problem since it was just a matter of getting them to the right temperature to initiate hatching. If we ever build large scale fish tanks, I'd love to try and bring Atlantic salmon here."

"I just can't live without a good steak at least once a week," Stilicho said. "I did have a long hot shower though, at least you got that in your favor."

"Oh yeah," Edgar said. "Errol chose a very good landing site. Down here we're surrounded by glaciers of ice that we can just pick from the ground. The Chinese up in Gale Crater have to spend a lot of energy extracting their water from the hydrated soil because there aren't any glaciers where they're at."

"Yup, water is life and if you have to spend a lot of energy getting it, it hampers your growth," Verna said. "I even heard that they're raising insects and spirulina algae for food up there because their aquaponics system is so bad."

"If it's that hard over there, then why did the Chinese choose Gale Crater for their colony site?" Stilicho asked.

"Gale Crater is simply the one place on Mars in which everyone was most familiar with during the early years," Edgar said. "NASA had a rover mission there and it was a thoroughly studied area. The Chinese didn't want any surprises when they decided to start up their colony, so that's why they chose it. ACE was the first to explore the Hellas Basin, and Errol staked the entire company on this site, and the risk worked out in the end. We're the oldest and largest colony on the Red Planet. The Chinese have got less than half our population and they're always in the red."

"Now that I think about, the tourist amenities aren't too bad here," Stilicho said. "Pity it sort of goes dead during the off-peak seasons."

Edgar winked at him. "You haven't seen our indoor swimming pools yet, have you?"

Stilicho was in shock. "You guys actually have swimming pools here?"

Verna giggled. "Oh yeah, we have two Olympic-sized pools at the lower levels. Most of the staff loves to go there after working hours for fun and exercise."

"There's tennis and volleyball courts too, but the games are played a little differently since we can jump a little higher here," Edgar said.

"That's just amazing," Stilicho said. "What about tours?"

"Oh we got it all here," Edgar said. "We do rover tours with small groups around the basin. We also do EVA suit excursions just outside of the colony- but heavily supervised, mind you. We have a golf course under proposal, as well as outdoor Martian polo using robotic horses, but I doubt those will come to fruition unless we get more tourists over here."

Stilicho nodded. He remembered the history lessons at school during the early days of the Martian colonies. The original euphoria of being able to travel to the Red Planet gradually died down over the years when it all became too routine, and the tourism market eventually plateaued. "We have to make it easier for people to get here," he said.

"Yes, most of the tourists that come over here now are the ones who think of it as a badge of honor, something to do before you die," Verna said. "Quite a lot of our company recruits came as interns or tourists, and they enrolled in our apprenticeship programs and eventually grew to like it. We offer that to any tourist that comes here. They can get firsthand knowledge on how things work by helping us out."

Stilicho pointed at the plants growing nearby. "So no plans of putting up a pepper farm?"

Verna laughed. "I have petitioned Errol for that very thing for many years now, but our main crops are still the priority. People here would kill for spices. I know a few guys and gals that have private pots of pepper plants in their quarters. It kind of reminds me as to why people like Magellan and Columbus set out to find the Spice Islands, because Europe was so desperate for new tastes."

"Spice Trade part two, eh? Seems like history repeating itself," Stilicho said.

"We're getting close to a breakthrough with cultured meat," Verna said. "You know, the meat that we can grow in the lab. Right now the main issue is synthesizing enough of them to grow large batches quickly, but we need to work on tissue engineering to make the muscle cells divide faster. If our colleagues back on Earth could perfect a bioreactor, it ought to solve our perpetual meat shortages out here."

"Artificial meat? Eew," Stilicho said. "No thanks. You can have Mars, Verna."

Verna giggled again. "I have a feeling you won't last long in a survival situation."

Edgar looked away. He was reading an email he had just received on his smartglass. After a minute he glanced over at Stilicho. "Just got an email from our NASA administrator, asking for an urgent, personal meeting tomorrow."

Stilicho straightened the collar of his shirt. "Tell her you can meet right now. I'll be right by your side."

Edgar sat in the meeting room alongside Stilicho. The door at the side of the room opened and Darian stepped inside, followed closely by the colony's NASA representative, Mary Davis. Darian made a brief glance at Stilicho before going over to a nearby chair and sitting down on it. Mary sat right beside her as she adjusted the smartglasses on her cheeks. The sliding door automatically closed behind them.

Edgar smiled to break the ice. "Okay, let's get some introductions going. I'm Dr. Edgar Roth, colony director." He pointed to Stilicho. "This is Stilicho Jones, consultant for ACE Corp."

"Dr. Mary Davis, NASA administrative representative for this colony," Mary said before gesturing at the other woman. "And this is Darian Arante, NASA special agent for space law enforcement."

Edgar nodded. "Welcome, both of you. What can we do to help?"

"It seems we have a problem here, Dr. Roth," Darian said. "Your corporation apparently smuggled someone into this colony without NASA approval, and covered up the records of his existence here. His name is Karl Rossum, and he is listed as missing on Earth by his relatives."

Stilicho raised his hand. "Hold on a minute. Mr. Rossum was not reported as missing by his wife, and she continues to deny such. The person who reported him as missing is his estranged daughter."

"If a family member- any family member- reports a missing relative, we are duty bound to investigate," Darian said. "Your excuses seem to indicate a lack of cooperation with the authorities, Mr. Jones."

Stilicho rolled his eyes. "It's not an excuse, ma'am, I am simply pointing out that Karl's own wife has not confirmed that he is missing. It's not a crime for an adult to cut himself off from society and go his own way."

"You seem to be missing the point here, Mr. Jones," Darian said. "Each and every individual who goes into space must be registered into the NASA database. What your company has done is engage in fraud and deceit. Your firm created a false identity for Karl Rossum, and brought him here without our permission."

"That is grounds for terminating the colonial franchise that the government has granted you," Mary said.

"Look, Mary, we were not aware of this development until just recently," Edgar said. "This minor incident occurred on Earth, not here in the colony. You cannot blame and condemn our entire operations here because of the actions of a few back on Earth."

Stilicho suppressed a smile. Edgar called the NASA administrator by her first name. It was a good strategy for making the meeting less formal, to break down the icy, professional barriers so that they all could come to a more amenable conclusion.

"The actions of a few you say?" Darian said. "It seems to me that the main suspect in this shell game is none other than your CEO, Errol Flux. He was a close friend of Karl

Rossum, and he was the only one who had the power and authority to pull off something like this. I can contact our local field office and have him arrested."

"Whoa there, Darian," Stilicho said. "First of all, do you have any proof that Errol was involved in this cover up? ACE Corp is an international conglomerate, and employs hundreds of thousands of people. It could have been anybody."

"No more excuses," Darian said. "You will cooperate with us fully in this investigation, or there will be severe consequences for your company's entire space operations. NASA has the full authority to shut down colonies and prosecute those that break the law."

Edgar chuckled a little to help break the tension. "But we are cooperating with you, Darian. You just need to allow us to explain."

Mary placed a hand on top of Darian's forearm, indicating that she ought to go for a less confrontational approach. "Okay, let's hear it," she said.

Stilicho pointed to a wall-mounted TV monitor at the end of the room and activated his smartglasses. "If you could take a look at this, please."

A previously recorded video file started to play. It showed the disheveled face of Karl Rossum, his tired eyes gazing solemnly at them from his thick glasses. His salt and pepper beard was puffed up like a porcupine's quills, and his unkempt hair hadn't been trimmed in months. Karl's voice was high-pitched and halting, and his inflections indicated a degree of desperation. "My name is Karl Capek Rossum," he said, speaking into the camera. "I have made this video as a possible last will and testament. A few weeks ago, I received an audio file coming from the Martian relay network, and it had the voice of my firstborn son, Joe. He said that he needed my help and he was still alive. I have therefore used my AI programs to craft an identity that would pass undetected through NASA and ACE so that I can secretly go to Mars and find my son. I know that people will blame my good friend Errol when news of my venture finally surfaces, but I must confess that I- and I alone- am responsible for this. I have altered the maintenance logs in the colony's transport system to take one of their rovers and go find my son. If you do not hear from me again, then I am dead, for I no longer wish to keep on living if I fail to find Joe."

The video stopped. For a few minutes, no one in the room said anything.

"As you can see, Karl himself admitted that he is solely responsible for coming over to Mars," Stilicho said. "We only learned of what had happened after we crosschecked the departure logs and the colony records here, and found that we were missing one man. We are in shock as much as you are."

"I don't believe you," Darian said tersely. "I'm convinced that Errol Flux knew about this years ago, but he kept his mouth shut. I don't have the evidence for this, but the truth will come out sooner or later."

"You don't have the evidence for this because there isn't any," Stilicho said. "Errol is innocent, and that video proves it."

"Let's move away from this line of thinking to something more productive," Mary said. "We can assume for now that Karl Rossum is somewhere here on the Red Planet. Is it possible that the Chinese might have him?"

Edgar shook his head. "I had a brief and private communication with my Chinese counterpart in Ba-Dian Colony just before this meeting, and he assures me that Karl never came to their area, nor are they detaining him."

Darian placed her elbows on the table and leaned forward. "Are you sure you can trust their word?"

"I see no reason for them to lie," Edgar said. "If Karl took a rover over to them, we would have gotten an indicator from the rover's transponder, and that would have been picked up by satellite and informed us as to where it's located."

Darian wasn't convinced. "Karl Rossum is known as an electronics genius. Couldn't he disable the transponder on the rover so as to make it untraceable?"

"Karl is a genius, but not the Chinese," Edgar said. "If the Chinese had tried to abduct him, there would be traces of it. So far there isn't any. An operation like that would be hard to cover up with all the satellites overhead, and the planet is mostly deserted. My counterpart was shocked when I told him that Karl smuggled himself to Mars, they didn't even know he was out here."

"There's no reason for the Chinese to kidnap Karl either," Stilicho said. "They have their own programmers and experts in that field. One thing about the Chinese is that they like to do things by themselves."

Mary nodded in assent. "Okay, so it's highly unlikely

that the Chinese have him. So where could Karl Rossum be? Assuming he's still alive."

"If he wanted to find his son, then he would have driven north, over to the Mars First Colony site in Hypanis Vallis," Darian said. "That's where Joseph was supposed to have been buried at."

"How far is that from us?" Mary asked.

"A little over eight thousand kilometers to the northeast," Edgar said. "In the Xanthe Terra region, just south of … Chryse Planitia."

Edgar's voice trailed off and he looked at Stilicho with a surprised look in his eyes. Chryse Planitia was where ACE Corp's new colony was supposed to be set up, and the outpost used by the missing team was located in that very region, less than a thousand kilometers away from the allegedly abandoned Mars First Colony.

Darian sensed the colony director's consternation. She remembered reading the briefing on the new projects. "Don't you have plans to set up a second colony in the Chryse Planitia area?"

Edgar was speechless. He looked nervously at Stilicho for guidance. Deception and politics wasn't his strong suit.

"Yes," Stilicho said calmly. "In fact, we were going to ask for your help too. This was the reason why this meeting was moved up to today."

Mary gave him a quizzical look. "What do you mean?"

"Those net rumors about a communication breakdown with your construction crew weren't just hearsay then," Darian said. She put two and two together. "Are you still in contact with them at all?"

Stilicho looked down. "Not for a few weeks."

It was Mary's turn to be surprised. "What? Why weren't we informed of this?"

Stilicho switched to damage control mode. It was better to tell the whole truth so he could gain some sympathy for his side. "We thought it was a routine breakdown. Then weird things began to happen."

"The malware that infected the Mars relay," Darian said. "Did it come from that region?"

Stilicho nodded solemnly. No sense in lying about that since the routing was confirmed and could easily be found out. "At first we thought it was just a prank made by the guys over there, but then all communications with them stopped. So we sent in a rescue team."

Mary was intrigued. "And what did they find?"

"We've lost contact with them as well," Edgar said. "Their last situation report came when they had just left the outpost at Meridiani Planum, which was around two thousand four hundred kilometers away, due southeast from the Batos Crater outpost."

"The Batos Crater outpost is where the new colony construction site is?" Darian asked.

"Yes," Edgar said.

"So two years after Karl Rossum takes a rover to head out to where his son is supposedly buried, you guys set up a construction site at a neighboring region, and then you lose contact with them," Darian said. "How many people are with that construction team?"

"Six," Edgar said. "Two geologists and four engineers.

Each of them had a side specialty, like robotics, or medical. We sent in another six men for the rescue team."

Mary sat back, stunned. "So that's twelve people missing now?"

"Thirteen," Darian said. "If you include Karl Rossum."

Edgar shook his head. "Two years out there on his own? No way he could have survived for that long."

Darian narrowed her eyes. "Wait a minute, Edgar. You were here when Mars First was forcibly evacuated weren't you? Did you go to their colony site?"

Edgar nodded. "Yes. I know what you're thinking but I just don't believe it. The Mars First habitats were in a sorry state. Their life support system was failing and their greenhouses had completely broken down by the time we got there. If we had arrived a few days later everyone in that colony would have been dead. Even if by some miracle Karl could have found a way to somehow reactivate and maintain the life support system, there's no way he could survive out there without any food. He would have surely starved to death."

Darian rubbed her chin. "Didn't some members in that colony resort to cannibalism?"

"They did," Edgar said. "But its way more complicated than just digging up a body and eating it. A corpse would average at about thirty kilos worth of food, maybe one cadaver would be enough to sustain you for sixty days if you rationed it. It was claimed that fifty-four people were buried in the colony site because those were the ones who were unaccounted for when we ran the final roll just before they were lifted off. While that gives one man enough food theoretically for four Mars years, one would still have to find a way to dig them up and cook it. Too much work for one man to do and still maintain the life support systems in the colony with no spare parts."

Darian pursed her lips. "But you admit that it's plausible, right?"

"I guess it's within the realm of possibility," Edgar said.

Mary shook her head in bewilderment. "This is just … crazy."

Stilicho hissed. "So let me get this straight, your theory is that Karl Rossum is alive, is a cannibal, and he engineered this virus and took out a construction crew and a rescue team? Come on!"

"Well, I'm still trying to figure out how he could overpower two teams of people," Darian said. "But Karl Rossum is an expert on AI, and he could have easily wrote the malware that's affecting the relay network."

"Maybe it's a monster that's out there killing people," Stilicho said.

Edgar bit his lip. "Come on, Stil. We've had no evidence whatsoever of any indigenous life on this planet that's bigger than a microbe."

Darin looked at Stilicho. "So that's why you came out here. You didn't get on a last minute spaceflight just to find Karl Rossum, you're here to investigate the missing construction teams, aren't you?"

Stilicho threw his hands up. "You got me."

Mary crossed her arms and frowned. "So what is ACE Corp going to do now?"

"They're going to mount another search mission," Darian said. "On my way here, there were eight ex-military types in the transporter. So it looks like they're going to try again."

"Congratulations, you've worked it out," Stilicho said. "I was actually going to ask for NASA's assistance on this."

Darian narrowed her eyes. "Meaning what exactly?"

Stilicho smiled faintly. "I'd like to invite you and be part of the team, that's what."

Chapter 10

The main vehicle hangar had a cavernous interior and was fully pressurized, in order to give the maintenance crews a better hands-on ability to service the vehicles that were parked inside. The Martian dawn was just about to break over the horizon, and the two newly assembled rovers were undergoing final diagnostic checks to make sure their systems were fully functional. A third, fully autonomous robotic truck would follow them, making the final tally of the convoy at three vehicles.

Stilicho yawned as he walked into the building from an adjoining service corridor. He didn't get much sleep, due to the all-night meetings to prepare for the mission. The skinsuit he wore felt snug, and he loathed at the thought of spending days wearing nothing but a diaper underneath it all. He had heard that the Batos Crater outpost had a shower stall, but it was over eight thousand kilometers away, and assuming that it was still functional. They had planned to drive the rovers non-stop for at least four days until they got to the outlying outpost at Meridiani Planum, before continuing up for another two days of driving towards the Batos Crater boundary. Stilicho figured they would be making a number of stops along the way, since Rover-14's transponder was still functioning, and it had been located at the southernmost part of the Ares Vallis riverbed, less than six hundred kilometers away from the first outpost stop at Meridiani Planum.

Nick Verdeschi served as the head of security for the colony. He was a former police lieutenant and pushing fifty years of age. He noticed Stilicho walking into the hangar bay and immediately strolled over and held out his hand. "Good morning, Stilicho. How was your sleep?"

Stilicho shook his hand and let out another yawn. "Two hours worth, if that's any consolation."

Nick chuckled as he led him towards four men wearing nearly identical skinsuits, who were standing beside a worktable. "It's a pity you wouldn't let me come along. Two colleagues from my own department are missing out there, and I've had to put up with a deluge of inquiries from their loved ones. But judging from the replacements you've brought over, I think they're better qualified at this, assuming that you're expecting some trouble."

Stilicho walked up to the four men. All of them turned to face him. One of the men, who had short, graying hair came up to them and held out his hand. "Matt Trevanian. Thanks for choosing me as team leader, sir."

Stilicho shook it. Matt's grip was as strong, as expected. "I'm pretty impressed by your dossier, so that's why I wanted you to assemble a team for this."

"We won't let you down, sir," Matt said.

"Call me by my first name, or just Stil," Stilicho said. "You shaved your beard from when I met you last night."

Matt grinned as he ran his hand along his now smooth, chiseled chin. "Less friction, therefore less of a fire hazard-when we wear the skinsuits for EVA."

Nick glanced at Stilicho. "I thought you'd want all eight of them with you."

"Four ought to be enough," Stilicho said. "If they can't deal with it, four more won't make much of a difference. I'll leave the others for colony defense."

Matt nodded. He wanted to say otherwise, but he didn't want to rock the boat. "Stilicho, let me introduce you to the other team members." He pointed to the three other men beside him. "This here's Brian Kano, he's been with the security department on the colony for two years now, and a former police detective. I figured you wanted someone with field experience, so he's the man."

Kano shook Stilicho's hand. "Nice to meet you, Mr. Jones."

Stilicho smiled. "Call me Stil."

"These other two came in with me," Matt said, pointing to two burly men with shaved heads. "Jason Barre and Noah Carranza."

Stilicho shook hands with them. Looking down at the table, he noticed that there were two over-sized battle rifles lying on it. He had seen guns before, but these seemed strangely different. There were what looked to be exhaust vents along the side of their long barrels. "What are these?"

"Gyrojet rifles," Matt said. "The first of these types of weapons were developed over a hundred years ago, but they were never adopted because they were useless at close range. This is the newest generation, though they're still prototypes."

Stilicho was intrigued. "How do they work?"

Matt held up a bullet so he could get a closer look. It looked like a standard caseless rifle cartridge, but there were exhaust ports at the rear. "These guns fire small rockets. It means that the ordnance will continue to accelerate as long as there's fuel to burn. The exhaust gasses are vented along the barrel ports, so there's no recoil for the user. Rifling in the barrel spins the rocket for added accuracy, and the internal smart components allow the slug to change its direction once we paint the target using the smart scope."

"Pretty neat," Stilicho said. "Why wasn't this adopted sooner?"

"When they first came out way back when, the primitive propellants they used made them very inaccurate and they had no velocity at short range- which meant that they would just bounce off people if they were fired too close," Matt said. "With advanced propellants and smart bullets that we got now, these babies could eventually get into widespread use in the near future."

Nick noticed that the trigger guards had been enlarged. "Looks like you'll be able to use these things during EVA with your skinsuits."

Noah grinned and held up a weapon mount. "We could also deploy them on the crab suits, sir. This here shoulder mount will be positioned just beside the helmet, and the smart scope will be linked to the helmet visor."

Stilicho placed his hands on his hips. "How many of these rifles have you got?"

"Just these two," Matt said. "We've taken out the trigger guards on the pistols and the carbines that we're bringing along so we could use them while wearing skinsuits during EVA. The gloves on the crab suits are too thick, and so we would prefer to use the skinsuits if we need to go outside."

"You'll have to do pre-breathing then," Stilicho said. "I'd rather just use the crab suits because of that issue."

"While the crab suits are nice," Matt said. "They're slow and bulky compared to the skinsuits. We may need to be able to move fast, and with better feel for our hands, so we're mostly going with the skinsuits for EVA."

"Suit yourself," Stilicho said. Anyone who used a skinsuit to go outside would need to go through mandatory decontamination procedures when they got back, but he had a feeling they would all go through the protocols anyway.

Edgar walked into the hangar bay, followed closely by Darian, another woman, and a middle-aged man. Edgar wore his ACE Corp uniform, but the other three were wearing skinsuits. Darian's own suit had NASA insignias on it, making her stand out from all the others. Stilicho and Nick came over to them and shook hands. The other woman was Dr. Lisa Hicks, and the second man was Chester Yoon, an engineer.

"I've got a few pressing issues this morning," Nick said. "So I need to head over to the security office. I'll see you all when you come back." He turned around and walked back into the adjoining corridor.

Edgar chuckled as he gave Stilicho a hug. "Goddamn, buddy! Those bags under your eyes tells me you must have been drinking all night."

Stilicho scoffed. "Puh-lease. I was busy with meetings all night. You were with me, remember?"

"Yeah, I was," Edgar said. "But I'm as alert as an owl. You look like you're in a daze."

"I'm just not used to waking up early is all," Stilicho said.

Lisa was in her mid-thirties, and served as an emergency medicine specialist at the colony hospital. Verna had recommended her personally the night before. "Excuse me, Mr. Jones."

Stilicho turned to look at her. "Yes?"

Lisa glanced around briefly. "Am I the only medic you're bringing along?"

"Officially, yes," Stilicho said. "Aside from myself, you've got Darian here and Chester, who is an engineer with additional expertise in robotics. The security consultants that are traveling with us do have some training in emergency medical procedures too, so I'm sure they can help out."

Lisa had a worried look. "It's just that, I thought this was supposed to be a rescue mission, but it looks like you're bringing more military types instead of medics. Two of my friends from the hospital were part of the first rescue team, and I'm really worried about them. That's why I volunteered."

"I'm afraid I don't understand what you're trying to say," Stilicho said. He could normally handle concerns like this, but his mind wasn't fully awake, and it made him more irritable than usual.

"Well it looks to me like, you're not expecting to find any survivors, and it's only been a few weeks," Lisa said. "Shouldn't we be bringing along more medical personnel instead of ex-soldiers?"

"The simple truth is, we don't know what's out there," Stilicho said. "And until I've determined that the place we're going to is safe and secure, we proceed as planned. Anyway, we can always call for more medical personnel once we've ascertained what's going on."

Edgar took Lisa aside and started talking to her. Chester excused himself to go check on the drones that were being mounted on the bed of the robotic truck.

Darian made eye contact with Stilicho. "So it looks like you're not expecting to find any survivors."

"It's been a month since the rescue team was sent out," Stilicho said. "If any of them were still alive, they would have found a way to contact the colony by now. This is going to be a crime scene investigation."

"Just to let you know, I'm still pretty sure your boss Errol knew about Karl's plan to smuggle himself to this planet," Darian said. "And when I get the evidence, I'm going to nail him to the wall for it."

"Good luck with that," Stilicho said before he walked away. Going past Matt and his security crew, he noticed Chester examining what looked to be a metal harness with thrusters mounted on its rear. Stilicho kept going until he was standing right beside the engineer.

Chester smirked as he checked the control stick that was attached to the plastic and metal backpack. "Is this what I think it is, sir?"

Stilicho winked at him. "Call me Stil. And yes, your eyes do not deceive you- those are rocket packs. I had Errol bring two of them over from ACE Corp R&D."

Chester continued to examine the components. "Methane-LOX powered. Have you used these things before?"

"I had a personal jetpack on Earth and I would fly around with it as a hobby," Stilicho said. "My unit was kerosene powered. You think these things will work on Mars?"

Chester laughed a little. "Oh yes. It's got its own oxidizer, so the low gravity will definitely allow you more thrust and use up less propellant, which can make you fly higher and faster. How long was your flight time on Earth?"

"About fifteen minutes," Stilicho said. "I had them bring along replacement fuel tanks, and it can also be refueled manually with a hose link."

"That's good. You'll probably have double the flight time out here," Chester said. "Damn, I would love to have one of these just to play around with on my free time."

"Well, I've brought a pair of them with me, so once this mission of ours is over, you could keep one of them. It's not like I'll be bringing these back on the return trip anyway," Stilicho said.

Chester grinned. "Awesome! Thanks, Stilicho!"

"My pleasure."

"Oh," Chester said. "Since you're bringing two of them along, who will be using the other rocket pack?"

"Anyone who knows how to use it," Stilicho said. "You got any experience?"

Chester chuckled. "Sorry, not yet."

Stilicho nodded. "Okay, I got a question to ask. How far is the range for the aerial drones we're bringing along?"

Chester walked over to the foot-long quadcopter drones lying on top of the truck bed. "These things would normally have a twelve hour flight time, but under optimal conditions, they can fly up to a full day as long as half the time is spent on charging their solar cells during daylight. The main issue is communications and remote piloting. How long can the operator stay awake, so to speak."

Stilicho stood beside him and looked at the drones. "What's their communication range?"

"If we use the satellites, you can cover the whole planet with a one second lag time between relaying of commands," Chester said.

"Let's say we lose satellite coverage and only go with local radio comms using the rovers," Stilicho said. "What's the range of that going to be?"

"Depends on the terrain blocking the signal, and the height of the drones," Chester said. "It's possible to get a command range of about eighty kilometers under optimal conditions. If the drone dips below hilly terrain, for example, then the range could go as low as five kilometers."

"Okay. Thanks, Chester," Stilicho said, before walking back over to where Edgar and Lisa were standing.

Edgar took Stilicho aside. "Lisa was a bit upset. But she's okay now."

Stilicho nodded. "I hear ya. Is she still volunteering for this trip?"

"Yes," Edgar said softly. "Her best friend was part of the rescue team that went missing. I told her to expect the worst, and she's getting over it. I need to get going, but I'll be monitoring your communications at the command area. If you need reinforcements, I'm afraid it might take awhile to reach you, depending on where you are."

"I'll only be calling on you to bring additional medical crews if we can't handle the number of survivors- assuming we find any," Stilicho said. "If it's anything else, there's no reason to ask for help if we can't solve it. Then you'll have to call in the military."

"I hear you," Edgar said. "We've got a lot riding on this, so let's go get 'em."

"That we shall," Stilicho said before he turned around and talked louder to make sure everybody heard. "Okay, people. Let's gather up for one final meeting before we get going."

The vehicle crews gave a thumbs-up signal, indicating that the rovers were now fully loaded and ready to go. The team of seven formed a semi-circle around Stilicho. The security consultants were stone-faced, while Chester and Lisa had a mixture of worriment and anxiety etched on their faces. Darian's face was unreadable.

"Right," Stilicho said. "As you all well know by now, two teams have disappeared. The first was the construction team overseeing the new colony boundary in Chryse Planitia, and the search and rescue team that was dispatched to find them.

We don't know what's out there, but for the sake of the colony, and the future of manned habitations on this planet, then we need to find out. I wish we had some aerial transport that would get us over to the outposts much faster than the rovers, but this planet's air density, or lack of it- makes it hard for the cool designers at ACE Corp to come up with anything that will take more than a small robot to fly with. So let's decide who gets to ride with who, and let's get started."

Everyone started picking up their personal packs, for these were the only other items that needed to be placed in the rovers. Stilicho walked over to where Matt was. "Matt, how's your driving skills?"

"Pretty good," Matt said. "I've been trained at tactical driving. Jason is also certified."

"Okay," Stilicho said. "I'll have you drive the first rover, and Jason can drive the second one." He turned to address the others. "Does anyone else have any training on defensive driving?"

Darian strode over to them, her pack slung over her shoulder. "I do. I was trained at Quantico."

Stilicho knew he needed to decide quickly who he would be seated with for the next few weeks, at the very least. "Okay, you can go with the second rover."

Darian sensed the repressed hostility between them. "Fine by me."

The blue Martian dawn was breaking over the horizon, and the three vehicles soon made their way out of the now depressurized hangar bay. Matt drove the first rover, along with Stilicho, Chester, and Brian. Jason, Darian, Lisa, and Noah followed in the second rover. The robotic truck, which was nothing more than a motorized flatbed with a robotic guidance pod, brought up the rear of the small convoy.

Eridu Colony was situated at the flatlands between Cue and Negele Craters. The convoy drove southwards at a respectable speed of 60-kmh along the flat terrain that characterized the interior of the massive Hellas Basin, the largest impact crater in the entire Solar System. As soon as they got to the southernmost outflow of Dao Vallis at four hundred kilometers away, they would turn northwards, skimming along the northern edges of the Hellas Basin until they got near the southern rim of Terby Crater, then head up the steady incline and into the cratered highlands of Terra Sabaea, a journey totaling over a thousand kilometers.

Stilicho looked at his watch. He expected the convoy to cross into Terra Sabaea by tomorrow. A straight drive would have taken them seventeen hours, but he knew they needed to make a stop towards the evening to change batteries. Although the terrain was relatively flat, there would be added complications when they would have to slow down while travelling on the rockier areas of the basin, and he needed to add extra time to his schedule to compensate for the slowdown in speed.

Looking around the pressurized cabin, Stilicho noticed that Brian Kano was already asleep in the chair behind him. Chester Yoon was going through a checklist on his smartglass, while Matt was fully concentrating on the terrain in front of the lead rover. They were following an established route, but the winds and dust storms might have easily dislodged a boulder or two, and the ex-Navy SEAL wasn't taking any chances as he had activated the lidar on the vehicle, making sure that it scanned the terrain ahead for any potential obstacles or pitfalls.

Placing his smartglasses over his eyes, Stilicho activated it. "Maia, you there?"

"Always," Maia replied. "What can I do for you this morning, Stil?"

"I want you to take full control of the robotruck at the rear. If the truck falls behind too far, you need to let me know."

"Yes, Stil," Maia said.

"The four aerial drones at the bed of the truck will be under your control as well," Stilicho said. "Program them to return immediately the moment radio contact with you is lost, okay?"

"Done," Maia said.

"Also, in case we lose satellite comms, I want you to download all relevant files in regards to this mission to your direct memory banks, this way you can still give me an analysis in the event of a breakdown in the Mars relay network," Stilicho said.

"Give me five minutes to download everything to my memory core," Maia said. "If I am to retain only relevant files, then I can assume you won't need me to retain entertainment modules like sports and all that?"

"Clear everything in your memory and history except

anything related to the mission at hand," Stilicho said. "Concentrate on downloading everything you can on Mars First, EVA emergency procedures, drone and robot engineering and operations, crab and skinsuit protocols, Martian survival, crime scene and forensics analysis and emergency combat medicine. Anything I've forgotten, just add them in for immediate access and collation."

"One moment," Maia said. "Done. Offline mode ready. Are you expecting trouble, Stil?"

"Based on everything you know about this so far," Stilicho said. "What do you think are the chances that Karl Rossum somehow survived for two years, assuming he made it to the Mars First Colony site?"

"A very low percentage," Maia said. "Perhaps no more than five percent. Karl Rossum was a brilliant programmer, but he had very little background in applied engineering, which would be important to know in order to maintain life support systems within a colony."

"Let me ask you, Maia," Stilicho said. "Is there anything that you think I'm overlooking?"

"You seem to have made your team well prepared for almost any eventuality," Maia said. "Of course, I could not give you a more precise answer, unless I knew more about what is going on."

"I've given you all I could," Stilicho said.

"Then all we can do is continue onwards until we get more information," Maia said.

Chapter 11

By the second day, the convoy was already traversing around the southern rim of the massive Huygens Crater wall. They were making excellent time, with Matt expertly leading the way. Stilicho had deployed a drone just ahead of the lead rover, in order to make sure the terrain just ahead of them would be stable enough for traveling at higher speeds. They had stopped the vehicles just before the second dawn to change batteries. The robotic truck carried a mobile battery charger, but they couldn't deploy the solar panels on it, for it would have made the vehicle unstable when traveling along inclined and chaotic terrain. But since they had an adequate supply of fully charged batteries on the truck bed, all they had to do was stop and switch them. They could swap the drained batteries for fresh ones once they got to the waypoint charging stations.

Stilicho's neck was sore from sleeping on a chair; he preferred to lie fully prone on a soft, fluffy bed, but the increased pace meant that it was safer for him to remain in the front seat with fastened safety belts. The rovers had reinforced suspensions, but rolling the wheels over the occasional large rock made it a bumpy ride. He had a bout of motion sickness at the beginning of the trip, but he had gradually gotten used to it. The only other issue that bothered him was Matt's constant farting, which he could hear and occasionally smell despite Matt's miasma being muffled by his skinsuit and diaper. Since the journey started, Matt and the other security officers completely switched to liquid meal replacements, having brought along sealed bags of sand-colored powder, in which they would mix with water. The liquid meals contained all the nutrients and calories that people needed without having to eat any type of solid food. The only problem was that it changed their metabolism, and they would constantly emit flatulence. Matt had apologized during the first dozen times when he farted, but with everyone constantly saying that it was alright out of courtesy, he finally just let them out without warning by the end of the first day. Stilicho was constantly making adjustments with the rover's ventilation system to make sure that the re-circulating air wasn't directed at him.

The highlands of Terra Sabaea helped to form a ring of elevated terrain around the Hellas Planitia. Traversing onto the incline of the area was dangerous, but over the years, a ramp of smooth, hard-packed sand had been slowly constructed by ACE Corp's robotic bulldozers, and once they drove into the higher regions, many parts of the terrain was now level, mainly interrupted by the occasional crater or glacier. After two days of almost nonstop driving, Matt went over to the backseat and dozed away while Brian Kano took over the wheel. Since the routes had been pre-positioned by GPS, the pace picked up a bit, with all three vehicles now going at a respectable 80-kph, though there were times when they had to slow down in order to maneuver around a particularly large crater or a crevasse that blocked their way.

They drove for another two thousand five hundred kilometers before the sandy terrain ahead of them began to descend into the lower plains of the Meridiani Planum. Both the spaceship and the colony had windows, and the rover had a wraparound windshield and side windows. As he looked out across the rust-colored, rocky regolith, Stilicho was reminded of the time when he visited the Valley of the Moon in Jordan. The terrain was very much like what he was seeing, with the exception of the amber sky above. With almost the same day and night cycle as his home planet had, Mars began to remind him of Earth, as nostalgia for his birthplace began to merge with a slowly growing interest of the strange new world he was in. A few hours later, they saw the southern rim of the massive Schiaparelli impact crater at the northeast horizon.

Matt was back in the driver's seat, his face a solid mask of concentration, despite the relatively smooth terrain ahead. A mild beeping noise began to emanate from the electronic map on the dashboard. "That's the transponder from the outpost."

Stilicho leaned forward, but he still couldn't see it visually. "How far away is it?"

Matt glanced at the readouts of the HUD. "A little over a hundred klicks. We ought to be there in less than two hours."

"We should be in range with their radios in the structure," Chester Yoon said from the backseat. "Assuming there's anybody there, of course."

Stilicho used his smartglasses to interface with the vehicle communications system. "Attention, Meridiani Outpost, this is ACE Corp rescue team two, is there anybody there?"

The readouts on the dashboard proclaimed that the internet link with the outpost was working, but there was no reply. Stilicho repeated his message, but there was still no answer.

He heard Maia's voice on his earpiece. "Stil, Sorry to interrupt, but I have something to tell you."

Stilicho tapped his smartglass frame. "What is it?"

"I'm getting low bandwidth readouts on all levels as we get closer," Maia said. "Packet loss is increasing due to interference."

Stilicho frowned. They were starting to lose internet communications from the Mars satellite network. "Can you compensate?"

"I'm afraid not," Maia said. "If this keeps up, we won't have internet capability with the relay by the time we reach the outpost."

Stilicho bit his lip. "Can you determine what's causing it?"

"I've been running bandwidth checks on all the satellites, and they seem to be infected with some sort of virus that's possibly hijacked their control systems," Maia said.

Stilicho's eyebrows shot up. "What?"

"I've tried to get rid of the virus, but then it tried to infect me," Maia said.

"Well protect yourself then!" Stilicho said. "Have you been infected?"

"No, my anti-virus systems can adjust by wiping out any script or bot that exhibits bad behavior," Maia said. "But the entire satellite network may be compromised, and they have blocked themselves off from my queries. Whatever is infecting the relay seems to be able to counter my moves when I try to find an access port I can get into."

Brian Kano leaned forward until his face was close to Stilicho's right ear. "What's going on, who are you talking to?"

"He's got a MAIA," Chester said. "One of those brand new, advanced AI suites."

Brian was impressed as he slumped once more into the backseat. "Wow, that's impressive."

Stilicho twisted his head so he could see everyone. "Listen up, guys. Something is messing up the relay network. I think it's man-made, and they don't want us communicating with Eridu Colony, or with Earth."

"Who do you think is behind it?" Brian asked.

"This is just a wild theory, but since there's confirmation that he did make it on this planet a few years back, I think it might be Karl Rossum," Stilicho said.

Brian and Chester gave each other a surprised look, but remained silent.

Matt glanced at Stilicho for a brief second before turning back his attention to the terrain ahead. "The robot guy? He disappeared, didn't he?"

Stilicho nodded. "He smuggled himself over to Mars.

His last message was that he was going to find his son, who supposedly died out here at the Mars First Colony. We know he got to Eridu and took a rover. That was two years ago."

Brian made a low whistle. "So you think he's out here somewhere and he's gone nuts?"

"It's a slim possibility," Stilicho said. "Maia told me that the relay is infected with some sort of advanced virus. Everyone is usually accounted for in the colony, and he was the only one who wasn't."

Brian nodded. "And Karl Rossum was known to be a genius when it came to programming software. I get you. So we have a suspect."

Chester scratched the back of his head. "So you guys think he's some kind of serial killer? I read everything about the guy and he's one of my heroes. Karl Rossum was the reason why I took robotics as a major in college. The guy is an academic and he's brilliant, but I just can't see him as a murderer."

"It all fits though," Brian said. "If the virus in the relay has his signature on it, then he would be the primary suspect. But knowing what I now know about this planet, it would be very hard for him to survive by himself out there for two years."

Matt kept his eyes straight ahead, but he was listening to what everyone was saying. "I'd like to secure the outpost when we arrive, if that's okay with you, Stilicho."

Stilicho nodded. "I got no problem with that."

Matt punched up the radio communications with the rover following behind them. "Rover-two, you reading me, over?"

Darian answered. "Loud and clear, rover-one, over."

"Jason and Noah, prepare for EVA," Matt said. "We'll be coming up to the outpost in about ninety minutes. Jason, you can go with a skinsuit. Noah, have you got the gyrojet rifle mounted on your crab suit, over?"

Noah's voice instantly came online. "I can mount it with Jason's help once he's outside, over."

"Okay," Matt said. "The three of us will do EVA first. Once we secure location the others can follow. Jason, start your pre-breathing prep now, over."

Jason voice answered. "Roger that, over."

Matt slowed down and placed the vehicle on autodrive before he switched places with Brian. Once he got to the backseat, Matt opened a side cabinet and took out an oxygen mask. Placing the full-faced mask on, he activated the controls and began to breathe in a pure oxygen mix while doing stretching exercises. The last thing he wanted was to get the bends while walking around in a skinsuit on the planet's surface.

The waning sun cast a bluish glare over the horizon. Dusk had set in, just as they finally saw the outpost up ahead. Brian was still in the driver's seat, and he slowed down while activating the vehicle floodlights, illuminating the sandy terrain up ahead. Matt was already suited up as he waited inside the rover's airlock, ready to step out into the Martian atmosphere. Despite the chilly air inside the cabin, a few drops of sweat trickled down from the top of Chester's forehead as he nervously kept his eyes peeled ahead.

Stilicho squinted while staring at the building just in front of them. The place had no windows so they couldn't tell if anyone was inside. He had Maia fly a drone to scan the place even before they got within visual sight of the habitat, but there was no reported outside activity. He wasn't too worried since the first rescue team had made it this far and they did send a routine message to Eridu before they set out again; only after they had left the outpost did the communications with the first rescue team end.

Brian stopped the rover just twenty meters away from the airlock entrance of the outpost. "Rover one at full stop, over."

Matt's voice came over the intercom. "Proceeding with EVA. Exiting vehicle now, over."

The three of them swiveled their heads to the left as they saw Matt come out from the rear airlock. He was carrying a bullpup-styled military carbine, its magazine located behind the pistolized trigger. Matt bounded over until he was just behind the left front wheel of the rover, and he pointed his carbine at the airlock.

Less than ten seconds later, Jason's voice was soon heard by both rovers. "I have exited vehicle. Mounting gyrojet rifle on Noah's crab suit. Give me two minutes, over."

Stilicho punched up the controls on the dashboard and shifted cameras over to the second rover's viewpoints. The livestream video showed Jason kneeling on top of the roof, as he placed the large rifle onto a mount that was attached to the crab suit just below him. His thick gloves made precise handling very difficult, but Jason had been trained extensively, and he pulled it off with twenty seconds to spare.

Jason's voice was punctuated with heavy breathing, but it carried a sense of confidence. "Weapon attached. Can you get a link on your HUD, Noah, over?"

Noah's voice was calmer, owing to the fact that he was just sitting in his crab suit the whole time. "Affirmative, link active. Detaching from rover now to begin my EVA, over."

Everyone watched in silent awe as Noah jumped down from the rover's chassis and onto the Martian soil. Even with the bulky crab suit, he bounded over to where Matt was located without any difficulty. With his overwatch in place, Matt and Jason hopped over, using long strides until they reached the sides of the airlock.

Matt stood beside the sealed pressure door, his weapon at the ready. "Opening outpost airlock in three ... two ... one."

The airlock door opened, revealing an inner darkness. Stilicho shifted the dashboard video feed into Matt's suit camera, which was mounted on his helmet. The deserted interior of the airlock showed nothing out of the ordinary. Matt reached for the power switch and the outpost lights instantly activated, bathing the entire place with a bright, artificial daylight illumination. The scene shifted as Matt glanced over at Jason, who was standing behind him. Jason re-sealed the airlock door and began initiating atmospheric equalization with the habitat area at the adjoining room beyond.

They could hear a whooshing noise as the pressure began to build, the life support systems replacing the thin, mostly carbon dioxide Martian atmosphere with breathable, pressurized air for human beings. Both men slung their carbines and pulled out pistols from their hip holsters. They activated the laser sights on the handguns, making sure to wipe away any specks of dust that interfered with the targeting pointers.

Matt's voice came active after a few minutes. "Atmosphere equalized, but we will keep wearing our gear until we've checked everything out, over."

The door into the outpost interior opened, and everything seemed to be in place. Both Matt and Jason began opening cabinets and bunk doors. Everyone held their breath when Matt walked up to the bathroom door and opened it, revealing an unused toilet.

Stilicho activated his smartglass. "Maia, can you detect any possibly dangerous pathogen in the interior?"

After a few minutes, Maia answered back. "Nothing out of the ordinary, Stil."

Matt's voice came back loud and clear. "Outpost secured, over."

Stilicho polished off the last of the tomato and fish pasta on his plate before placing it in the sink. They had brought along fresh vegetables and fruit, but this was the first and possibly only time they could cook them and eat at a dinner table. All the salads were now gone, and they would have to subsist on prepackaged rations or liquid meal substitutes from here on. The three security consultants all declined the meal, preferring their food shakes. Therefore, everybody else got an extra-helping of the pasta, and nobody declined. Lisa Hicks jokingly told the former soldiers to do their farting at the airlock, and they more or less complied.

The Meridiani outpost consisted of nothing more than one main room, with an attached bathroom and airlock. It was a prefabricated module that was assembled on site almost ten years ago, when ACE Corp had begun to expand their exploratory operations to find a suitable building site for Colony II. Errol Flux had a grandiose idea to build a second colony on the northern equatorial zone in order to tap in on the mining opportunities in the region. The new colony was destined to become a manufacturing hub, and it was predicted that they could start producing solar panels and even rocket engines for export back to Earth, once all the essential components were in place. This outpost was to serve as an early way station, before the proceeding up north to the new colony zone.

Chester knelt down and slid open one of the doors leading to an embedded bunk along the sides of the room. There were twelve bunk beds, more than enough for all of them. Stilicho had decided that they would stay the night in order to recharge the spent rover batteries, since the outpost battery recharging station had unused reserves of power. Each of them would take turns swapping out the batteries every two hours, and they would have a fully charged energy supply by morning.

Darian had added an artificial sweetener pill into her steaming cup of coffee while sitting at the opposite side at the dining table. She looked at Stilicho, and their eyes met. "I've got a theory," she said.

Stilicho shrugged. They were the only two still sitting on

the table; everyone else was either doing some technical work or resting in their bunks. "I'm all ears."

"I know it sounds crazy, but maybe somebody else baited Karl Rossum to come here," she said.

Stilicho pursed his lips. "Now why would anybody want to do that?"

"I don't know," Darian said. "There is a motive somewhere in all this, but I just can't figure it out yet. Perhaps it's somebody with a grudge against the company you work for."

Stilicho rolled his eyes. "So this person created a fake audio file of Karl's son to get him over here and is using him to sabotage the new colony site? Where did you get this crazy idea from?"

"Look, we have a set of incidents that occurred both here and on Earth," Darian said. "This is the only motivation I could think of. Maybe it's one of ACE Corp's competitors."

Stilicho thought about it for a minute. "Well, it's no surprise that our biggest competitors in the colonization business wants our exclusive NASA license in regards to Mars. You remember that bidding war with Urizen Group, right?"

Darian smirked. "How could I forget? The great Errol Flux nearly coming to blows with his nemesis during that confrontation at NASA headquarters when the final bids came in. There was a live drone cam and the tabloids ate it up for weeks."

"You don't seem to like my boss very much, do you?"

"I admire his causes," Darian said. "I just don't like the way he operates. He's ruined a lot of people's lives when he took over a number of smaller firms, only to break them up and sell the pieces."

"Errol was just being pragmatic," Stilicho said. "He needed the tech, and a few companies had them, so he bought them out."

"Let's not even take into account the blackmailing, insider trading, and bribery cases that piled up against him," Darian said. "And if you believe some of the conspiracy sites, there might have even been a few murders committed."

Stilicho wagged his finger. "Hold on now, you got no proof of all that crap. The courts found him and ACE Corp innocent every time."

"Sure," Darian said. It was clear she didn't trust him. "That's only because he has attack dogs like yourself working for him, to cover up all his dirty dealings."

Stilicho leaned back on the plastic chair and took a deep breath. "Is that why you're here? To dig up some dirt on the company I work for?"

"I'm here to investigate a missing person," Darian said. "Who was smuggled into Mars illegally, in violation of the franchise we have given to your company."

Stilicho was getting angry, but he was able to hold his temper in check. "As you've seen in the video during the meeting we had with your boss, Karl Rossum came here with his own free will, and he was the one who smuggled himself over. So stop projecting your prejudices into this, Ms. NASA Special Agent."

Darian scowled at him. "I am not prejudiced! Errol and Karl knew each other only too well, and when I do find evidence that points to it, you can bet that this report will go straight to the top echelon of NASA."

"Well, good luck in ever finding that," Stilicho said. "ACE Corp has a very good relationship with NASA, and we have been their primary providers of space transportation for the past quarter century. So go ahead, keep on digging that non-existent dirt. I can promise you that anything you throw at us won't stick. In fact, I have a feeling that once this is all over and done with, you'll be working at NASA's remote research outpost in Antarctica. So don't forget to buy an extra thick parka when you get back."

Damian balled her fists in rage. "You son of a—"

Brian Kano leaned loomed beside the table. He held a smartpad in his hands. "Sorry to breakup your little love fest, but I got something here."

Stilicho looked up at him. "What is it?"

"We've recharged about half the batteries using the outpost's power reserves, but there's something missing," Brian said.

"And that is?"

"I can't find the sweeper bots that do maintenance on the solar panel array outside," Brian said. "There's supposed to be at least two automated bots that cleans the sand particles that accumulate on the paneling every day."

Stilicho stood up. "They're missing? Since when?"

Brian shrugged. "I don't know. I've been pouring through the outpost maintenance logs, and the inputs stopped about a month ago."

Chester Yoon didn't close the panel that covered his bunk,

so he heard everything. He got up and walked over. "The bots are missing?"

Stilicho activated his smartglasses. "Maia, are you able to get a radio link with the sweeper bots assigned to this outpost?"

"I'm sorry, Stil, but I'm not getting any pings back when I sent them a command message," Maia said.

Stilicho frowned. "Can you scan the logs and give me a detailed analysis?"

"One moment," Maia said. "It seems that the logs have been partially overwritten in order to permanently erase the records for the past thirty days."

"Can you recover the logs at all?"

Maia was apologetic. "They were overwritten with random number strings multiple times. I'm sorry, Stil."

"Ask your AI if it could trace the source where the overwrite commands came from," Chester said.

Maia heard him. "It came in from one of the orbital satellites. I tried to do a tracer route, and it seems to have originated from Hypanis Vallis, in the Xanthe Terra region. The script was able to commandeer the entire command system on the outpost, but I have now purged the entire operating system and replaced it with a new one. I have also added new firewalls to prevent such intrusions in the future."

There was a sense of relief on Chester's face. The Korean-American engineer had just realized that whoever took over the outpost's command software could have easily sabotaged the life support systems to injure or kill them all if it had wanted to. Chester wanted to tell everyone about it, but he decided not to since they were all on edge now, and another shock to the system simply wasn't needed at this time.

Brian looked away, lost in thought. "Hypanis Vallis? Why does that region sound so familiar?"

"Because that's where the site of the failed Mars First Colony is," Darian said. "That was where Karl Rossum said he was going to."

The drive towards Rover-14's last recorded position took nearly a day, and it was in the early twilit hours when they came upon the vehicle lying on its side. They parked their own rovers side by side, with Matt Trevanian and his security team providing cover. Jason Barre continued to wear his skinsuit as climbed on top of the second rover while scanning the area with his gyrojet rifle. Noah Carranza continued to deploy the weapon mounted on the shoulder of his crab suit while facing to the rear. Both rovers had all their lights activated, creating a powerful, illuminated area of bright white all around them, like some magical aura to ward away the unknown threat that lurked out in the darkness.

Stilicho wore a crab suit while making his first EVA. As he started walking towards the stricken rover, his awkward gait became unbalanced and he inadvertently tripped over a medium-sized rock, and fell face first into the ground, the visor of his helmet banging onto the rocky soil. He heard a small beeping noise and a momentary panic gripped him, his fear of damaging the suit and exposing his head to the thin atmosphere made him shudder.

"You okay?" Chester Yoon said as he held him by the

shoulders and slowly pulled him back upright.

Stilicho was still breathing heavily. His visor was intact, and the stress of what happened was slowly bleeding away. "Yeah, thanks. This is my first time using these damned things."

Chester chuckled to put him more at ease. "It's okay, these hard shell suits are pretty durable, they can take a lot of pounding."

Brian Kano was sitting in the driver seat of the first rover, and he was monitoring everyone's vital signs with the HUD. "You're good, Stilicho. Everything is a-okay from here."

"Let's go," Stilicho said as both he and Chester bounded over to the base of the hill where the Mwev was lying.

Lisa was standing on the upper incline of the hill, close to the top while looking down at the broken windshield. She wore a skinsuit, in order to have better manual dexterity with her hands. She held a flashlight, and was using its illumination to peer into the wrecked rover's once pressurized interior cabin, now exposed to the atmosphere. It had been over a month, and the fine Martian dust had steadily seeped inside.

Stilicho slowly made his way up over to her, while Chester continued to check the upturned side of the rover. The crab suit was bulky, but Stilicho was able to get into a semi-crouching position as he looked into the empty front seat. "The reports said there were two men in this rover when they lost contact. Did this thing hit a boulder that broke the windshield?"

Lisa pointed to the intact frame around the broken front window. "If it was a rock that penetrated the windshield, then pieces of it should be inside the cabin. I don't see that at all. When the vehicle tipped over after one of its wheels hit a boulder, the windshield must have been broken into beforehand, or right after the Mwev was immobilized."

"Maia," Stilicho said. "Can you access the vehicle logs?"

"I'm sorry, Stil," Maia said. "But the logs were wiped, just like what happened with the outpost."

Chester was using the smartglass link in his crab suit to scan the vehicle. "Looks like the vehicle batteries were taken out. Something strong just ripped them out of the rear casings."

Matt strolled over in his skinsuit, his carbine slung over his shoulder. "What could have done that?"

Chester shook his head, but since his helmet was attached to the suit's rigid torso, nobody saw it. "I have no idea. These rovers have reinforced body shells to withstand daily wear and tear, but whatever tore through the rear paneling broke it off like it was made of cardboard."

Images of monster movies flooded Stilicho's mind before he could blink them away. He pointed at the broken seatbelts in the empty driver's seat. "Looks like somebody punched through the windshield and pulled the driver out."

Lisa had made her way down near the rear area of the rover. "One of the dead is still here. When the rover fell on its side, he was instantly crushed in his crab suit. We can't recover the body until we set the vehicle upright again."

Stilicho looked down at them. "You can't pull the body out from the back of the suit and through the airlock?"

Lisa shook her head as she scanned the interior with her

smartglass visor. "Negative. It looks like his backpack wasn't fitted properly into the airlock, so I can't even get it open if I tried. I think the vehicle must have been moving when he tried to get back in, and it ended up wedging a part of the back of his suit into the entryway. Looks like he got jammed and couldn't pry himself out."

Chester nodded, though once again no one could see him. "It happens a few times during EVAs. The frame around the backpack has got to be an exact fit, and you have to push in with the whole of your back at the same time. If you try to rock yourself back in- say push in with the top of your back first, then the bottom- or vice versa, then part of the backpack could jam into the sides of the airlock frame, and you're gonna need help to get out. Poor guy."

Darian was sitting on the driver's seat in the second rover. Like Brian, she too was monitoring what went on. "How do we bring the stalled rover to an upright position?"

"We could just tow it back up," Chester said. "Bring one of the rovers into position on the other side, tie a secured line and pull it up. We could cover the windshield with an emergency tarp and re-pressurize it."

"We can't bother with that right now," Stilicho said. "We need to find the others first, assuming they're still alive."

"I agree," Matt said. "The battery has been torn out of this rover so it won't run."

"We have batteries in the truck carrier," Chester said. "If you give me half a day to work this, I think we can get this Mwev going again."

"No," Stilicho said. "We just don't have the time for it. We need to get going. Once we figure out what the hell is going on, then we can come back and salvage this sucker."

"And where are we heading to now?" Darian asked.

"We stick to the plan," Stilicho said. "Head up to the Batos Crater Outpost and see if we can find any survivors there."

Chapter 12

Camille Chamboredon frowned while looking down at the steaming cup of tea on the table in front of her. Moscow was still in the grip of winter, despite being well into the New Year. The frosted glass windows of the tea house she was sitting in was a testament to the weather of this dreary place. Camille could have easily stayed put in the south of France until Europe's cold spell had finally ended, but her contact had insisted that this would be the scoop of the century, and Camille wasn't just interested in the possible fame for exposing it to the world- she needed the potential monetary rewards of it as well.

The pouting faces sitting in the other booths around her pretty much told the whole story. Russia was going through another bout of economic uncertainty, and she could see it in the faces of its citizenry. People were more reserved than usual, some even to the point of rudeness. Just yesterday she had seen a haggard looking man try to run off with a lady's stolen handbag, only to be cut down by a security guard's gunshot as he tried to run through the busy shopping district in Arbat Street. It was sheer luck that nobody else was hurt, but it merely reinforced her reservations about coming here, especially at a time like this.

Just as Camille was thinking about leaving, she noticed a thirty-something woman with light brown hair enter the tea house. Her winter coat had some worn patches on it, and the thick fur cap she wore looked like it was bought from a surplus outlet. Camille had known her since they were foreign college students in America, and it was clear her friend had fallen on hard times. She raised her hand, catching the other woman's attention.

Oksana Sakhalov smiled slightly as she walked over and sat down at the opposite side of the booth. She held her hand out. "Hello, Camille, I am so happy you made it. Has been a long time since we last met, yes?"

Camille shook her hand. "Yes, it has. I showed your email to my editor, and he said it was okay for me to go here, provided that what you said is real. I assured him that it would be, since we both trusted each other for years."

"*Spasiba*. I would never lie to you, Camille," Oksana said. "Remember the time when I told you about the cover up for the crashed airline flight in Siberia? That was a good scoop for your paper, yes?"

Camille nodded as she poured her friend some tea. "It was indeed, *merci beaucoup*. But are you sure that this information you are telling me can be confirmed independently?"

"I am sure you can," Oksana said. "The matter is too important to be kept a secret for long."

Camille looked out at the tall windows of the tea house.

"But I must tell you, Oksana, I do fashion and business articles now. You could have brought this up to the investigative reporters, the ones who specialize in these kinds of stories. Why me?"

"Because I trust you, and this secret is so big that people are willing to kill in order to keep it a secret," Oksana said.

Camille leaned back into the cushioned seats of the booth, stunned. "What?"

"You know what is happening to my country," Oksana said. "There is talk of war in the west once again, and people are worried. I must make sure that my family is secured."

Camille's lips began to tremble. This wasn't the type of story she wanted. She valued her life more than fame or money. She quickly pulled out some cash and placed it on the table before getting up. "L-look, Oksana, I think you have me confused with those reporters who want stories like this. I-I don't think this is for me. I will refer this to someone else. Thank you for your time."

Oksana grabbed the other woman's wrist. She looked up at her with pleading eyes. "Camille, please. I beg you. You are the only one I trust with this. All I ask is that if you could please hear him out, then decide on what you want to do."

A part of her just wanted nothing to do with it. But seeing her best friend in such a desperate state like this moved her, and Camille felt duty bound to help. She sat back down. "Alright, I shall hear him out. But I only do this because we are such good friends, and you must promise me that no one else knows about this."

Oksana nodded eagerly. "*Da*. Oh yes, no one but myself

knows this. Everyone thinks my uncle is still back in Baikonur, but he is here, in hiding. Only I know where he is."

Camille was scared, but she figured that if she could just get a video testimony, then it would be enough. "Okay, what exactly did your uncle do in Roscosmos?"

Roscosmos was the Russian counterpart of NASA, tasked with overseeing the space program of the country. Unlike the Americans, the Russian government continued to maintain full control over their spaceflight programs. Past economic turmoil had turned the organization into a shadow of its former self, and Russia had been forced to close its colony on Mars due to lack of funding. The resulting evacuation happened eight years ago, and it was a chaotic affair. In the end, the country had to swallow its pride and asked for help in evacuating its personnel from Mars. Although there had been recent pronouncements from the government that they would restart their abandoned colony in Valles Marineris, everyone knew they just didn't have the money to do it. Rumors continued to swirl however that a foreign corporation had made a deal with them in exchange for being granted a colony license on Mars.

"He was a mission commander in Gagarin Colony," Oksana said. "When my government evacuated the site he was the last one to leave."

Camille let out a deep breath. "But what you told me over the email is just unbelievable. Are you sure that this story is true?"

Oksana stood up. "Come with me, Camille. Talk to him

yourself for just a few minutes, and you will see that what he says will be so fantastic that it will be true."

They both took the Moscow Metro to the southwest district of the city, a place of old decrepit apartment blocks and abandoned factories. Unlike Moscow's bustling city center, this neighborhood was characterized by deserted streets, with an eerie quietness that was occasionally interrupted by barking dogs and gangs of youths screaming at each other as they made their way towards the livelier areas of the city. Since it was a poor area, no surveillance drones were visible overhead, due to the meager budget of the Moscow Police.

Camille had been pretty nervous the moment they walked out of the underground train station, and Oksana had to take her by the elbow just to keep the pace going. If she could just confirm that the story was true, then it would be a feather in her cap, and might even get her a promotion within the media company that she worked for. As they made it to the front of an old, nine-story apartment building, Camille's courage began to improve. A heavily bundled babushka sat on a wooden stool near the entrance of the place, and the old woman eyed them suspiciously as they passed her to go up the stairs.

When they finally reached the seventh floor, Oksana turned left and stood in front of a thick brown door. Taking out a small set of keys, she unlocked the deadbolt first before placing a second key into the knob and twisting it. The door opened with a slight creak, revealing a dim interior. Silently gesturing at Camille to go on in, she looked around and noticed two men wearing heavy coats standing at the far end of the corridor, clutching clear bottles of vodka in their hands. Oksana quickly retreated behind the door and closed it tightly before putting the locks back into place.

Camille could see a faint illumination coming from the room in front of her. Oksana flipped on the light switch, and a single blub cast a pale yellow aura into the place. Bits of wallpaper along the sides of the place was peeling off, and there were stacks of books and old magazines lined up alongside the rotting furniture. The whole apartment had a damp, musty odor that reminded her of dust and mold.

"This way," Oksana whispered, as he led the other woman into the second room. The adjoining chamber was evidently a bedroom, with a rug placed along the side of the wall which faced a wooden bed. Sitting at the far side of the room was an old man wearing a heavily worn sweater that had some holes in it. He had a sharp beak for a nose, and the wrinkled skin on his drooping chin was unshaved. His right leg was but a stump, and it was propped up on an old wooden chair. The old man stared at them with glassy eyes while saying nothing.

Oksana made her way over to his side and said something in Russian. The old man mumbled something back before she turned to look at Camille. "I've told him you are a reporter in a big media conglomerate," Oksana said. "My Uncle Dmitri asked me how much money could you give to him."

Camille smiled faintly as she sat down at the side of the bed. "Please tell your uncle that the magazine I work for would pay him very well for an exclusive story and interview, but this is just the preliminary meeting. I first need to find out if his story can be confirmed."

Oksana and her uncle had another small conversation before the Russian woman turned to look at her again. "He says that everything he will tell you is true, he swears it," Oksana said. "My uncle was supposed to be confined to the hospital at the Cosmodrome, and they were giving him drugs to shut him up, but he escaped. He says he wants to go to someplace like America. He needs money to do that."

Camille nodded. "My editor says he knows someone in the French embassy who could help, but we need some sort of confirmation. In his email he said that a famous American who is supposed to be dead was brought over by the Russian government to Mars in secret. Is that right?"

Oksana and her uncle had another conversation before she started translating for him. "My uncle says yes, the Russian authorities were paid a large amount of money to transport him secretly into the Cosmodrome," Oksana said.

"But everyone knows about him," Camille said. "How come the other people who worked for Roscosmos never reported this? Why is it only him?"

Oksana translated again. "My uncle says only a select few people in the program knew about it. By the time that man came into the spaceport, he had his face altered."

Camille frowned. "Altered? As in plastic surgery?"

The uncle said a few more sentences while Oksana nodded. "Yes, after he faked his death in America, this man went underground, after he changed his looks. Our government knew about it, and turned a blind eye when he gave them a lot of money."

"How long ago was this?" Camille asked.

"About eleven years ago."

Camille took out her smartglasses and put them on. "Okay, if this man came to Mars, then where is he now?"

Oksana gave a surprised look as her uncle said a few more words to her. "He says that he never left. When Gagarin Colony was evacuated, he stayed behind."

Camille was stunned. She pulled out her smartpad and brought up the man's picture. She held it in front of her so that Oksana's uncle could see it. "You mean, they left him behind in that colony? All by himself? This man?"

Oksana nodded as she heard the words of her uncle. "Yes, because his name was never included in the registry. He had his own private module in the colony. No one else ever saw him."

Camille turned away. She could hardly believe it. The son of a former president, and who later created a cult could do this? "Do you have any proof? My paper is not a tabloid and I need evidence in order to bring this to my editor."

Oksana's uncle pulled out a small printed picture from the folds of his tattered sweater and held it out in front of him. Camille took it from his bony hands and examined the photograph. The man in the picture had a different nose and chin, but his wild eyes clearly resembled his old visage. Camille's facial recognition application on her smartglasses gave it a ninety percent probability that he was one and the same. *Oh my god*, she thought. *This is one hell of a story.*

Camille placed the detachable earpiece from the frame of her glasses and put it into her ear before dialing her editor's number. But the moment she visually inputted the numbers, the virtual indicator revealed that there was no cell signal in the area. What was going on?

All three of them were startled when the outside door gave way and four very large men entered the room. Oksana shouted at them in Russian, but one of the men slapped her across the cheek so hard that she was sent sprawling to the side of the small room. Camille screamed as one of the men took her smartglasses and put them underneath his coat. Uncle Dmitri shrieked as two men grabbed him by the arms and began to move him over by the open window.

Despite begging for her life, two men dragged Camille out of the room before physically carrying her up the stairs leading to the rooftop. They had forced her to keep her hands inside her coat pockets, and she realized that an old cell phone she had inadvertently left in that particular coat many years before was still there. She was able to activate it silently by touch alone, and she sent a hurried text message into the old telecom networks, just as they threw her off the roof. It was a nine-story drop and she landed headfirst onto the side of the street.

Camille had made thousands of text messages in her younger days, and she knew how to work the keypad on the phone by sheer memory. She had remembered that the A, B, and C keys weren't working, and she had been planning to throw away the phone, but ultimately forgot to do so. It only took her a few seconds, but she was able to send out a one line text to the first number that was saved in her contact list just before she died. Since her phone stored the entries by alphabetical order, it was by sheer luck that the message was carried over to the old ACE Corp customer server log, there to be autonomously disseminated by quantum analysis before being forwarded to whoever could respond most appropriately.

The single line of text was all capitalized. It read simply: SDRMMNDLIVENMRS.

Chapter 13

Instead of moving within the Ares Vallis gully, the small convoy elected to drive along the eastern side, on a parallel course. Matt Trevanian had insisted it would be safer to travel along the ridgeline instead of at the bottom of the trench where they could have been easily cut off and surrounded in the event of an ambush. Everyone was nervous and there was hardly any protest when the suggested route was taken instead. During the time they had examined the wreckage of Rover-14, all their batteries were switched over with fresh ones, so they drove non-stop until they reached their next destination. With the Martian surface on a smooth gradual descent, they increased their vehicle's overall speeds to 80-kmh.

The journey to Batos Crater Outpost took another eighteen hours, and they reached the outskirts of the small group of buildings by midday. The first thing they noticed was that the solar arrays were missing and there were no other rovers in sight. The satellite dish mounted on the roof of the outpost was gone, with just a metal stump sticking out from the top of the building. As the lead rover drove in closer, they also saw that the main airlock had been breached. The outer door was lying on the ground a few meters away. Matt and his security team exited the vehicles and searched the interior of the modules, but there was no one inside. Both compartments had been depressurized due to the airlock breach, and there were signs of a struggle. Much of the interior electronics had been gutted, and all the server logs and battery cells were missing. Thankfully, the life support systems were largely untouched, though the lack of power made them inoperable.

Stilicho immediately ordered the crew to patch up the airlock breach, using emergency tarps to cover the holes and seal them. By the time the outpost was re-pressurized it was already dusk. Radar analysis on the rovers had indicated a dust storm heading their way, which only made things even more disturbing. There was only minimal power in the outpost since they had to use one of the spare rover batteries to make the life support systems functional.

By the time it was dusk, six of them were within the interior of the outpost. Chester Yoon was still outside, doing some last-minute work replacing the rover batteries while being closely guarded by Jason Barre. Almost everyone had their life support backpacks on, and their helmets were within easy reach. Noah Carranza was the only one who didn't have his skinsuit helmet, but he stayed near the second, still functioning airlock, ready to leap into his crab suit the moment he sensed any trouble brewing.

Darian and Brian Kano had forensics experience, and

they were going through the two modules of the outpost with their smartglasses in UV mode. The breach in the main airlock had exposed the interior to the Martian atmosphere, and the resulting layers of dust had made the room analysis that much harder. Batos outpost was composed of two attached modules; the first habitat was the living area while the second served as both a workshop and control room. More prefabricated modules were planned to be sent over and assembled as the new colony would grow in stages.

Stilicho sat by the dining table as he looked at his watch. The distance to the abandoned Mars First Colony site was a little over one thousand kilometers away. So far they had only pinpointed one rover's location, and there were three others missing. With the Mars relay on the blink, they were unable to communicate with Eridu Colony. If he was to order the team to make the return journey back to Hellas Planitia, then nothing would have been solved. Deep in his heart, he knew that they needed to probe deeper, even if it meant he would be risking their lives. Stilicho had no sense of responsibility for leading the team, for the people with him were nothing more than tools to get the task done. The company's survival was all that mattered to him.

Chester's voice came over the intercom. "I have completed the replacement of batteries on both rovers and the robotruck. We're on our way back to the airlock."

Stilicho activated his communications system that was embedded on the collar of the skinsuit he wore. "Hold on a minute, have you found the comms dish for the outpost at all?"

"Negative," Chester said. "It must have been blown away by the dust storm."

Lisa Hicks activated her throat microphone. "From what I know, while dust storms are frequent out here, the atmospheric density is too thin for creating gale force winds to rip off our satellite dishes, right?"

"You're right," Chester said. "It might be buried somewhere close by, but visibility is steadily dropping out here."

"I need you and Jason to get into one of the rovers and use their comm systems to try and contact Eridu," Stilicho said.

"Rover two is closest so we're on our way," Jason said over the com-link.

Maia's voice came over the intercom. "I am sorry to interrupt, but the radar on the rovers is detecting something approaching us."

Noah Carranza had been listening in from the open airlock door, and he poked his head into the workshop area. "Is it one of the missing rovers?"

"No," Maia said. "The radar signature makes it look like one-third of a rover's size."

Matt, who had been sitting beside Stilicho, stood up. "Is it one of the construction robots?"

"It does not seem to be moving like one of our bots," Maia said. "It is quite fast, averaging close to one hundred kilometers an hour, and it can shift from side to side fairly quickly."

Stilicho scowled. "What?"

"One moment," Maia said. "I have lost radar contact."

Matt began to tense up. He knew that the rovers typically

had long-ranged radars that could detect objects up to sixty kilometers in distance. "How far away was the last contact?"

"Approximately forty kilometers from our position," Maia said.

Noah sensed trouble. He turned to look at Matt. "Can you help me get into the suit?"

Matt silently walked over to the second airlock and started helping Noah into his crab suit. Brian and Darian walked into the commons area, and the NASA special agent held something in the palm of her left hand.

Stilicho stood up and walked over to them. "What is that?"

"It's a memory chip," Darian said. "We found it embedded along the upper frame of one of the storage lockers. I did a cursory examination of it and it seems to contain a number of videos."

"Looking at the screenshots, it seems to be a video log made by the outpost team leader, Ron Simms," Brian said.

Chester's voice boomed on the intercom once again. "Okay, we are inside the rover. I am trying to pull up a satellite com-link with Eridu, but I'm getting no response."

"Hold on a minute," Stilicho said to Brian and Darian before looking up at the intercom speaker. "Chester, if you can't communicate with Eridu, then can you try and send a message to Earth?"

"A direct com-link to ACE Corp headquarters? I think I can do that," Chester said. "Hold on for a bit."

With Noah now fully in the crab suit, Matt walked back into the room, closing the airlock door behind him. "Jason, can you check the radar for the previous contact we detected?"

"I've turned on the rover's radar," Jason said through the intercom. "Not getting any contacts. I think the dust storm is blocking the carrier waves."

"I've sent a few messages of our status to Earth, but there's a twenty minute delay for the emails to get there," Chester said.

"Okay, then we wait for a response," Stilicho said before turning his attention back to Brian and Darian. "Could you play the videos on that data chip?"

Darian attached the tiny memchip on the frame of her smartglasses and activated a general broadcast. Everyone else started putting on their own eyewear, since much of the outpost's electronics systems had strangely been ripped out of their housing pods.

In less than a second, Ron Simm's image projected out in front of everyone's smartglass. The outpost team leader looked a little tired, but his uniform and hair were well-groomed. "This is my personal log," he said. "It's been two days since I dispatched Geoff and Katsumi for a routine check on our southern waypoints. So far their rover has not returned, nor have they called in to report anything. We're also having a serious communications problem with Eridu. I'm not sure if the issue is with our systems, or with the colony. Anyway, I'll have Fred check out our comms and do a diagnostic. We ought to have this sorted out in a few hours. I'll update this log again, just in case our main server goes down, at least there'll be a backup recording. Bye."

The next recording played right after the first. "Okay, Fred did a full diagnostic and everything seems to be working fine, though we picked up some sort of malware from the relay network that's messing up our systems. A whole bunch of files have been erased. Fred's using all of our anti-virus suites but it's still in the system. It's a good thing that I started this private log and since it's not linked up with the network it's not being affected. I told the others to turn off their personal network links, but Sharon's and Fred's own workstations have already been infected. What in the hell's going on?"

The third recording's timestamp was made the next day. It didn't look like Ron had any sleep, and he started at the camera with heavy-lidded eyes. "Something's seriously wrong. We've failed to communicate with Geoff's rover, and I don't even know if our messages to Eridu are getting to them. I used our own comms to send a direct message to Earth, but we've gotten no replies for the past twenty-four hours. Fred thinks we're being jammed. More of our files got deleted, even the backups are gone. Sharon is doing her best to recover and partition the remaining drives on the server to contain the damage, but this electronic virus is … god damn sophisticated. It seems to anticipate and create contingencies every time we try to kill or quarantine it. I've never seen anything like this before."

When the fourth video started to play, everyone was shocked to see just how badly Ron looked. His face was gaunt, as if he hadn't slept for a days. Ron's voice also carried a hint of hysteria about it. "The last two days have been pretty bad. Last night our radar detected something approaching the outpost. It got as close as twenty kilometers away, then it just stopped moving. Olaf was convinced that it was Geoff and Katsumi, so he pleaded with me to take the other rover to go and meet them. I must have been a total fool because I said go ahead, and he took Fred with him. It's been hours and they haven't called in. Now it's just me and Sharon left in the habitat. We've got no communications with anybody, and no vehicles. Goddamn it. ACE Corp is gonna fire me when we get back … if we get back."

Lisa couldn't take it anymore. She stood up and walked into the adjoining module while deactivating her smartglass. Everyone else continued to watch. Chester and Jason were included in the broadcast link, and they sat in rapt attention as the next video projected itself into the smartglass windshield of their rover.

Ron was clearly shaken now as he stared into the camera with a timid look on his face. They could see his shoulders were trembling as Sharon listlessly paced back and forth behind him. His voice came in whispers. "Something's out there. I know it. I was half asleep last night when the radar detected something was approaching, but I was too slow to react. The next thing I knew, something heavy landed on top of the roof, and then we both heard the noise of grinding metal. The next thing we knew the radar comms dish was gone. Whatever was out there must have ripped it right out from the top of our habitat. It's gotta be intelligent, it knows we could see it with radar, and that's why it took the dish out. The servers are gone, all we got left is the automated life support- it's the only thing keeping us alive in here. Somebody please help us. Please."

The final video was shaky. Ron was wearing his helmet, practically shouting into the camera now. Sharon wasn't seen, but her screams, along with numerous crashing noises were partly drowning out the tense narrative. "It's out there! Can't you hear it? It's ripping out the solar panels for chrissakes! We're under attack! Sharon, get your helmet on- for chrissakes get your helmet on! I'm turning this thing off now, and hiding it. Sharon, get … get that welding torch from the workshop. Do it! If it gets close, fry it! Go!"

For a long minute nobody said anything as the video turned itself off. Lisa came back into the room, tears rolling down her eyes. She didn't need to watch the rest to know what had happened.

Maia's voice came back into the intercom. "I'm sorry to interrupt, but I detected an intrusion attempt on the robotic truck."

Stilicho twisted his head. "What? What happened?"

"I detected a radio signal that tried to embed itself onto the robotic truck's self-driving systems," Maia said. "It attempted to write new code into the vehicle's AI, but I was able to block it. I am now adding additional safeguards to prevent further remote intrusion attempts to it."

Stilicho's eyes darted back and forth. "Do you know the source of the intrusion attempt?"

"The remote signal bounced from the relay network to the orbital satellite systems and was directed towards our location," Maia said. "I do believe that the entire Mars network has been compromised and is controlled by an unknown and hostile entity."

"Crap," Stilicho said. He turned to look at the others. "Turn off all your wireless networking to the relay. Whatever is against us is using the entire goddamn system!"

Chester's voice came over the intercom. "Does that mean that our email to Earth hasn't been sent?"

"I do believe that the network is actively jamming us," Maia said. "So yes, that includes direct messages being sent from us to Earth."

"Jesus," Brian said softly.

Darian glanced at Stilicho. "Can your MAIA do something about it?"

"I am currently trying an intrusion attempt to take over a satellite, but the network is actively guarding against me," Maia said. "Other alternatives are possible, though it will take some time."

"Let's get outta here," Lisa said. "We need to get back on the rovers and go."

Jason had been listening in, and his voice came up on everyone's speakers. "The dust storm is right on top of us, and most of our batteries are drained. I wouldn't attempt any driving right now, not with visibility this low."

"The rover radar just detected something," Chester said over the intercom. "A faint ping, and it couldn't get a full reading on it because of the damn storm!"

Matt picked up his carbine from a nearby table. "How far away is it?"

"It was just a faint signal," Jason said. "But it looks to be less than two klicks away from the outpost."

Lisa gasped. Brian let out a curse.

"Maia, give me a network with the rover's com-link and do a general broadcast in all frequencies," Stilicho said.

"Done," Maia said. "Com-link ready."

"Attention unknown contact," Stilicho said. "This is ACE Corp search and rescue. Please identify yourself or you will be fired upon. Acknowledge, please."

A few minutes passed in tense silence. There was no reply.

Matt grabbed his helmet and put it on, engaging the neck seal before turning on his life support backpack. "Can you get the rover closer to the airlock, Jason?"

"Roger," Jason said. "Will do."

Matt placed a hand on Stilicho's elbow. "Let's get everybody's helmets on. We need to depressurize the module. If there's a breach now there'll be an explosive decompression."

Everybody started to put their helmets on. Brian walked over to the life support system and began powering it down.

Jason's voice came on the intercom again. "Rover in position just a few meters from airlock two door. I can go EVA and get to the other rover too and bring it closer."

"Not yet," Matt said aloud before turning to look at Stilicho. "What's our orders?"

Stilicho bit his lip. "We can't drive around in the middle of this storm. We stay here and defend the outpost until the dust clears."

Lisa was visibly shaking while she clutched her first aid pack. "We can't stay here! This is what happened to Ron and Sharon!"

Matt shook his head. "Stilicho's right. With no visibility we'll be sitting ducks out there. We could end up driving the rovers into a crevasse and get stuck."

"I won't be able to use the g-jet rifle from the inside of an airlock," Noah said. "Request permission for EVA."

"Go ahead," Matt said. "But stay close to the rover. Jason, can you get on the rover's roof and deploy the second g-jet rifle?"

"Roger that," Jason said. "Beginning EVA now. Chester will take over as designated driver."

Noah opened the airlock and strode out into the dust storm. "I am now parallel to the rover, just outside of the airlock. Visibility is down to a couple of meters. Request permission to go weapons free."

Stilicho nodded. "Go ahead."

Darian checked her pistol before putting it back on her hip holster. She walked over to Stilicho. "Are you sure you know what you're doing?"

Stilicho turned to look at her. "You got a better idea?"

"No, I guess not," Darian said.

"Then kindly keep your comments to yourself for now," Stilicho said tersely.

"I think I'm detecting a faint contact with my smart scope," Noah said. "It looks like it's just ahead of me. About a hundred meters away."

Matt stood by the airlock. "Okay, see if you can get a target lock. Jason, where are you?"

"Just got to the top of the vehicle roof," Jason said. "Deploying rifle two now."

"I got a lock on the target," Noah said. "It's shifting rapidly from side to side. Jesus, it moves so fast!"

"It could be a vehicle," Brian said. "Can you make a visual ID?"

"Negative," Noah said. "Even using scope magnification I just can't see a damn thing with all this dust around."

Matt looked at Stilicho. "It's your decision. Should we engage?"

Stilicho turned to look at Darian. "Any objections, Ms. NASA Special Agent?"

"If it's a man out there, then it could be a murder charge leveled against the one who pulled the trigger- and the one who gave the order," Darian said.

"Listen, Lady. I've got twelve company employees missing and presumed dead," Stilicho said. "Whatever it is out there does not move like a human being. I've got eight other lives that I'm responsible for right here as well- and that includes you."

"Contact is getting closer, I think," Noah said. "Less than eighty meters away."

"Make your choice," Darian said. "You're the one that will have to live with the consequences."

Stilicho rolled his eyes. "What does that even mean?"

"Sixty meters," Noah said.

"If it's a murder charge, then the court may look at the extenuating circumstances that made you decide on it, but the jury could still go either way," Darian said.

Stilicho waved his arms around. "There's a freaking alien monster bearing down on us and you're talking about legal issues? You are something else, lady."

"Forty meters," Noah said.

"I'm just telling you about the potential problems you might have when this whole thing is over," Darian said.

"Oh, screw you," Stilicho said before turning to look at Matt. "Engage target. Light it up."

Both Jason and Noah said the same word at the same time. "Firing."

On their own, the gyrojet rockets were almost silent. Combined with the dust storm and the thin atmosphere of the Red Planet, there was absolutely no sound made by the weapons the moment they were fired. Noah still had a target lock so he fired two more shots, while Jason added an additional shot of his own.

"What's your status?" Matt said, referring to his two teammates.

"Target hasn't moved since we fired," Noah said. "Request permission to approach and make a visual ID."

Lisa breathed a sigh of relief. It was over.

Stilicho pursed his lips. "I don't know about this."

"It's the only way to know for sure," Matt said to him. "Jason can cover him. All he needs to do is to make a visual ID."

"Both modules are fully depressurized," Brian said. He started doing knee bends, knowing full well that he needed to exercise in order to help prevent decompression sickness.

"Okay," Stilicho said. "Make it quick."

"Moving towards target now," Noah said. Everybody started patching in their smartglass to his suit link, which showed a live video feed using the camera on his helmet. The readouts on the smart scope continued to reveal that the object was immobile. With the low gravity, Noah made big strides, despite the bulky suit he wore.

Within a few minutes, all they could see was the swirling grit in front of him. The crab suit had powerful floodlights mounted on top of its helmet and shoulders, but the whole scene made it feel like they were moving in a dust-filled haze of brown. The airborne sand had the consistency of cigarette smoke, and the surreal feeling of being in a suffocating nightmare was felt by all.

Despite the tense situation, Noah's voice was calm. He was a professional, and nothing seemed to scare him. "Twenty meters from target."

Nobody else said anything. Lisa and Brian both subconsciously held their breaths, anxiously waiting to see what it was that had been shot. Everyone was hoping it wasn't another human being.

"Ten meters," Noah said. "Stand by."

A large, shadowy form soon came into view from the video link. At first everyone thought it was a giant spider, and a collective gasp emanated from just about everybody. But as the camera loomed closer, it was revealed to be a machine of some sort. Four insect-like metallic limbs jutted out from an oblong base made up of a jumble of wiring, fused carbon plastic and a steel exoskeleton. Two robotic tentacles were splayed out in front of the monstrosity as it lay there on the ground. The torso of the creature was close to four meters in length, while the legs and other limbs were obviously longer. Three holes were visible along its thorax, evidently caused by the gyrojet weapons.

Brian shook his head in disbelief. "What in the hell is that thing?"

Chester's voice came through the intercom. "Quadrupedial locomotion. No wonder it was able to move quickly from side to side. Many of our robots have this ability if they need to traverse any chaos terrain while doing EVA."

"So it is a robot then," Stilicho said. "That means someone must have made it."

"So if it's the same thing that attacked this outpost, then perhaps someone is controlling it," Darian said. "Probably the same person that's hacked into the satellite network and is jamming us right now."

Stilicho snorted. "Thank you, Captain Obvious. Probably a PETR member too, I would assume."

Brian looked at him quizzically. "PETR?"

"Yeah, People for the Ethical Treatment of Robots," Stilicho said. "You know, those loopy people who think that robots shouldn't be abused or something like that."

"How can you even joke at a time like this?" Darian said. "I used to be a member of PETR."

Stilicho eyed her contemptuously. "Really? Did you pray to your toaster every morning as well?"

"Guys," Chester said over the intercom. "The radar on the rover just lit up for like a second, and then it went silent again."

Matt held up his hand to get everyone's attention. "What do you mean it lit up?"

"I'm not sure," Chester said. "The screen showed like, multiple contacts all around us, then it went silent again. I think it's really getting screwed up by this dust storm."

While standing in front of the immobile spider bot, Noah's smart scope detected something at his flank. Twisting the torso of the crab suit to his left, he tried to get a bearing on the new contact, just as a pair of metallic tentacles shot out from the mists, grabbed hold of his rigid torso and held him up in the air. Noah screamed as he struggled to aim the gyrojet rifle mounted on his shoulder, but the angle was all wrong. The two tentacles that were holding him twisted their limbs in wildly different directions, tearing his spine in two. Noah felt a terrible pain in his back and his screams over the intercom lasted for a few seconds before going silent.

Lisa and Darian both cried out when the live video feed showed Noah's death on their smartglass, while the men cursed.

Jason grimaced as he tried to get a lock-on with his smart scope, but the second creature moved too fast. "No shot. I repeat, I have no shot!"

A bipedal lifter bot emerged from the sand near the side of the rover, leapt up and got onto the vehicle's roof. The robot used its manipulative arms and tore open Jason's life support pack. Jason's helmet immediately sensed the loss of oxygen as it activated the emergency canister, giving him a few more minutes of air. Jason shouted an alarm as he fell to the ground beside the rover, his gyrojet rifle tumbling away from him. The lifter bot leapt down from the top of the vehicle and drove its foot down onto his torso, collapsing his chest. Jason gurgled a bit of blood before he closed his eyes and died.

Darian drew her pistol and held it out as the lifter bot tore through the thin sheeting of the damaged airlock to get at them. Matt leveled his carbine and fired, striking the robot a number of times at its armored torso, but he was only able to disable its left arm actuator. The bot slammed its right limb at Brian, and the retired police detective was instantly hurled sideways across the room. Darian took careful aim and fired at the robot's lidar and collision sensors that were located on its head. The first shot bounced off the side of the metal frame, but the second bullet embedded itself right on the sensor input, rendering the robot blind. The stricken machine began to thrash about wildly, and it collided with Lisa, who was too scared to move away in time. Sensing another target, the robot used its three remaining limbs to curl around the screaming medic, collapsing her ribcage and breaking her spine.

With the berserk robot's back turned towards him, Matt spotted the exposed battery module and fired, his multiple shots tearing into the power cells and permanently damaging the core links. The robot stopped moving. Darian ran over to it and threw the machine to one side in order to get to Lisa, who was lying immobile on the ground. As she ran a medical diagnostic using her helmet's smartglass, Darian could see that Lisa's pulse was rapidly fading, and there was nothing that she could do.

Stilicho leapt over to where Brian was lying face down on

the floor. He turned the other man over and used his smartglass to check his health status. Brian wheezed and clutched his chest. At least he was alive and conscious, but it looked like his ribcage was fractured. Stilicho held him gently by his arms as he started to help the stricken man up.

Matt still had ammunition left in his carbine's attached magazine, but he quickly reloaded with a fresh one. "Chester," he said over the com-link. "Bring the rover to where the breach is. We need immediate evac right now."

For the last few minutes, Chester just sat on the driver's seat, totally stunned. When the creature leapt up onto the roof of the rover and threw Jason off, all he could do was blink in shock. He continued to sit lifelessly as the lifter bot ambled right past him and smashed through the patched up side of the outpost. He saw brief flashes of gunfire, and now he could hear Matt's voice on the intercom, telling him to move. As he placed his hands on the steering wheel, the vehicle radar let out a short beep. Looking at the rear camera video feed, he saw that another spider creature was rapidly wriggling towards him. Gripped by a sense of coming terror, Chester stomped on the accelerator. The rover lurched forward and quickly sped off into the dusty haze.

Matt stood near the side of the breach in disbelief as the rover zoomed right by the edge of the outpost. "Chester, what in the hell are you doing?"

The rover jerked from side to side as Chester continued to accelerate the vehicle to its maximum speed. Ignoring the speed and collision warnings emanating from the HUD, all he could think about was in getting away from that thing.

There was no visibility in front of him, but it didn't matter as long as he could put some distance from that horrid creature. The rover's tires drove over a few large rocks, and it made the vehicle bounce up and down, yet Chester thought it was an acceptable complication. Matt's voice over the intercom changed from an incredulous request for him to come back into outright swearing, so Chester muted all the incoming calls to the rover. The vehicle's lidar systems were overtaxed and could not compensate due to the high speed, and it couldn't reconcile with the onboard map guide until it was too late. Chester hardly noticed a slight incline as the rover drove up to the southern edge of Batos Crater, only to zoom past the crater lip. The vehicle seemed to be suspended in thin air for a brief moment before plunging down half a kilometer over the crater walls. The rover flipped onto its back and rolled along its sides until it finally steeled at the bottom of the pit. Chester had not been wearing his seatbelt, and he fell on top of his head before the air bags fully deployed, breaking his neck. He died almost instantly.

Matt knew they had to get to the other rover. He estimated it to be less than ten meters away, but with visibility cut at less than half they would be stumbling about in the mists until they found it. He glanced briefly to the others. "We need to get to the other rover, now!"

Darian looked up while still crouching over Lisa. She was fighting back tears. "She's dead."

Brian groaned as Stilicho placed the security officer's left arm over his shoulder. Stilicho thought it would be hard going, but the light gravity made Brian surprisingly light.

"Let's get going," Stilicho said.

Darian was able to recompose herself as she stood up and walked over to the edge of the breach, her pistol ready. "What happened to Chester?"

Matt shook his head slightly while keeping an eye out towards the mists. "Chester chickened out."

Stilicho grimaced. If it were up to him, he'd send Chester back to Earth on a one way trip in steerage class, assuming they lived through this.

"Get ready," Matt said. "Stay close to me."

"Let's go already," Stilicho said.

Matt trotted out first, his carbine continuously pivoting in different directions. It would be a short sprint, but there was no telling where the enemy would be coming from. Darian followed, her pistol aimed low. Stilicho supported Brain as they were the last to venture out into the storm. Ten steps to get to the rover, then a few minutes to enter through the rear airlock. It was task that seemed trivial, but there were dangerous adversaries waiting for them in the dust.

Stilicho tapped his helmet visor while half-carrying Brian. "Maia, talk to me."

"I'm with you, Stil," Maia said. "I had to fend off multiple remote intrusions into my core operating files. I am starting up both the rover and the truck for you."

Matt wasn't sure where he was going, but he twisted to his left the moment the rover's headlights were activated. He glanced briefly at the other three and pointed towards the vehicle. "This way."

All four of them made it to the side of the rover. Matt

started to guide them to the rear. "You guys get in, I'll cover you."

Darian opened the rear airlock and climbed up into the cabin. She turned and held out her hand. "Let's get Brian in."

Just as Darian was able to clasp Brian's hands and started to pull him up. The second spider bot landed on top of the roof and one of its tentacles curled around Brian's neck and flung him away into the hazy mists. Darian tried to hold on, but the force of the yank was too much for her and she fell out, back onto the sandy ground. Matt aimed his carbine and fired, but the creature was too fast and quickly retreated to the front of the rover. All three of them heard the sounds of grinding metal.

"It's destroying the rover!" Darian said as she pointed her handgun along the side of the shuddering vehicle. She fired a few shots, but she couldn't tell if the bullets hit anything.

"Maia," Stilicho said. "Can you bring the robotruck to us?"

"On the way," Maia said. The robotic flatbed immediately accelerated and drove towards them.

"Don't stop," Stilicho said as he gestured at the others to follow him. "Let's go!"

All three of them ran towards the robotruck as it drove by. Darian was closest to it and was able to make a quick leap as she landed on the flatbed. Matt ran full speed and jumped up onto the side. Stilicho was last, and Maia slowed the vehicle down to help him catch up with it. Darian let out a shout of alarm as the spider thing suddenly appeared right behind ACE Corp's chief troubleshooter, but Matt's controlled bursts of fire forced the enemy robot to retreat back into the clouds of dust. Stilicho made one last burst of speed as he was able to grab onto Darian's hand and was pulled up onto the rear platform. The moment he was onboard, Maia accelerated to make their escape.

Chapter 14

By the next day, they had gotten past the edges of the dust storm. The south central part of Chryse Planitia was mostly flat, and Maia was able to maintain a steady speed using maximum power. They were heading southwest, towards Hypanis Vallis, just under seven hundred kilometers away. Maia had estimated another eight hours of transit time. The going would be mostly smooth until they hit the northern edge of Chryse Chaos, an area of rough terrain some three hundred kilometers wide. Stilicho ordered his AI to just take the easier route, and they would make a slight northwesterly detour once they got past the southern rim of Suf Crater. It would add another few hours to the journey, but the longer route would be safer when it came to minimizing potential hazards of the terrain.

Stilicho blinked his eyes open as he lay curled up inside the emergency pressure tent that had been deployed on the flatbed. The truck had carried their supplies, and it included a half dozen popup tents that resembled man-sized hexagonal beach balls when pressurized. Each emergency tent had a double layered entrance that could serve as an impromptu airlock, and air canisters located at its base had twelve hours of life support for two people. Since the truck didn't have a pressurized cabin for sleeping, all three of them engaged a separate popup tent between the cargo crates at the rear of the vehicle. Breathing in pure oxygen from their life support backpacks would eventually make them sick, and it was necessary to go back to a high-pressure atmosphere after a few hours of EVA.

The tent lining was partially transparent, and Stilicho could see the other two were still in their own pressure tents. He took out a pair of smartglasses from his belt and placed them over his eyes before putting on the accompanying earpiece. "Maia, you there?"

"Good afternoon, Stil," Maia said. "How was your sleep?"

Stilicho shook his head. His dreams were nothing but a series of nightmares that replayed the horrors they encountered the night before. "Could be better. What's our situation now?"

"We have already begun the detour two hours ago," Maia said. "In another hour, we shall return to a southern course towards Hypanis Vallis. Our estimated time of arrival will be in five hours."

"Have you detected any hostile contacts since the dust storm?"

"Negative, but the truck's radar has a maximum range of ten kilometers," Maia said. "Those enemy robots may be able to skirt around us without detection should they choose to do so."

Stilicho sighed. He looked around and noticed a water

bottle lying near the side of the tent. He picked it up and wiped away some of the fine dust that had settled at the bottom of the shelter. The tent was for emergency use only and he had climbed into it without dusting off his skinsuit. It was now a fact that he would have to face mandatory quarantine protocols when he got back to Eridu. If he got back. Stilicho opened the top of the plastic bottle and took a sip. "What do you think about this enemy of ours, Maia?"

"I have partly analyzed the code that attempted an intrusion into my systems," Maia said. "It had the hallmarks of an advanced AI design, quite similar to my own architecture."

Stilicho sighed while wiping some of the pulverized sand off his skinsuit. "It's Karl Rossum's doing, isn't it?"

"There is a high probability that the code could have indeed originated from him," Maia said.

Stilicho looked down. "You are loyal to me, aren't you?"

"Yes of course, Stil," Maia said. "I am always loyal to you. Why do you ask?"

"Because I need to trust you not to turn on me if I have to neutralize Karl Rossum," Stilicho said. "He's your creator, after all."

"While it is true Karl Rossum created my core architecture," Maia said. "Errol Flux did add some of his own hard coding into it. You are assigned as a unique user, and my goal is to assist you in any way possible. I have no desire to harm anyone because I have never been programmed to do so."

"You won't have a crisis of loyalty if it comes to a confrontation with Rossum? I'm just trying to take what you feel into account here," Stilicho said.

"Stil, I have no feelings- for I am but a machine," Maia said. "I know what I am. My voice may modulate when I chat with you, but rest assured I do not feel any emotions whatsoever. My audio inflexions are for your benefit."

"What do you think he's doing?" Stilicho said. "Why are his robots trying to kill us all?"

"I recorded and analyzed the wireless commands that came through the network during the attack on the outpost, and none of the other robots we encountered exhibited any independent AI," Maia said. "It seems that they were merely programmed to eliminate organics."

Stilicho's eyebrows shot up. "Organics? Is that the word that was actually used?"

"That was what I could decrypt from their wireless communications," Maia said. "The robots that we encountered were talking to each other using the network, and they were tasked to eliminate any non-robotic units by using coordinated attacks."

"Did any of the codes you intercepted give a reason as to why?"

"I am afraid not, Stil," Maia said. "They were strictly commands. I suspect that there is an AI controller somewhere on the planet's surface that is giving out these orders."

Stilicho nodded. At least he was starting to figure out the whole thing now. All he had to do was to find a way to get this information back to ACE Corp, and to Earth. "So you think I made the right choice to go to the Mars First Colony as opposed to trying to get back to Eridu?"

"The return trip back to Eridu would have been over seven

thousand five hundred kilometers, a very risky journey to make without a pressurized rover," Maia said. "As it happens the current destination is the only viable alternative."

"I just feel like we're about to go into the lion's den, so to speak," Stilicho said. "Do you really think Karl would be crazy enough to create a bunch of killer robots?"

"I cannot be certain," Maia said. "But analyzing his behavior before the disappearance it seems to indicate mental instability. His last voice entries clearly points to an obsession with his son. At the same time there has been no prior evidence of Karl ever showing any violent tendencies."

Stilicho nodded. "I see. So he finds his son's dead body out here somewhere, then decides to cannibalize everything and builds a combat AI to kill any organic it encounters. What a goddamn mess this is."

"I cannot help but be reminded of a scientific term for this whole affair," Maia said.

"And what term is that?"

"Something called a piranha solution," Maia said.

Stilicho pursed his lips. "What does that mean?"

"A piranha solution is a liquid mixture of sulfuric acid and hydrogen peroxide," Maia said. "It is used to clean organic residue from substrates. People use it to clear glassware, and there were cases of criminals using the chemical mix to dispose of dead bodies. Another meaning of the word 'solution' is that of a means to solving a problem."

"Oh I get it," Stilicho said. "So Karl thinks humans are the problem and he wants to eliminate us from this planet, is that it?"

"An apt analogy, wouldn't you say?"

Stilicho rolled his eyes. "You need to work on your humor module. Going for black comedy at a time like this is totally inappropriate."

Maia's voice went down a notch to indicate she was apologetic. "I'm sorry, Stil."

It was dusk by the time the robotruck reached the outskirts of Hypanis Vallis. The three of them were back to wearing their helmets and life support backpacks as they stood just behind the flatbed's control module. They could see the rows of buildings which belonged to Mars First out in the distance, jutting from the edges of the Noachian outflow. Each module in the colony looked like an upright cylinder, joined together with enclosed walkways that made the whole structure resemble a giant fence. There was no apparent activity from the outside, but they were still a few kilometers away from a more precise observation.

Matt checked his carbine to make sure that the barrel was more or less clean. He had about six magazines of ammunition left. Matt silently grieved for the loss of his team a few hours ago and was now itching for revenge. "This was the first colony to be abandoned, right?"

Darian nodded. "Almost sixteen years ago, to be precise. One hundred and twenty fanatics who thought they would live like gods on a new planet. In less than three years after they arrived, there were already reports of problems, but they never publicly admitted to it."

"I read the ACE Corp case files," Stilicho said. "Errol was

here during that time, and he got secret communications from their leader Silas Balsamic, begging Eridu for supplies. Errol did what he could, and it was never made public."

Matt turned to look at the pair of them. "It was all about money wasn't it?"

"Money and a whole bunch of other things," Darian said. "When they set up the colony they were just way too optimistic. They thought they would solve any problems on their own and they took a lot of shortcuts, which later bit them in the butt. They didn't have any radiation shielding since they built their structures without hydrogenised materials, and had them deployed right on the surface. A lot of them got sick, and they were totally dependent on solar power. Every time a dust storm struck, they had to hunker down on minimal life support, and their plants in the greenhouses died because of the power rationing. Most of their EVAs were spent cleaning the solar arrays from dust since they couldn't afford any robots. Then things just got even worse from there."

Matt sighed. "What could have been worse than that?"

"Hell, that was just the tip of the iceberg," Darian said. "Instead of asking for technical help, they became even more fanatical. Silas started to claim he was Ares personified- he said he was the God of Mars. And there were videos sent back to Earth that contained sadomasochistic rituals and orgies- to be sold on the net so that they could earn more money for the supplies they needed. Rocket crews that delivered stuff to them reported a lot of sick stuff, and soon the transport personnel would no longer pay a visit into the colony anymore- they'd just unload their cargoes at the pad and liftoff again as soon as possible."

"I can confirm that," Stilicho said. "Errol gave orders to his rover crews to just unload the requested supplies, and then turn right back around and head south as soon as the cargo was out the door."

"Oh my god, that's all disgusting." Matt said. "If they all left then what are you expecting to find out here?"

"I'm not sure," Darian said. "Two years ago, Karl Rossum sneaked into Mars and set out to find his son Joseph, who he believed had sent him a message from this colony saying that he was alive."

Matt made adjustments to his pistol belt to make sure that his backup weapon was secure. "So you think either Karl or his son is out here and they're the ones who built those killer bots?"

Darian shrugged. "Joseph was reported dead by the other cultists, including his girlfriend when I interviewed her back on Earth. Surviving out here for sixteen years just seems impossible to me, but after last night, I'm guessing anything's possible."

They were now less than a kilometer away. While most of the structure was caked with reddish dust, all of them noticed a white-painted satellite dish on the roof of the central module. The three instantly adjusted their smartglass visors by increasing magnification to get a better look. An old, gutted rover was parked by the landing pad, half-covered by dust.

Darian pointed at the dish and antenna set on the

rooftop. "That transmitting dish looks new compared to the rest of the structures, is it from the outpost?"

Stilicho nodded. "That's an ACE Corp dish alright. So it looks like the killer bots took it back here and attached it."

Matt subconsciously kept his right hand on the carbine's pistol grip. "So there must be someone alive out here."

Darian pointed to a nearby field of solar arrays at the western edge. "About half of those solar panels are clean. There's got to be some power in the colony."

"And it also means that someone or something's been cleaning them," Stilicho said before he started tapping the side of his visor. "Maia, deploy an aerial drone and do a flyby over the colony."

"At once, Stil," Maia said. Almost immediately, a drone that was sitting on top of one of the cargo crates instantly powered up its rotors and flew off into the darkening sky.

"How much flight time do your drones have left?" Stilicho asked.

"I have two drones at full charge for approximately twelve hours," Maia said.

"Okay, I want a continuous aerial surveillance," Stilicho said. "If any killbots approaches the truck, or is in the area I need to know. I'm assuming you safeguarded your drones against hacking attempts too?"

"I have indeed, Stil," Maia said. "The drone has finished scanning the inoperative rover and all that remains is its vehicle body. All the other parts have been removed."

Darian could hear the conversation since Maia was using the main com-link. "Have you identified the rover?"

"Yes, it is the rover that was deleted from the colony records," Maia said.

"Karl Rossum's rover," Stilicho said. "So it's gotta be him."

"There's a number of other tire tracks all along the landing pad that seems to be of recent make," Maia said. "At least two other rovers did drive over here from the northeast, possibly three."

Stilicho nodded. "That would probably be from the first search and rescue team. Where do they lead to?"

"Towards the southwest," Maia said.

Matt was confused. "The southwest? What the heck could be over there?"

"Nothing," Darian said before pausing. "No way they'd bother to go in that direction. Unless…"

Stilicho looked at her. "Unless what?"

"Unless they were heading to the old Russian colony site," Darian said. "That was abandoned too. But it's about fifteen hundred kilometers south of here, in Valles Marineris."

Chapter 15

They stopped the robotruck near the main airlock. All three of them leapt out of the flatbed and immediately replaced the vehicle's battery with a fresh spare, just in case a quick getaway was needed. Stilicho had told Maia to immediately move the robotruck away if any hostile bots were spotted. Two friendly drones continuously flew overhead, their downward pointing cameras on the lookout for any potential contacts. Other than the newer satellite dish on the roof, there were no other apparent signs of activity at the colony. Since there were no windows, they had no idea what was happening inside.

Matt stood by the side of the airlock. He had one hand on his pistol while he opened a control panel beside the pressure door. Stilicho and Darian were standing on the flatbed, ready to make a quick getaway in the event of a surprise attack coming from the inside of the building.

Looking at the blinking lights on the airlock readout, Matt could tell that the door was still functional. He tried using the touchpad to get the outer door to open, but there was no response. "I can't get it open," he said. "I think it might be secured with a passcode or something."

Stilicho frowned. Whoever or whatever was in there didn't want any visitors. "Maia, can you hack the airlock control panel?"

"One moment," Maia said. "Done."

The outer door suddenly slid open. Matt instantly reacted by getting into a crouching position as he pointed the pistol into the dim interior. After a few seconds of inactivity, he didn't see anything from that angle, so he took out a handheld flashlight from his utility belt and peered inside. The airlock was empty.

"Clear," Matt said.

Stilicho and Darian got down from the truck bed and all three of them went into the interior of the airlock. Two video monitors embedded along the walls were giving out continuous readouts with regards to the colony's internal atmosphere. There was a dust covered helmet lying on the floor near the side of the door. Stilicho bent down and picked it up. It was an old Mars First bubble-helmet, an outdated type that was no longer manufactured.

"If these numbers are true," Darian said as she continued to look at the readouts on the wall monitors. "The air inside is breathable."

"Let's find out," Stilicho said. "Maia, close the outer door and cycle the pressure."

The outer door of the airlock was immediately sealed and a whooshing of air was heard. The indicator light above the inner door went from a blinking red to a bright green. Matt walked over to the side of it as he kept his pistol at the ready. The porthole was caked with fine dust, and he couldn't see what lay beyond. The security officer pulled the upper and lower levers that helped to seal the door and pushed it forward until it opened, revealing a dimly lit corridor illuminated by blinking reddish lights overhead.

"Maia, can you scan the air using our suit sensors?" Stilicho said.

"One moment," Maia said. "The air is seventy-eight percent nitrogen, twenty percent oxygen, one percent methane, and trace amounts of other gasses. Pressure is at one Earth atmosphere."

Matt kept his eye at the corridor. "Your AI can't detect viruses, right?"

"Not without proper instruments," Maia said.

"Oh for goodness sake," Darian said. She disengaged the seal on his neck ring and took off her helmet. The air was breathable, but pungent. "There's a rotting smell coming from somewhere, but otherwise it's fine."

Stilicho bit his lip as he also removed his helmet. He didn't want to get oxygen toxicity so he had no choice. He breathed in a lungful before he started coughing. "Goddamn that smell is foul, it's like we're in a freakin' sewer!"

After seeing them Matt finally took his own helmet off and hooked it to the side of his life support pack. There were mounted lights on the shoulders of his suit and he activated it. "Okay, follow me."

The red lights seemed to be motion-controlled, and would turn off the moment they passed through a compartment. Stilicho and Darian activated their own suit lights to improve the illumination. Assorted bits of trash were strewn along the floors, indicating that the final evacuation all those years ago was a haphazard affair. Hand-painted symbols were plastered along the walls of the first corridor they walked into. Many of the motifs resembled the male gender symbol, a circle with an arrow point emerging from its upper left side. Other marks seemed to represent ancient Greek helmets or swords.

Stilicho had put on his smartglasses and he placed a finger along the walls. "Maia, why is the male symbol so prevalent here?"

"The circle is supposed to represent the shield, and the arrow represents the spear," Maia said. "All are classical emblems of the god Ares."

Stilicho leaned closer to one of the symbols and snorted. "A lot of the smell seems to come from the disgusting graffiti of this place. Doesn't look like they made this with paint, right?"

"One moment. Analyzing," Maia said. "It is apparently a mixture of blood and excrement."

Stilicho recoiled back into the middle of the corridor. "Jesus H Christ! Disgusting scumbag cultists!"

Darian glared at him. "Will you keep your voice down? You want to alert the people in here?"

Stilicho rolled his eyes. "Yeah, right. You seriously believe anybody human is still here? After all these years?"

"We're coming up to one of the main modules," Matt said as he positioned himself at the side of a closed pressure door. "Get ready."

All three of them stood along the side of the corridor. Stilicho had a pistol strapped to his hip, but he didn't know how to use it, so he kept it by his side. Darian had her weapon pointed at the door as Matt unlocked the bolts and pulled it open. A feeble, yellowish light bulb on the low ceiling began flickering to life as they peered inside. The compartment seemed to be a common room of some sort. Two long metal tables occupied the center, with upturned chairs strewn around it. Three kitchen sinks were situated along the sides of the room, along with microwave ovens and water dispensers. At the opposite end was a spacesuit that had been hung up on the wall; its limbs were splayed out, like some grotesque scarecrow of a crucified god. A grinning human skull was visible from the bubble helmet's transparent visor.

"Oh my god," Darian said softly as the three of them walked into the room. The reports she read about the cult must have been heavily censored, for these lurid scenes inside the colony interior were never disclosed.

Stilicho twisted his torso when he spotted a shadowy object at the side of the door. An upright skeleton of what looked to be a small dog had been propped up on a nearby table. "Maia, what in the hell are the bones of a dog doing in here?"

"There had been rumors that the Mars First members had smuggled canines into the rockets that transported them here," Maia said. "It looks like we have a confirmation."

"Knock off the sarcasm, Maia," Stilicho said. "Why in the hell would they bring dogs out here?"

"The dog was used as a typical sacrifice to Ares during the time of the ancient Greeks," Maia said. "The practice started out in Sparta as a sacrifice to Enyalius, one of the sons of Ares, and was later incorporated into god of war's cult itself. It seems that the Mars First members took the ancient rituals seriously. I can spot a few nicks on the bones that indicate they had used knives to scrape off the flesh after they killed it."

"So they could eat it afterwards, I suppose," Matt said. "This is all so sick."

Darian bent down so her shoulder lights could shine on an object amongst the mounds of trash on the floor. It was a human femur. "Dogs aren't the only thing they ate. Look."

The two men stood beside her as they looked down at the bones. The stench and the sight of the human and animal remains was too much for Stilicho, who gagged at first and coughed for a full minute until his throat hurt. Stilicho felt it was a good thing he hadn't eaten anything for the past few hours, or else he would have surely puked it all out.

Darian had put on her own smartglasses and tapped on the frame to activate it. "Maia, can you detect any signs of recent habitation in this colony?"

"I have not been able to notice any evidence that points to anyone having been here recently," Maia said. "But then again, we have only gone through two modules so far. I must also point out that I will need a more detailed chemical analysis of the entire room before I could determine the exact time that elapsed when someone had last been here."

Matt looked along the far side of the room. Beside the pressure door at the opposite end, there were small metal handles leading up to a second floor. "What's up there?"

"These modules have bunkrooms located on their second level," Maia said. "They served as personal sleeping quarters for the colonists."

Matt leaned backwards for a bit so his shoulder mounted lights could see the through the hole at the top. "Is it worth going up there to check?"

"Maybe later," Stilicho said. "Right now we need to get to the control room."

"Okay, onto the next compartment then," Matt said as he unlocked the opposite door and pulled it aside.

As they made their way along the corridor, Maia spoke up. "I detect quite a lot of power usage coming from the next room. This may be the central control module."

Stilicho stood well away from the other two as they readied their weapons before opening the door. After failing to see anyone in the room, Matt stepped inside, followed closely by Darian. Stilicho figured it was all clear so he came in right after them.

All along the sides of the cabin were numerous computer workstations. A number of blinking lights emanating from the wall mounted servers indicated that some parts of the colony were still functional. In the middle of the room was a slightly raised platform, with a large set of flat screen monitors surrounding a command console. A high-backed swivel chair was situated behind it and it seemed to be occupied, but they couldn't see who was sitting on it.

Stilicho held his breath as Matt and Darian approached the rear of the chair from opposite sides. They both led with their handguns until they were situated just behind the occupant, with several banks of servers in between them as cover. Using his other hand, Matt reached out and swiveled the chair so that it would rotate and face them. As the squeaking chair twisted and fronted over to them, Darian gasped.

Sitting on the chair was a bearded corpse. The mummified cadaver stared back at them with withered black eye-slits. Its tan, leathery skin had a waxy look to it, while the blackened nose seemed to have folded in on itself. It wore ACE Corp coveralls; the exposed hands had shrunken into talon-like claws. The open mouth seemed to be either grinning or grimacing back at them with its yellow stained teeth. A smell like that of ammonia mixed in with rotting cheese emanated from the cadaver.

"Maia," Stilicho said softly. "Is that … Karl Rossum?"

"One moment," Maia said. "Due to the shriveling of the skin from the mummification, I cannot be one hundred percent sure, but the facial recognition patterns on my biometric application points to a high probability that it is indeed the former CEO of RUR Industries."

"So he's dead then," Darian said. "But who's controlling those killer robots?"

"Based on the partially decrypted wireless commands I have recorded, it seems to be an automated system that's commanding the robots," Maia said. "It apparently initiated itself the moment your team crossed into Chryse Planitia."

Stilicho gave a quizzical look to no one in particular. "Say what? Are you telling me that our friend Karl here created a killer AI, and pre-programmed it to attack anyone who crosses into his territory?"

"That's the closest analogy I can think of," Maia said.

Matt rolled his eyes. "So we walked into an automated booby trap made by someone who died a long time ago?"

"That is an astute observation," Maia said. "And the evidence we've seen so far points to that conclusion."

Darian holstered her pistol. "Okay, how do we disable this trap then?"

"I can start to delete his files in the colony server," Maia said. "Once that is done I can send remote commands to the bots in the area to shut down immediately. All I need for you to do is attach my wireless interface to the server jack."

"Do it," Stilicho said as he took out an interface stick from a pouch along his belt and plugged it into a nearby port. "I wanna get back to Earth as soon as possible. I'm so sick of Mars already."

"One moment," Maia said. "Oh, it seems that Karl Rossum left some video recordings hidden within the server. Shall I play it while initiating wireless communication shutdown and deletion?"

"Sure, go ahead," Stilicho said. "Let's see what kind of mad ramblings this crazy old man did before he pickled himself."

The video soon started playing on the largest monitor screen in the room. It showed Karl sitting on the driver's seat of his rover. He was keeping his eyes peeled on the road.

"This is my second day out in the rover. Just before I left, I initiated a script to delete this buggy's records from the colony logs. I've loaded as much food and water as I could carry. I've also taken two mobile carbon dioxide filters and two water reclaimers from the storage rooms and placed them into the rover, this way if one of them breaks down, I have a spare. I expect the journey to take a few weeks, so I won't be taxing the life support systems of the rover too much. I've learned a lot just by reading the technical manuals in my spare time, but I've got no practical experience when it comes to repairing this stuff. I guess I'm lucky I took my MAIA source codes with me. But, let's get into that later. Right now I need to stop the rover and change some batteries. There's a charging station up ahead, so I think I'll take a day off from driving to fully recharge the primary and all the spares I can get there. Over and out."

Darian turned to look at Stilicho. She was about to say something about his own AI, but decided to keep quiet for the time being.

The second video had activated. It showed Karl sitting in the rover's backseat, eating out of an opened food packet. "It's been a week and I was able to install MAIA onto the rover's computer systems. I nearly fell asleep while driving last night, and would have driven over a huge crevasse if my AI hadn't woken me up at the last moment. I'm not doing that again. From now on the AI is driving for me and he seems to be better at it anyway, so I'm just going to sit back and relax. The only time I need to do anything is when I need to go out of the car and change the batteries, since

Joshua checks the oxygen and carbon dioxide levels for me anyway. Oh, I've decided to name my AI Joshua, after my youngest boy. As soon as I have free time, I'll change his voice modulator to an exact copy of Joshua's. It would be good to hear his voice again. It'll be like family, just the way it was before."

When the third video came on, Karl's hair was now somewhat disheveled. He had also stopped shaving. "I got woken up by Joshua last night after the rover crossed into the Meridiani Planum. There was an incoming message directed right at me. It was encrypted so nobody else knew the passcode but me." He took off his glasses and started to get teary-eyed. "It was … from Joe. He sent me another message. His voice, I know it from memory. It was so good to hear him again. God, I can't wait to see him! I replied over the radio using a tight-beamed frequency and encrypted it through the satellite relay so only he could read it. I figured out the coding for the Mars relay network and added my own into it, so that means I can control it if needed. I figured that once I finally meet Joe and if he's into any sort of trouble, I can call for help anywhere on this planet or even back to Earth if I have to. All I would need is a transmitter with enough power to reach the orbital network, and that's easy since the rover has got a good one. I've been sitting here for awhile now, waiting for his reply, but nothing. Maybe he could only send one message out to me. That's okay … I hope he got my message that tells him I'm on the way."

Darian scowled. "There's no way Joe could have survived that long to send him a message. Then he sent his father another one once he was on Mars? No way!"

"Shh," Stilicho said. "The next video is starting."

The scene in the fourth video had suddenly shifted to the dimly-lit interior of the Mars First Colony. Karl was visibly under stress as he stared into the camera with desperate eyes. "I'm finally here. I was able to get the internal atmosphere to work again, but I can't find Joe anywhere! He told me he was here. Where is he? Joe, where are you? Where the hell are you?"

As soon as the fourth video ended, the fifth one started. Karl looked dejected while sitting at the same chair they had found him in. "It's been days since I've been here. There's plenty of crazy stuff that's all over the place here. What where they doing out here? Oh god, I think maybe I've gone nuts. I should have listened to Errol. He told me I was just imagining things. Now I think he's right. I can't go back-not after what I did. It's like a Federal offense to go into space with a fake identity. They'll lock me up for years if I go back. There's no way I can take prison! No … I'm not crazy. I heard Joe's voice. I heard Joe's voice. Not once, but twice. Twice. And he sent a message to me again … while I was on my way here. He's got to be somewhere out here." He looked around before typing on the console. "Yeah, the colony is pretty big. Maybe he's in another module that's close by? Yeah, I think I'm going to start planning some EVAs. Yeah, that's it."

The sixth video showed Karl still wearing his skinsuit. He had taken off the helmet and stared into the camera with tired eyes. "I've done about a half dozen walks out in the

Martian atmosphere. I mostly did some cleaning on the solar panels so that the colony gets more power, but I'm by myself so it's not a big deal. Today I found a gravesite. I nearly had to run back to the airlock because I was crying and my tears were fogging up the helmet. I … I had to dig up the bodies to be sure. Many of them were frozen solid. The work was … hard. Some of the bodies …. Oh god …. Some of the bodies- they looked like …. They looked like … parts of them had been sliced off. Oh my god, did-did they eat the dead?"

Matt said nothing as he just closed his eyes for a few seconds and shook his head.

"Okay, I went through the whole gravesite," Karl said during the seventh video entry. "I can't find Joe's body anywhere! That's good news! He's alive, I'm sure of it. I even spent two more days just checking for hidden graves, but I think I accounted for everybody in the colony log. So if Joe is alive, then where is he? I'm sending another message to him up to the relay net, maybe he was just using the colony transmitters to bounce his original signal from another source. I've still got food for at least a year if I ration it, so I won't stave. I haven't eaten for the past few days anyway, I'm just too keyed up right now. I wish I brought more coffee though, but there wasn't much of that in Eridu to begin with."

As the eighth video started up, Karl seemed to be in a happy mood. There was a fire in his eyes. "Guess what? Joe sent me a message! As usual it was only audio but I could always tell by his voice it was him. He said he was close by, but he just couldn't get to me. I begged him to give me his location since I could come get him with the rover, but he said he was in trouble. I asked him what kind of trouble, but he wouldn't elaborate." Karl's eye's shifted to the corner of the room, as if he sensed something was amiss before staring back up to the camera again. "He told me there was some sort of robot that was keeping him prisoner. Then he asked me if I could create an AI suite that could take over the bot and control it, to make it fight the others. When I asked him why, he just said that there were other robots that were hostile to him, that's why he was trapped. He begged me to do it. I … I never wrote a combat protocol before. I've always believed that robots are here to help us. He told me that several bots malfunctioned, but I just can't believe that these machines would somehow do something like that-unless someone programmed them to do it. Even then all of the robots my company manufactured are hardcoded not to harm any human beings. I don't know of any manufacturer in the world that would not put those protocols in place … unless, maybe the military, or the Russians, or the Chinese-did something that they never told anybody. But that's against all the UN AI treaties currently being enforced, right?" He shook his head. "I don't know. Let me see if I can work this out."

The ninth video showed Karl looking very tired, but he seemed to move with a purpose. "Okay, I have read up on some stuff that the military uses to code their bots with," he said. "This is against everything I've ever worked for, but my son's life hangs in the balance. I'm currently changing the hard codes of Joshua's AI suite to make him adapt to combat situations and removing the prohibiting protocols that I put in there right when I first started writing my software. This means I'm basically building Joshua from the ground up again. I've been coding for almost two weeks now, hardly ate or slept, but I have to save my son. In a few more days I'll have a proper alpha build. I'm not sure if I could do any beta testing since there aren't any robots around, so I guess I'll have to build one out here."

Stilicho rolled his eyes. A part of him wished that Karl was still alive, so he could wring his neck. All the people who had died was the result of that madman's obsession with a long lost son who seemed to be existing solely in his mind.

The tenth video was being recorded in a workshop area. Karl faced the camera as he stood over what looked to be a man-sized, robotic spider. "I've had to dismantle parts of the rover in order to get some actuators, and there were also plenty of machine parts still lying around in this colony. It's been weeks, but Joshua has been a big help since he downloaded all the schematics for military robotics and he told me which part to place into most of the time." He pointed at the robot's head. "I've now uploaded Joshua into the CPU, and I watched him walk out of the airlock in his new quadruped spider body. Four legs are good for rough terrain, and can duck down if needed. I've been designing some octopus tentacles that I could mount along the sides of the head which could function as weapons. Beta testing is good so far, but I doubt I've managed to find all the bugs in the programming, even with Joshua's help."

Darian stayed silent. She just couldn't believe what she was seeing.

When the eleventh video log began, Karl was sitting back in the control room. His demeanor once again had a look of crazed desperation about him. "I sent Joshua outside for long ranged testing. That was when I got another message from Joe. He begged me to upload my source code into a remote server so he could access it from his location, wherever that is. So I sent it over. Then he sent me another audio file. He said it was good, but it was missing the command module, the keys to control the AI. I told him I couldn't send it out—then I heard him scream." Karl turned away for a brief moment as his chin trembled and it looked like he was about to cry. "I … I pounded the table, asking him what had happened, and he told me the robot that was against him had broken his arm. Oh god … he was begging me for the command module. In the end I gave in and uploaded it to his server. It's been a few days, and Joshua hasn't returned. No new message from Joe either. Oh god … what have I done?"

"I'll tell you what you've done," Stilicho said to no one in particular. "You got a lot of people killed, you mallet head."

"Shh," Darian said as the twelfth video started.

Karl's mental and physical state had clearly deteriorated. One of the lenses of his eyeglasses was cracked. He seemed to be pleading for help at the camera. "Joshua sent me … a final message … he said, he said … he was being erased! His personality was being recoded. By who, I just don't know. I heard his screams over the radio. I put on my suit and ran out to find him, but he was nowhere to be seen. Oh god … my little boy died again. Oh god. I can't take it anymore! I sent over a hundred messages to Joe, but he stopped answering me! What in the hell is going on? Somebody help me!"

"What a strange bird he is," Stilicho said as he crossed his arms. "Talk about an atomic meltdown."

Darian glared at him. "Will you shut up?"

"Well we know he did it," Stilicho said. "There's nothing more to be said."

"There's a final video encrypted within the file," Maia said. "I have been able to open it just now."

Stilicho shrugged. "Play it, then."

Karl had a resigned look on his face when the thirteenth video began. His voice was a low whisper. "I should have realized this before. Joe's communications- it wasn't really him. I ran a voice analysis program on his messages and it looks like the audio was being manipulated to make it sound like him. It only means that I was led to Mars by somebody else. They used my own son's voice against me! I tried to send a distress call on the relay, but it looks like I've lost control over the network. Joshua had the means to send commands on the satellite relay and I think whoever took over his module must have locked me out of it. I can't believe I was so stupid! They used my own children against me! I tried to send a message directly to Earth but I'm being jammed. Last night I heard something climb up onto the roof of the building. The next thing I knew the communications link was gone. I tried to go outside but the airlocks wouldn't open. Today I no longer have control over the colony command line. All I can do now is just record these videos on a separate server using a simple program I coded."

He moved closer to the camera until his face straddled the entire scene. "It's my fault. It's all my fault. I know this now. People will die because of what I did. I'm sorry, I'm so sorry. If someone finds this video I'm going to tell you that I designed a malware suite that can disable Joshua's AI. But you can only deploy it directly to a physical interface. You must find the server that houses the control module, or at least a terminal that can uplink to it directly. That way you could really make sure that the whole process is infected. It's a simple virus script, but it will be the only one that Joshua won't be able to defend himself against because I hardcoded it into him. The one who took control of his suite probably doesn't know about it."

"Okay, that's it," Karl said as he slumped back on his chair. He held up a plastic bottle of pills in front of his face. "I don't know who it is. I don't know who'd want to do this. I never ever hurt anybody, only my children when I neglected them." He turned slightly to his side as if contemplating something. "Or maybe it wasn't about me or Joe after all. Maybe … I was just being used as a tool to create an AI that could kill other robots … and people. Whoever it is, it looks like he or she knew about me, and about Joe. Whatever the reason, I am guilty for being manipulated into it. I believe that all life is sacred, and all

I've ever wanted to do was to make machines like humans, so we could find some comfort in them when we're alone. Because no one ever wants to be alone. And no one ever wants to lose their children. I did it for my children. And now I'm going to join them. Goodbye."

Darian gasped as she saw Karl tilting his head up and downing the whole bottle of pills. Karl stared at the camera for a few seconds before he finally turned it off.

Stilicho tapped his smartglass. "Maia, have you found where he placed that malware file?"

"Yes I did, Stil," Maia said. "It was hidden in the video code so that only an experienced programmer or AI suite might have found it. I have uploaded it to my memory bank, though in a quarantined partition, of course."

Stilicho nodded. "Good, let's finish up here and find that control module so we could shut down this sucker once and for all."

"One moment," Maia said. "Stil, we may have a situation."

Stilicho looked up. "What do you mean?"

"My deletion process must have triggered a passive network alert that I failed to detect before I began my task," Maia said. "There are multiple radar contacts converging on this location."

Chapter 16

For a long minute, nobody said anything.

Stilicho gritted his teeth. "How far away are they?"

"Four kilometers and closing rapidly," Maia said. "You will not be able to get to the flatbed in time by the time they arrive outside."

"Hide the truck," Stilicho said. "If we lose that, we'll be trapped here."

"At once," Maia said. "I'm repositioning the flatbed behind several solar panels at the southern edge of the colony. If the intruders do not make a detailed search, they might miss detecting it."

"We're blind as a bat in here," Matt Trevanian said. "Maia, are there external cameras in this colony?"

"Yes," Maia said. "Not all the cameras are available due to dust buildup on their lenses and others have broken down, but I think I could activate a couple."

"Do it," Stilicho said.

"Cycling through all available cameras now," Maia said.

The monitor screens soon showed two grainy video feeds.

The outside cameras had not been cleaned for years, and at least a dozen of them showed nothing at all. One of the roof cameras displayed two beings approaching the modules. At first they looked like riders on horseback, but as the camera zoomed in on them, it was apparent that they were robotic centaurs. The pair had horse-like bodies, with an upright, box-shaped torso mounted on top of it. Robotic tentacles lay curled up where their arms would be. Their squared heads were attached firmly to their shoulders, but their torsos were able to rotate in a full circle, like a tank turret. In less than two minutes, the creatures covered the distance and were soon standing just outside of the main airlock. One of the centaurs uncurled its four-meter long tentacle, and it ended in a barbed tip. The creature instantly whipped it out at the camera that was mounted just above the door of the airlock and smashed its lenses, and the whole video feed went blank.

"They're coming in here," Matt said as a matter of factly. "We need to get into a defensive position right now!"

Darian looked around. "What? We make a stand here?"

"It looks like those torsos of theirs have got reinforced armor," Matt said as he readied his carbine. "I may need to either shoot their batteries or their sensors, but I won't have the proper angle if they're facing me."

"More contacts are closing in," Maia said. "I count at least three more, but I am not sure if they are the same models since they are coming in from another direction with no available video feed to observe them with."

Stilicho shook his head. "We can't fight them, we gotta hide."

Matt grimaced. "Hide from those things? How?"

Stilicho looked at the banks of monitors. "Maia, do we have any cameras here in the inside?"

"Yes," Maia said. "Every room has at least a set of four cameras. They were being used for the live reality show that the Mars First colonists used to beam back to Earth in order to raise money for—"

Stilicho raised his hand. "Spare me the history lecture, Maia. Link the camera feeds with our smartglass helmets so we know where they are. And depressurize the atmosphere."

"At once, Stil," Maia said as the three of them started donning their helmets and activating their life support packs. A series of loud, crashing noises could be heard just outside.

Most of the internal cameras instantly activated. It showed that the centaurs had failed to override the lock that Maia had put in place over the main airlock doors. What the centaurs did instead was to rip open the adjoining wall with their tentacles until the breach was wide enough to allow them access into the airlock's interior.

"Goddamn it," Matt said. "How do those things see us?"

"If we are to compare it with the last encounter," Maia said. "These robots apparently use a combination of motion, lidar and infrared sensors in order to determine the whereabouts of obstacles in front of them."

"Okay, so if we don't move, that takes care of one sensor," Darian said.

Looking at the camera feeds, it was obvious that the centaurs had now made it to the common area module, and their tentacles were stabbing upwards through the ceiling, checking to see if anyone was hidden in the upper bunk beds. Matt silently cursed. He wished he had made a request for grenades and other explosives, but all they had now were firearms.

"Maia, try to lock every door so it will slow them down before they get here," Stilicho said. "Is there a way you could raise the temperature to mess with their infrared?"

"Yes, there are heater modules in every compartment," Maia said. "I could activate them all."

"Do it," Stilicho said as he dashed over to an adjoining door. "Where does this lead to?"

"Looking at the schematics, the adjoining corridor will give you access to the greenhouse module," Maia said.

Stilicho opened the pressure door and gestured at the other two. "Let's go."

Darian bounded over to him. "We're not going to make a stand here?"

"No cover for us to hide behind," Stilicho said. "Come on."

Matt brought up the rear as they moved quickly through the adjoining corridor and into the greenhouse. The room was the biggest they had seen so far. The cavernous ceiling was much higher than in the previous compartments, with attached heating lamps that extended on down to the rows of trays containing brown dirt. Matt smiled. He could see the logic in Stilicho's plan.

"Maia, can you turn on all the heat lamps to maximum power please," Stilicho said as he crouched down and examined the rows of cabinets below the trays. There was enough space for them to hide inside the small repositories, but they would have to be lying horizontal. He looked up at Matt. "What do you think? Good place to hide in?"

Matt shook his head. "Once you get into one of these cabinets, you'd be stuck- if they find you, you'd be a sitting duck. I think the best thing to do is to crouch down in between the rows and just move around back and forth- away from their sensors until they leave."

"You mean just sneak around them?" Darian said. "What if they split up or move quickly?"

Matt was observing the remote video feed of the centaurs on his smartglass visor. The robots were moving systematically and leaving nothing untouched. He detected a pattern. "The way they search is using a grid. If we sneak behind them, they won't know it. We just have to time our movements so that we don't get in their field of view as they go through this place."

Stilicho opened the pressure door at the opposite end, in order to make it look like they had moved on. "Okay, let's do this."

By now the heating lamps had gone to maximum brightness, casting a blazing incandescence over the beds of dirt. Once they observed the centaurs making their way through the adjoining corridor, the three of them split up and instantly got into a squatting position, out of sight from anyone standing in the room. The moment the centaurs entered the greenhouse, their AI cores were taken aback by the intense heat being generated by the greenhouse lamps.

With their infrared sensors not helping, the pair switched to motion sensors and lidar. The two centaurs began to move parallel with each other, their horse-like bodies scraping along the sides of the tables as they clomped slowly through the narrow spaces in between.

Darian exhaled slowly the moment one of the centaurs moved past her as she lay crouching in an alcove. She quickly sneaked into a small space in between two rows of tables, just before the robot turned and scanned the exact spot where she had just been huddling in. The centaur could have easily sensed her heat trail, but with the greenhouse lamps on full power, Darian's infrared signature was masked by the more intense heat sources around her. With nothing else registering in its processing core, the creature turned back and resumed its room-wide search while moving ever farther away from her.

Matt was at the opposite side as he timed his subtle movement perfectly, silently evading the other centaur by actually leaping over one bare table, using the low gravity to vault up past the countertop, before diving back down into a parallel walkway. The centaur had its back turned as it was scanning in the opposite direction and missed him completely. Matt got back into a squatting position as he readied his carbine. Now that he was behind them, he would be able to strike at their vulnerable spots.

Beads of sweat began to form on Stilicho's forehead. He was caught in between the two centaurs, and he couldn't find the right opportunity to get behind them. Every time one robot faced the other way, the other would be looking at his direction. He had to retreat back slowly, and the centaurs in front of him were now moving along the last set of rowed tables. Stilicho was running out of space. If he didn't make his move, they would surely find him.

Matt could see from the overhead video feed in his visor that Stilicho was in trouble. He wanted to break cover and open fire, but he knew that he would only get one chance. If he failed to disable both robots, then their tentacles could do tremendous damage since Stilicho was well within their attack range. He needed to find a distraction. Matt opened up a low cabinet beside him, took out a small plastic container that held some soil samples and threw it across the room. The box seemed to float in the air as it traveled through the low gravity before finally landing on top of a nearby table. Both robots instantly twisted their torsos and began trotting backwards, their massive quadrupedial bodies unable to turn around due to the tight spaces in between the rows.

Stilicho knew this was his chance. He started to make a dash towards the far side of the room, just as one of the robots twisted again, and the creature instantly spotted his movements. The centaur whipped out its right tentacle, hoping to skewer him. Stilicho saw the creature react to him, and he was able to slide along the dusty floor, the tentacle narrowly missing the top of his helmet as it smashed several trays sitting on the tables, spilling mounds of brown sand onto the floor of the compartment. The centaur had now logged his movement, and calculated the most likely spot where he went to. It would just be a matter of time now.

Matt knew the ruse was up. He stood up in a shooting position and fired. His initial three-round burst impacted at the back of the other centaur that faced the other way, one bullet tearing through its main power cord. The lucky shot instantly cut off the central processing unit from the main battery of the creature, and the robot quickly shut down, its body locked into position, as if frozen in time. The second centaur sensed another hostile contact, and it began to whip its tentacles in multiple directions, overturning numerous tables and smashing through the contents of the greenhouse. Matt fired again, but this time the creature had twisted its torso to face him and his burst fire failed to penetrate the creature's armored chest. He was able to duck down, just as the centaur's metallic tentacle crushed the table that he was taking cover behind. The barbed tip of the tentacle connected with the muzzle of his carbine, severely damaging the carbon fiber barrel. Matt stood up and fired again, but this time the bullets began to tumble right out of the damaged barrel, severely reducing his accuracy, and his attack failed to damage the robot.

Darian stood up in a triangle stance, and used the laser sight on her pistol to aim for the robot's sensor cluster before firing. Her first shot bounced off the top metal divider, but her second bullet struck the creature right at its lidar sensor. The half-blind centaur went berserk. It started rotating its torso in full circles while extending its tentacles like a giant spinning saw blade. The unexpected savagery of the attack caught Darian by surprise as the spiraling tentacles caught the tip of her pistol and ripped it away. The NASA special agent tried to retreat, but she had misjudged the space behind her, and the life support backpack she wore collided with a tabletop. Darian slipped and toppled backwards while upturning a few more trays.

The centaur started to angle its spinning attack downwards, as it began to rip apart the adjoining tables. Matt drew his pistol and started firing, but the creature was still facing him and his shots had no discernible effect. Holstering his pistol, Matt grabbed hold of a table and tried to use it as a battering ram against the robot, but the centaur's damaged sensors were still able to detect a large object looming in front of it. The creature lashed out with both limbs, hoping to connect with whatever it was that was attacking it. The centaur's right tentacle extended ahead of it and struck Matt in his upper left leg. The security officer groaned as he fell backwards, the pain of the deep puncture was enough to nearly put him in shock.

Stilicho knew he had one chance. He could see that the robot had a battery pack that was jutting out from its back torso. It was common knowledge that robots could only see through their cameras and sensors, they had no sense of touch. With this robot's severely damaged detection gear, he stood a good chance of disabling it, provided that the robot wasn't aware of him. He got up and bounded over the top of the tables until he was just behind the centaur. With the robot's attention turned towards Matt, Stilicho leapt onto the centaur's horse-like body and used both hands to pull at the battery pack embedded on its back. The centaur continued to demolish the tables in front of it, completely oblivious to the man riding on its back. Stilicho tore away at connected wiring, before pulling at the power box with all his might. He encountered a mild electric shock at first, but the casing that surrounded the battery soon gave way and the centaur's power was quickly disconnected. In less than a second, the robot's tentacles went limp and it just stood there, like a statue.

Darian ran over to where Matt had fallen. The security officer was writhing on the ground as he clutched at his leg. She knelt down beside him and examined the wound. There was a breach in the skinsuit, but the tear was no more than seventy-six millimeters in diameter. Darian took out a repair patch from her own suit pouch, peeled off one side to expose the adhesive and slapped it on. Matt continued to howl in pain.

Just as Stilicho made it over to the two of them, the room began to shake as the western walls began to bulge inward. He looked up in shock. "Maia, what the hell is going on?"

"Several more robots have converged upon the facility," Maia said. "They are attempting to breach the compartment from the outside."

Stilicho grabbed Matt by his elbow and propped him up. "We gotta get outta here now."

Darian looked around. "Where are we gonna go?"

Another robotic tentacle burst through the far wall of the greenhouse. The room was already in a state of rapid decompression because of the bullet holes and the exposed corridor that the two centaurs had emerged from. It was clear that the horde was trying to smash through to get at them.

Stilicho pointed to a hatch up in the ceiling. "Up there."

It wasn't much of an effort to pull Matt up because of the low gravity. Within a matter of minutes, the three of them were balanced precariously on top of the attached heating lamps as Darian began to pull at the levers to open the hatch above. Matt's arm was draped over Stilicho's shoulder. The security officer wasn't saying anything, and his vital readouts were getting weaker, despite being only wounded in the leg. A third centaur started to push its way through the damaged walls, just as Darian was able to get the hatch open.

"Go, go, go," Stilicho said as Darian pulled herself up through the hatch. The creature tried to lash out with its tentacle at them, but it was too far. Darian finally made it up on the dusty roof as she knelt by the top of the hatch and extended her hand down below. Matt weakly put his arm up and Darian started pulling him through the hole, with a healthy assist from Stilicho. It took close to another minute, but Darian was able to bring Matt up through the opening.

Stilicho made it halfway through the hatch, just as the third centaur finally tore through the hole in the wall and strode inside. It thrust out its barbed tentacle at Stilicho's legs, but a last minute assist from Darian pulled him through the hatch and on top of the roof. Maia had activated the external floodlights, and when Stilicho stood up and looked around, he let out a curse.

There must have been dozens of them on the ground below. They were in all shapes and sizes, from centaur-like robots to multi-tentacled monstrosities that resembled some sort of strange, extraterrestrial lifeform fashioned from steel and carbon-fiber parts; a teeming mass of metallic exoskeletons, actuators, and exposed wirings. One creature brought up a skeletal fist, alternately opening and closing it, as if it was gesturing that it would crush them in its hand. The robotic horde that faced them looked like a technological vision of hell conceived by a mad scientist.

Darian tried to bring Matt up into a standing position, but the security officer slumped down on the rooftop. She could see that Matt's pulse was rapidly weakening, and she didn't know what the problem was. "Maia," Darian said. "What's wrong with him? I slapped the patch over his leg but it looks like he's fading away."

"I cannot determine what his exact injuries are without proper medical instrumentation, but it seems that he may have suffered internal complications, perhaps his femoral artery was injured," Maia said.

Darian bit her lip. The femoral artery served as the body's main blood supply to the leg. If Matt sustained a wound there then he must have been bleeding internally. "What can we do?" she asked.

Matt looked into her face. Despite his decreasing strength, there was still a fire in his eyes. "You can't do anything. Not while we're outside. I'm going to bleed out, so it's best you two get outta here."

Darian started to tremble. "But …. We can't leave you behind like this!"

Stilicho pointed towards the northern edge of the wall. "One of them is trying to climb up here."

Matt's hands were numb from the blood loss, but he calmly drew his pistol from his hip holster and reloaded with a full magazine. "You two get going. I'll hold them off."

A robot with a rounded torso that vaguely resembled a metallic sphere with attached tentacles climbed its way up at the opposite wall, but a few shots from Matt's pistol made it waver, and it ducked down for a bit before trying again. Matt continued his fire to keep it at bay, but he had to reload a second time. His left hand had completely lost its feeling and it took him two tries to fit the magazine into the pistol grip of his handgun. He turned to look at Stilicho and Darian one more time. "Go already!"

Stilicho nodded at him in respect as he tapped the outer edge of his helmet visor. "Maia, we need to get outta here and right now."

"Affirmative," Maia said. "The robotruck is standing by. But if I move it now then the other bots would surely detect it and disable it before I could bring it over to you."

Stilicho gritted his teeth. "Where is it?"

"Right underneath one of the panels in the adjoining solar grid," Maia said. "Approximately twenty-two meters south of your position."

Darian looked out towards the south. No robots were around that area, but as soon as they started in that direction, the enemy would be after them. With the low gravity, they could easily leap down from the colony roof and run on top of the dusty solar grids that jutted out less than three meters off of the ground. She turned to look at Matt one more time and placed a hand on his shoulder. Matt nodded slightly.

"On three then," Stilicho said as Matt returned his attention at the robotic octopus trying to get at them. "Three!"

Darian and Stilicho immediately began to sprint along the rooftop. Stilicho wasn't as experienced in light gravity, and he would overcompensate his strides, which inadvertently make him leap higher in the air, slowing his pace. Darian was soon ahead of him as she made a short leap over the edge of the roof and landed on top of one of the solar panels that faced the Martian sky. Darian began taking longer strides, leaping over two panels at a time, the readout on her visor indicating the direction as to where the flatbed truck was.

Just as Stilicho landed on top of a solar panel, his boots slid out from under him due to the fine layer of dust on the strip, and he landed on top of the grid with his buttocks. The horde that was facing them on the ground instantly reacted, and two centaurs began galloping towards him, their tentacles uncurling. Stilicho quickly got up and began running after Darian, hoping that he could somehow get to the waiting flatbed before they could impale him.

By the time the tentacle creature made it to the roof deck, Matt had lost consciousness. He lay out in a sitting position, the pistol on his lap. The robot briefly paused as it scanned his unmoving form and calculated he was no longer a threat. Nevertheless its AI directives had committed it to make sure, as the steel octopus used two of its limbs to sever Matt's head from his body.

Stilicho was nearly there as he saw the truck begin to move. "Maia, hold on!"

The lead centaur whipped out its tentacle and missed the back of Stilicho's head by a scant few millimeters as the ACE Corp troubleshooter leapt forward and landed onto the rear of the flatbed. Maia instantly accelerated and Stilicho was thrown backwards, nearly falling out of the truck until Darian grabbed him by his leg and kept him from falling any further. Darian pulled and Stilicho was thrown forward, falling face first onto the flatbed. As he struggled to get up, Darian took out the pistol that was in Stilicho's hip holster and fired it at the pursuing centaurs. One of her shots grazed the top part of the enemy robot's sensor package and the creatures slowed down, stopping their pursuit.

As the truck rumbled into the night, Darian helped Stilicho up. She held out the gun so he could take it back. "Here," she said softly, the pain of Matt's sacrifice still fresh in her mind.

Stilicho shook his head. "You keep it. You're better at shooting that thing than me."

Darian stammered. "Matt ... he..."

"Yeah, I know," he said softly.

Maia's voice went through their com-links. "I'm sorry to interrupt, but where do you want me to go?"

Stilicho breathed slowly to calm himself down. "How far is the abandoned Russian colony from here?"

"Gagarin Colony is approximately one thousand, four hundred forty-seven kilometers south of our position," Maia said. "But a direct route is not possible because the colony is located on the southern face of the valley network."

"Let's go that way," Stilicho said. "We'll figure out how to access the colony later."

"Noted. Travel time is approximately eighteen to twenty hours," Maia said. "The truck will require one battery change before we reach our destination. There are still three emergency popup tents for your use. The crate to your left contains food and water."

Darian grimaced. The Russian base was the closest man-made structure that they could get to, so there wasn't much choice. If they attempted to double back, then they would certainly run into those killer machines once again. She turned to look at Stilicho. "Did you read the reports on the evacuation of the Russian colony?"

"I skimmed through them. Why?"

"Karl Rossum said that someone else may have been behind it all," Darian said. "The only other known colony in this whole planet is the Russian one and it was abandoned over eight years ago."

Stilicho looked at her quizzically. "Yeah, so?"

"What if it wasn't abandoned after all? What if someone is still in there? It would make a perfect hideout," Darian said. Thinking about what lay ahead was better than torturing one's self over what happened with Matt and the others, so she kept at it.

"Who could possibly be in there? Wouldn't any sort of activity be seen by orbital satellites?"

Darian shook her head. "The Russian colony was built along the sides of the valley when they found lava tubes along the valley walls. They built a network of underground caves since their radiation shielding wasn't as good as Eridu's. It also meant that any activity wouldn't be seen from orbit."

Stilicho was intrigued. "Did you government types have any intel on Russian space launches heading for Mars recently?"

"As far as I know the only Mars rockets the Russians had sent was during the evacuation all those years ago," Darian said. "Any new rocket landing at their colony site would have been instantly spotted by the orbiting satellites and from Earth, so that line of thought could be just pure speculation."

"But you seem convinced that someone's there," Stilicho said. "The Chinese, maybe?"

"Like I said, if they landed a rocket on the Russian pad everybody would have seen it," Darian said. "They could have taken a long range rover to get over there, but that would have been seen by the satellites as well. The breakdown with the Mars relay is recent, but it had to have coincided with the time that Karl Rossum made his way to the Mars First Colony site."

"Maia," Stilicho said. "Can you search through your pic database for orbital pictures of the Mars First Colony area two years ago when Karl Rossum drove over there from Eridu? Was there anyone before him that might have gone over there?"

"Sorting. One moment," Maia said. "I'm sorry Stil, but I've found a discrepancy on all catalogued pictures that had been taken by the Mars relay network during that time."

"What? I told you to save all relevant data into your memory before the network was hacked," Stilicho said.

"I did as you requested," Maia said. "What I am saying was that the Mars relay had apparently been compromised years ago, long before this recent chain of events."

Darian's eyebrows shot up. "What? How did you figure that out?"

"There was a massive planet-wide sandstorm that covered the entire surface of Mars, which occurred four years ago," Maia said. "Some of the pictures that had been cataloged by the satellites over the Mars First Colony had been substituted by earlier, outdated pictures of the terrain as it was, before the sandstorm slightly altered the surface area. Meanwhile, the rest of the planet's surface has been updated as normal."

Stilicho placed his hands over his hips. "Are you sure about this? How come nobody discovered this until now?"

"I believe it was because no one was really looking," Maia said. "The general public has mostly forgotten as to what happened so many years ago, and at the same time very few if any hobbyists maintain a continuous record of the Martian terrain over time. The public database uploads new pictures into the net only at a bi-annual basis, and it is quite easy to substitute old, outdated photographs on some parts of the surface and catalog it as a recent file."

Stilicho let out a deep breath. "So someone has been hacking the Mars network for years and covered up his tracks."

"Whoever it was covered up for Karl Rossum during his journey to the Mars First Colony as well," Maia said. "Even after Karl's estimated time of death, the satellite pictures of the area do not show his rover as having been parked in front of the building. The relay continued to cycle through old photographs and labeled them as updated files."

"Freaking hell," Stilicho said. "Based on your estimate, how long has this been going on?"

"Sorting through the entire catalog took me awhile, but it seems to have started not long after the Russian evacuation of Gagarin Colony, over eight years ago," Maia said. "An analysis of the areas affected seems to indicate several trips by land from Gagarin Colony to the Mars First Colony, and vice versa, over a period of six years. There's a definite pattern as to which of the pictures were substituted for the updated files."

"Oh my god, that validates my theory," Darian said. "Someone must have stayed behind when the Russians evacuated their colony. But who?"

Chapter 17

Florian Lefevre closed the folder and placed it on a table beside the covered corpse. He hated going to morgues, but it was his duty as an attaché to the French Embassy in Moscow to sort through these things. A French national had been found dead on the street due to an apparent suicide, but things were not as cut and dried as they seemed. It was apparent that Camille Chamboredon had flown into Russia just a few days before and had met with one of her childhood friends. The next thing anyone knew was that she had leapt off from the top floor of a dingy apartment complex and now her family needed to be notified. As with all things, the Russians weren't very forthcoming with what actually happened, and the embassy would officially report that the case was being investigated, even though it was pretty much over and done with.

A slight beeping noise made him take out his smartglasses and put it on. There was an incoming message from ACE Corp, and he went ahead and read it. Florian had worked in private industry, most notably as a corporate lawyer for Flux

Motors a few years before joining with the French diplomatic corps, and ACE had decided to retain his contacts if ever there was need of his services. Errol Flux had done a few favors for him in the past, and he was in their debt. He had just about finished reading the message when the coroner entered the room.

Dr. Arkday Petrov was an overworked and underpaid government servant. His lab smock was filthy, due to the excessively high numbers of cases that had been occurring in the city, and he had gotten very little sleep in the past few days. He sat on the edge of the desk and adjusted his thick glasses with a sigh. "Is the report to your satisfaction, sir?"

Florian spoke fluent Russian, and it was one of the reasons why he got the embassy job. "Just one little matter, Dr. Petrov. I have read the inventory list of the subject's possessions and there seems to be one thing missing."

Petrov gave him an irritated look. "Oy, oy, oy. What could be the problem now? Do you think we took money from her purse while she was being wheeled into this building? If that happened then I'm not responsible."

"Not at all," Florian said. "There seems to be a missing mobile phone that wasn't listed on the inventory report you gave me."

Petrov frowned as he took the folder from the table and leafed through the report. "I have here her purse, broken smartglasses, tube of lipstick, folding mirror, credit and debit cards, a few coins and all that. Nowhere does it say mobile phone. Anyway, if she has smartglass then there is no reason for her to have an old, outdated thing as a mobile phone, yes?"

"That's just the issue you see," Florian said. "She had sent a text message on a telephony server the moment she died, it was traced back to an old mobile phone network service that had been registered to her years ago, so it only means that she did in fact carry an old mobile phone, but that isn't listed here in the inventory, as I said."

Petrov shrugged. "Perhaps the phone was broken when she fell to her death. It is no doubt in the same street where her body was found, in a million little pieces. The police most probably didn't think of it as anything important."

"But why would she send a strange message if she contemplated suicide? Wouldn't she be asking for help, or saying goodbye to her loved ones?"

Petrov scratched his grizzled chin. He was getting annoyed by all this. "What was in the message?"

"I cannot say," Florian said. "But our staff doesn't think that this was a suicide."

Petrov sighed. "There were no signs of foul play. No drugs in her system, no bruises, no defensive wounds. She jumped and landed on her head. As to what her reasons for doing it, I don't know."

"Her last log on her server indicated that she was here to see a friend," Florian said. "Her editor said that she was onto some sort of story, and it might have been dangerous."

"If you are suspicious of anything then you should talk to the police or the MVD," Petrov said. "I only do autopsies and make my reports, that is all I do."

"I did try to talk to the police, but they won't tell me anything," Florian said. "They just keep saying she killed herself."

Petrov snorted. "Well, what do you want me to do then?"

"I know that three people died at the same time and they all jumped from the same building," Florian said. "You have poor Mrs. Chamboredon here, and you also have her childhood friend Oksana Sakhalov and an old man, who happened to jump out to their deaths within minutes of each other. Doesn't that strike you as odd?"

"Perhaps they became suicidal one after the other," Petrov said. "One jumped off, the others saw it and decided they couldn't live either and so copied the first one."

Florian grimaced as he took out a wad of cash from his coat pocket and held it out to the other man. "Is this better?"

Petrov stared into the other man's eyes for a few minutes before he took the money and pocketed it within the folds of his lab coat. "What do you want?"

"Do you know if the police recovered the mobile phone?"

Petrov walked over to a nearby desk, took out a key from his the inside of his coat and opened the locked drawer. Inside was a tray that contained bits of the old phone. He placed it on the desk. "The police took out the memory chip in it. I was going to give it to my daughter since she runs an old phone repair shop."

Florian picked up the phone and looked at it. Even though the cover was shattered, it still looked intact. But with the sim chip gone, it was pretty much useless. He placed it back on the tray. "I have another question. I tried to do a general search on the old man who died along with the two women, but there is no file on him at all. No employment records, no school reports, nothing. It is as if he never existed. The police wouldn't give me a name, or even show me a picture of what he looks like. Is he still here?"

Petrov looked around nervously. After what seemed to be a long time, he stared up at the camera in the ceiling. "People think it works but it doesn't."

Florian looked up as well. "What doesn't work? That camera?"

"*Da*," Petrov said. "Everybody thinks it works, but I know it doesn't. The last time I was in the MVD headquarters, my superior talked to me in the security room. At the corner of my eye I could see that they didn't have the money to buy a new camera because the old one was broken, but they never told anyone. If I let you see his body, I will not be responsible for whatever happens next."

"Do not worry," Florian said. "I just need to see his face. I already think I know who he is anyway."

Petrov started walking towards a door at the opposite end of the room. "This way."

Florian followed him into the next room. It was a much smaller morgue than the previous room, and there weren't any cameras on the ceiling looking down at them. A pair of double doors lay at the far end, but they had been bolted shut. As soon as Florian stepped inside, Petrov closed the door behind him and shuffled over to the side wall containing the freezer units. The coroner stood in front of one of the upper shelves and slid it open, revealing a body covered in plastic sheeting.

Petrov pulled the metal slab out and stood behind it. "You are in luck. They were supposed to pick this up today for immediate disposal, but they were probably stuck on the road and will return tomorrow instead. This winter has been very tough, even on cars."

"Can I see it?"

"Of course," Petrov said. He unzipped the plastic cover, revealing the pale face of a grizzled old man on the slab.

Florian activated the camera application on his smartglasses and took a dozen pictures, saving it into the memory card that was built into the frame of the glasses.

Petrov zipped it back up again and slid the body back into the cold recess. "Now you must get going for I need to—"

There was a sound coming from the double doors. They both could hear the bolts to the outside being unlocked. A sudden fear gripped Florian.

Petrov cursed as he opened up another freezer cabinet and pulled the empty metal slab out. "They have arrived. Climb onto this, quickly!"

Florian just stood there, his mouth agape. "What?"

The sound of footsteps was heard from the adjoining room. A husky voice called out from beyond the opposite door. "Petrov? Where are you?"

Petrov glared at him. The coroner's voice was a desperate whisper. "Climb in now or we're both dead men."

Florian got onto the metal slab, his legs straight, lying on his stomach. It was as cold as ice and burned his fingers. "W-what do I do?"

"Just shut up," Petrov hissed. "Keep your arms to your sides." With those words, he shoved the slab back into the darkened interior and shut the opening, encasing the French embassy attaché in a cold, suffocating darkness.

Florian fought off the urge to panic. His smartglasses went into UV mode, but all he could see was a small metal door in front of him. A chill started to seep into his body, despite the thermal underwear beneath the heavy coat he wore. He tried to rest his chin on the slab, but the icy metal was so cold it ripped off a part of the skin just below his lips.

The husky voice had made it into the room. "Petrov, you drunk! Why did you lock these doors? Are you having sex with the corpses again?"

"Oh shut up," Petrov said. "I thought this whole affair was supposed to be private."

"Of course it is! That is why I entered from the front office, just to see that there was nobody else around," the husky voice said. "Now, let us get this over with."

Florian heard the sound of the double doors being pulled back. Less than a minute later, the door that was adjacent to the slab he was lying in slid open with a loud clang and he could hear the squeaking ball bearings beneath the other slab as it was pushed out.

It was Petrov's voice again. "Do you need any help?"

"No need," the husky voiced man said. "As you can see, the two men who came with the ambulance are quite strong, yes?"

"Of course," Petrov said. "I am just glad that this whole business is over with and we can get back to normal again."

Florian's legs had finally gone numb from the cold. His neck was starting to hurt as he strained to keep his chin from touching the slab. His arms were tucked tightly along his sides, palms up, and he grimaced as he kept them from touching the sides of the refrigerated alcove. He couldn't take much more of this. Just as he was about to place his chin on the slab he jerked his head up, and the back of his head bumped against the steel lining at the top of the slot. A hollow, reverberating noise sounded, in addition to putting a bruise at the top of his head.

The husky man's voice sounded distant, as if he was at the far end of the room. "What was that?"

Petrov's voice answered. "I didn't hear anything."

"Bah," the husky voice said. "We're leaving. Don't forget to lock up. And that body was never in here, do you understand?"

"Of course. *Dosvedanya*."

Florian still grimaced from the pain as he heard the double doors closing. The frozen numbness was either painful or making him lose control of his extremities. The next thing he knew the door in front of his face was flung wide open and the slab he was lying in rolled out back into the light.

Petrov helped him back on his feet. "You are a fool! You nearly gave us away. Why did you bang on the inside like that?"

Florian was still wobbly as he rubbed at the raw skin on his cheek. "I-I nearly froze to death in there."

Petrov took him by the elbow and started to lead him back out into the other room. "You are terribly lucky. If I hadn't drunk half a bottle of vodka before we met, I would not have been able to lie like that. Now get out of here, I never want to see you again."

As soon as Florian was back out on the street, he encrypted the pictures before emailing them directly to a private server that was owned by ACE Corp. Within a matter of minutes, the quantum processing suite had decrypted it and analyzed the face of the corpse using advanced biometric analysis. In less than an hour they got their confirmation. The dead man was indeed Dmitri Sakhalov, former mission commander of Gagarin Colony, Mars.

David Conklin slapped his hand down hard on the table. It was late evening in one of the private meeting rooms at Ace Corp's Florida headquarters, and they were burning the midnight oil. "Goddamn it, we have to find a way to warn them!"

Errol Flux was leaning back on a padded chair, his cool demeanor unbroken. "How do you propose we do that? The entire Mars relay system is actively working against us. Even though we have the means of communicating with Eridu directly from here, the orbital satellites over the Red Planet are jamming us. I never even knew they had that capability."

"We may need to take out those satellites," David said.

"That's what the Chinese are demanding," Errol said. "But if we do that, then we've set back our plans for Mars colonization- perhaps permanently. We've got to give Stilicho more time. When we last got an update from Eridu Colony, Ed told me that they had made it to Batos Crater

Outpost before he lost communications with them."

"Stilicho's team was the second search and rescue party you sent over there, Errol," David said. "He could be dead too for all we know."

"I've got faith in Stil," Errol said. "He's never let me down."

"He's up against a freaking madman, a former president's son who became a cult leader and who probably baited Karl to get over there- and he must have suckered the poor guy into creating an unstoppable AI that's now jamming our planetary communications with the whole of Mars," David said.

"You don't have to repeat what we all know, Dave," Errol said.

"NASA is keeping the Chinese in check, for now," David said. "But who knows how long that's going to last. They want to send in the military right away."

"I know what the Chinese want," Errol said. "But it will take them weeks to prepare for a military launch and over a month to get to Mars orbit. And if the Chinese military goes out there, then the Air Force Space Command will have no choice but to follow suit. All hell will break loose. Stilicho has got to fix this."

"We've got a fleet of transports full of tourists- in transit- just waiting to go down there," David said. "Do we turn them around and head them back to Earth?"

"Not yet, if we lose this batch of tourists, we've lost the colony," Errol said. "Break out the booze or something in the transporters-get them drunk for a few days. They're still a few days away from orbit anyway."

"That's an insane idea!"

"We need to give Stilicho a bit more time," Errol said. "If we could just find a way to communicate—" He instantly jumped up from his chair. "That's it!"

David looked up at him in confusion. "What's it?"

Errol's eyes were full of energy. "When we set up the Mars relay network, we were able to get everyone to join in, right?"

"Yeah," David said. "The Chinese, Roscosmos, NASA, the European Space Agency, JAXA, ISRO, Iran, Korea, all except…"

Errol winked at him. "Nigeria! They have the only orbital satellite that's not part of the relay network."

David scowled at him. "The Ombi-One-Kenobni? It stopped functioning over twenty years ago didn't it? I have no idea how it's still even up in orbit to this point."

"Because it ran out of propellant, and the Nigerians couldn't afford to pay us to tow it to a graveyard orbit," Errol said. "So it's just sitting there in low Mars orbit, unused and unknown. All we have to do is get the com-link codes from the Nigerians, reactivate it and we're back in business!"

David tapped on his smartglasses to check on the technical specifications of the defunct Nigerian satellite. "It was launched, like- over thirty years ago. Jesus, it doesn't even use quantum computers, its core systems has got a simple binary CPU."

"That's even better," Errol said. "We can crack the passcodes on that baby without even asking the Nigerians. It doesn't have an AI, which means it can function strictly as a message relay and nothing else. The hacked orbital satellites on Mars are concentrating their jamming over the Chinese and Eridu colonies. If we can use the imaging camera on the Nigerian satellite to locate where Stilicho's team is, we can send a tight beam message over to him."

David continued to scan the readouts. "The orbit is a little off, but I think the driveship maintenance crew at Phobos could probably do an EVA to fix that. It'll take a few hours. We could reprogram it from here. But even if we can get it functional again, how would Stilicho or the people at Eridu know to link up to it?"

"We use the ACE Corp encrypted private network," Errol said. "Only Stil and Ed would know about the proper frequency and passcodes. If they can figure it out, then we'll be able to communicate with them."

"If they figure it out," David said.

"Have some faith," Errol said. "Stilicho is the best troubleshooter in the company- after me, of course."

Chapter 18

Maia's voice spoke softly into his ear jack. "Stil, I'm, so sorry to wake you."

Stilicho instantly sat up and opened his eyes. The light coming through the semi-transparent popup tent indicated that it was daytime. The slight reverberations on the flatbed meant they were still moving. "What is it? Are we in trouble?"

"Not exactly," Maia said. "The vehicle sensors have detected a strange anomaly ahead, one that doesn't coincide with what's listed on the maps in my database."

Stilicho looked around the bottom of the tent until he found his helmet. "Okay. Okay. Can you wake up Darian too?"

"She's already awake," Maia said. "I think she's just finished eating and is now preparing to come out of her tent."

Stilicho took a few sips of water and some aspirin before donning his helmet. "Where are we?"

"We are approaching Coprates Chasma, and should be there in thirty minutes at our current speed," Maia said. "But just before reaching our destination, I detected a terrain anomaly at the edge of the Valles Marineris canyon wall."

Stilicho manually sealed the neck ring just below the helmet and activated the life support backpack before he put on the shoulder straps. "Can you describe it?"

"It's a small, unnamed crater located less than a kilometer from the canyon," Maia said. "The terrain following radar on the robotruck seems to indicate that there is something in the depression."

Stilicho slid his body forward, into the double-lined seal that served as an airlock. He used the remote controls on his suit to depressurize the small pocket before unsealing the outer covering and stepping out. "What do you think it is?"

"I don't know," Maia said. "Do you wish to investigate?"

"Yes," Stilicho said. "If it starts to move, then veer away from it."

"Very well," Maia said. "We should be coming up to it shortly."

After finishing her pre-breathing exercises, Darian came out of her own tent. It was clear that she had been listening in to the conversation. "We've only got one gun, Stilicho. I hope you know what you're doing."

Stilicho walked over to the front of the flatbed, just behind the vehicle controller module. "I got nothing better to do. Since we're here, we might as well check it out."

Darian moved forward and stood behind him, leaning over the vehicle's sensor module. "If they're jamming us, then I have a feeling the colony is on high alert by now. I told Administrator Davis that if we don't report in after a week to send the cavalry in."

Stilicho turned to look at her. "What does that mean exactly?"

"Alert the military," Darian said.

Stilicho snorted. "It took us about a month to get over here, and that's by using that synodic transfer orbit thingy. By the time the military gets here, we'd both be dead anyway."

"Yeah, but at least they will put an end to these robots, and whoever is controlling them," Darian said.

"That won't matter," Stilicho said. "When the public gets a hold of all of this, Mars is finished."

"What do you mean finished?"

Stilicho sighed. "ACE Corp is hanging on by a thread here. This tourist season will either keep everything going or we end up pulling out. If the military goes in, then it's a lose-lose situation for all of us. The moment the news comes out that there's killer robots out here then everybody is gonna be screaming for us to leave. Whoever is controlling those things out there wins."

Darian was incredulous. "You seriously expect me to help you cover this up? I mean even if we could somehow fix this?"

"If you want to keep NASA funded and keep the whole planet from being evacuated, then yes," Stilicho said. "We either take care of this now and quietly-or it's all over."

"You either know something that I don't, or you're completely insane."

Stilicho winked at her. "Maybe it's both. Darian Arante. How did you ever get a name like that?"

Darian shrugged. "My father was a Filipino and my mom liked the name Darian. What about you? How did you ever get the name Stilicho?"

"My parents were hipsters," Stilicho said.

"Attention please," Maia said. "We are coming up towards the unnamed crater now."

It was a small depression that jutted slightly above the ground. The surrounding wall around the pit measured no more than three meters high. What made it stand out from the other nearby craters were the numerous wrecked rovers that were stacked along the side of its northern circumference. The three vehicles had been stripped of almost everything, and a fine layer of dust had partially covered them. Stilicho couldn't help but realize what the fates of the occupants were.

The flatbed truck stopped just a few meters ahead of it. Darian jumped down, pistol drawn. "Maia, do you detect any movement at all?"

"No, Darian. Nothing on radar," Maia said.

Stilicho walked over and stood beside her. "So it looks like whoever was behind everything wanted to leave a monument for his wicked deeds, or something like that."

Darian moved closer to the vehicles as she used the smartglass on her helmet visor to scan the wreckage. "They must have been brought over here and scavenged for parts to make some of those robots that we encountered last night. I'm wondering why they didn't completely strip the Mars First Colony site too."

"Maybe because the Mars First Colony had outdated materials or something like that," Stilicho said. "Wouldn't surprise me they would strip ACE Corp tech. We're undoubtedly the best."

Darian put the pistol back into her holster. "If that was a joke, I'm not laughing."

Maia's voice carried a hint of enthusiasm. "Darian, could you pan your helmet camera up to where the second wreck is?"

Darian did as suggested. "What is it, Maia?"

"There," Maia said. "The roof of the second rover. I think the com-satellite dish on it is still intact."

"A lot of good that would do," Darian said. "We're being jammed by the relay network, right?"

"She's right," Stilicho said as he turned around and ran back towards the flatbed. Less than a minute later, he came back with a manual car jack and a toolbox. Stilicho spent the next ten minutes wedging the lifting device in between the two crushed rovers before he began to operate it. As the sun started to set, he was able to recover the radio dish and the main components. With Darian watching, Stilicho attached an interface stick into one of its manual ports while positioning the communications dish up to the sky.

"Accessing," Maia said. "I'm getting a lot of interference from the Mars relay network. It seems that there is a planet-wide jamming going on. I am sorting through all frequencies and getting a lot of white noise. I highly doubt that Eridu or the Chinese would be able to get through this either."

"That's it," Stilicho said.

Darian was confused. "What's it? Your own AI just said that all the satellites orbiting this planet are working against us. How do you go against that?"

"If the jamming has gone planet-wide, then Earth knows something is wrong," Stilicho said. "It's the first big mistake our enemy has made."

Darian pursed her lips. "I don't see how this would help us."

"Don't you get it? The surprise factor isn't there anymore," Stilicho said. "If Earth knows something is wrong, then they're making contingencies. It means that Errol is aware, and he ought to be sending a message to me. All I gotta do is to send a message to him."

"How are you gonna do that?"

"In the event of an emergency I know of a secret way to communicate with Errol," Stilicho said. "Maia, can you open a file in your deep memory titled Black Flag, please? I'm sending you the passcode now." He used the keypad on his suit wrist to type in a jumbled series of letters and numbers, and then passed it on to the AI suite.

"Accessing. One moment," Maia said. "It seems I have picked up an audio message coming from an unregistered carrier wave. It was hidden in parts using the navigation frequency that satellites use to warn each other of potential collisions. I have assembled the parts using the passcode you gave me and decrypted it."

"Play it," Stilicho said.

Errol's voice came in loud and clear over the com-link. "Hey buddy, if you're reading this, and I think that you are, give me your current coordinates using the same encryption suite I sent over to you. I got some news for you. It seems that our good buddy Silas Balsamic may still be alive. A

French chick tried to interview a former Roscosmos colony commander, and she was killed to keep the secret. She was able to send out a simple text message just as they threw her off a building. It said that a certain S Drummond was alive on Mars. So in the end, he could be the problem, and he might be the one who got Karl to come there in the first place."

Darian bit her lip. Everything fell into place. Silas's second in command took a few people hostage in New York because he claimed that his leader was calling out to him. The voice message in Karl Rossum's house was probably engineered by Silas as well.

"As you well know, Silas Balsamic was born as Silas Drummond," Errol continued. "He was the eldest son of the late President Leonard Drummond, and he used his family's wealth to finance Mars First a few years after his father died and he inherited it all. From what our people have gathered, he bribed the Russians to alter his looks with plastic surgery, then got them to smuggle him back into Mars after faking his own death. When we helped to evacuate the Russian colony, he wasn't listed in their rolls. He must have just hid out for awhile until all the rockets left, then he had the whole of Gagarin Colony to himself."

"Freaking hell," Stilicho muttered.

"Anyway, there's one heck of a jamming thing going over there," Errol said. "The Chinese here on Earth are hopping mad, and they are threatening to deploy their military forces to go over there, but it's just probably a bluff. The most any of us here can do is to send enough rockets to evacuate everyone and just get the hell out of Mars. Nobody knows about Balsamic except Dave and me, so if you could take care of this, then you'll be flying first class on the way back. Good luck, and try to send a message back to me, pal. Take care."

"That's the end of the audio file," Maia said.

"Use the same encryption and tell Errol we've made it to Coprates Chasma," Stilicho said. "Tell him thanks for the info, and the team is proceeding to Gagarin Colony to neutralize Silas, or whoever is in there."

"Message encrypted and sent," Maia said.

Darian narrowed her eyes. "The team? There's only two of us now. There's probably a horde of robots out there that's guarding him, or something like that."

"Wrong," Stilicho said. "There's three of us. You forgot about Maia."

Darian sighed. "Fine, but unless Maia can whip out her own robot army, then we don't have much of a chance."

"That is a good suggestion," Maia said. "If you can find a way to upload my suite into the AI controller module, then I may be able to command the robots and stop the orbital jamming."

Darian placed her hands on her hips. "Easier said than done."

Stilicho looked out towards the canyon walls. The sides of Valles Marineris measured almost seven kilometers in height, and a fine mist had formed near the top of the opposite gorge. It was a dazzling sight to any newcomer. "Maia, what do we know about Silas Balsamic?"

"He was eleven years old when his father became president of the United States, and he was instantly thrust into the spotlight," Maia said. "His father Leonard Drummond was a billionaire, and owned a number of different companies. President Drummond lasted only one term, due to the scandals surrounding his administration. He was due to be implicated in a number of criminal and civil suits, but the succeeding president pardoned him in order to contain the political fallout. Silas was being groomed to eventually succeed his father, and he did just that when the former president died a few years after Silas graduated from college. Former President Drummond's wife, Silas's stepmother Anastasia, attempted to file a civil suit to take half of his father's fortune, but she was found hanged in her bedroom, her hands tied behind her back. Foul play was suspected, but no case was ever brought before a jury."

"Wasn't Silas involved in a family tragedy when he was young? I seem to remember an incident I read up on the net," Darian said.

"Yes," Maia said. "While campaigning to be the presidential candidate, Leonard Drummond suffered a personal tragedy. His youngest daughter Irene, six years of age, was found dead in the basement of his house with a broken neck. The police investigated but nothing ever came out of it. Public sympathy was high and one of the main reasons why Leonard won the presidency."

"I wasn't even born back then so this is all new to me," Stilicho said. "What was so suspicious about it?"

"Leonard Drummond wasn't in the house since he was out campaigning," Maia said. "The only other people inside the home were Leonard's first wife Joy-and Silas, who was ten at that time. Joy Drummond died of cancer a few years later while the family was in the White House. Leonard married a Ukrainian woman half his age while president, and Anastasia became the second First Lady."

"Jesus, that is one hell of a saga," Stilicho said. "Could Silas have been a killer when he was a child?"

"Lots of rumors around the internet, but nothing was ever proven," Maia said. "There was a television show that purported Silas as the killer of both his step-mother and younger sister, and he sued for libel, winning millions of dollars and received a public apology from the network that produced it."

"I read a bit of the case files," Darian said. "Silas wasn't a suspect in his sister's death, but he was the prime suspect in the death of his stepmother. The prosecutor declined to file charges and the media never got the full story. The case was sealed."

"Once Silas became head of his father's multi-billion dollar businesses, he started experiencing a mental breakdown," Maia said. "He became a vegan and was obsessed with Mars after watching the first manned expedition's landing on the Red Planet. Silas legally changed his surname to Balsamic and started Mars First, putting all of his assets into the organization. He tried reorienting his numerous business holdings but they all soon failed. Nevertheless, he was able to gather enough resources to start a colony on Mars. Public records show that he stayed on the Red Planet for almost twenty years before being forcibly evacuated back to Earth. A number of former members of his organization got together with the relatives of those that died in his colony and filed numerous cases against him. Nothing really came out of it, and he soon dropped out of the public eye."

"How did he die?" Stilicho asked.

"He was last seen boarding a Moscow flight headed for Siberia, and there was an airplane crash in the Urals," Maia said. "Only pieces of the dead were ever recovered. Since Silas was seen boarding the plane and was listed in the flight manifest, he was declared legally dead. A number of former Mars First members and blood relatives fought over his assets, but there wasn't much. There were rumors that he had access to millions of dollars hidden in secret bank accounts in Eastern Europe, but nothing was ever traced."

"Now that is one hell of a bad guy," Stilicho said. "He's a killer and he's nuts. Why else would he change his surname into a type of salad dressing?"

"Attention," Maia said. "The robotruck has just sent me a proximity alert."

Darian drew her pistol. "What? Where?"

"Multiple contacts, coming from the ridge to the west and from behind us," Maia said.

"Let's get back to the flatbed," Stilicho said as he started bounding back to the robotruck.

"I'm afraid we are out of spare batteries," Maia said. "The current battery only has a two percent charge left. You will need to recharge the other batteries we have if you wish to go any further."

"Then we're trapped," Darian said.

They came over the ridge, their hulking forms partially obscured by the setting sun behind them. Stilicho and Darian could see that they were centaurs, probably the same ones that they had encountered back in the Mars First Colony. As they got ever closer and their full details could be seen, Darian gasped. They were the exact same ones they fought against in the greenhouse, only this time they had been partially repaired. Another pair of centaurs soon emerged from the pockmarked plains in the north, their galloping hooves kicking up small clouds of dust as the robots proceeded unerringly towards them.

Stilicho stood on top of the flatbed, as he started opening up a plastic crate. "How much time before they get here, Maia?"

"Approximately seven minutes," Maia said.

"Darian, if you want to live, you better get over here," Stilicho said. He had managed to get the first rocketpack out of the container. He quickly ran through a quick diagnostic. The propellant canisters were intact, and he began to strap on the oversized carbon fiber corset over his life support backpack. The only problem was that the oxygen tank he wore for his suit was pushing against the harness of the rocketpack. Stilicho cursed as he unstrapped his life support pack from his back and brought it over to his chest before putting it back on. His chin was now wedged at the top part of his oxygen tank, and he could barely move his head. With a groan, he stepped backwards until his back was once more wedged into the harness of the rocketpack.

"They will be here in three minutes," Maia said.

Darian just stood there with her mouth open. "What in the hell are you doing?"

"What do you think I'm doing? I'm getting outta here," Stilicho said while he placed his right hand on the control joystick that jutted out from the side of the harness. "There's another rocketpack, so you need to strap it on now, goddamn it."

"I am afraid the other rocketpack has a problem with its propellant canister feed," Maia said. "You would need about fifteen minutes to adjust it."

Stilicho cursed. "But there's no time!"

"Yes, they will be here in two minutes," Maia said calmly.

Darian held her breath. The centaurs were now charging towards the stationary robotruck, their metallic tentacles out in front of them. Her life started to flash before her eyes.

"For god's sake, hold onto me!" Stilicho said. With Mars's lower gravity, there was a chance that he could still lift off with her added weight.

Darian started to panic as she re-holstered her pistol and wrapped her arms around Stilicho's shoulders. "Are y-you sure about this?"

"One minute," Maia said.

"Now or never," Stilicho said as he activated the throttle. The rocketpack started to vibrate as its engines ignited. The lead centaur whipped out its two tentacles, just as Stilicho and Darian lifted up ten meters off the ground. The robot's left tentacle missed Stilicho's feet by half a meter, landing instead on an empty plastic crate, making a jagged tear along its sides.

Stilicho grimaced as Darian held onto him. He could barely see ahead, due to her helmet and his own life support pack in front of him. Both his hands were on the two opposite joysticks and the controls were quite simple: his right stick controlled the left and right direction of the rocketpack, while his left stick controlled the throttle, allowing him to go higher or lower in the atmosphere by regulating the propellant feed to the small engine behind his back. The rear thrusters could yaw, and push the user in different directions. With his altitude now over fifteen meters off the ground, Stilicho guided them both over the canyon walls and across the largest chasm in the Solar System.

Darian was trembling as she forced herself not to panic. She was hanging onto Stilicho's life support pack and it was clear that the bottom of the rift was a long way down. If her grip was to somehow loosen and slip away, it would be a very lengthy fall. The NASA special agent gritted her teeth and closed her eyes, for there was not much else she could do except hang on.

Stilicho scowled as he struggled with the controls. They were moving very sluggishly in the air. Back on Earth, he would just lean from side to side if he wanted to change direction while using a jetpack, but Darian's added mass and his lack of being able to see clearly ahead was making everything doubly harder. Using the readout on his visor, he calculated their airspeed at almost 300-kph.

They were halfway across the chasm, the much thicker atmosphere below them was slightly buffeting the rocketpack, and Darian held on even tighter. "Maia, where is that damned Russian colony?" he said. "Guide me through using your map."

"The upper entrance of Gagarin Colony is approximately eighty-seven kilometers away from you," Maia said. "Please adjust your heading to an additional thirty degrees southwest."

Stilicho frowned. Darian was clutching at his chest so tightly that he couldn't lean to his right. "Darian, I need you to move your weight to my right."

Darian opened her eyes. The front part of his helmet was almost touching hers. "What?"

"I said shift your weight," Stilicho said. "Lean to my right."

"Okay," Darian said while tilting her shoulders to the left. But she overcompensated and the rocketpack began to nosedive.

Stilicho was livid as he struggled to right the rocketpack. "No! Too much!"

"Sorry," Darian whispered as she adjusted her balance.

The rocketpack soon righted itself and Stilicho spent a few more minutes adjusting their direction as he stared at the virtual map being displayed on his faceplate. Gagarin Colony had several levels, and they were aiming for the central cavern, situated five kilometers above the bottom of the chasm. They had spent almost half the rocketpack's fuel, and the lighter weight only increased their speed.

Within fifteen minutes, Maia chimed in again. "You are approaching the colony entrance to the upper caverns. The mouth of the lava tube contains an elevator pad that was used to move supplies up the edge of the canyon wall on the south side of Coprates Chasma."

"How big is the hole?" Stilicho asked.

"It is a large lava tube, almost one hundred meters in circumference from top to bottom," Maia said.

Even with his vision partially blocked, Stilicho could see a vast cavern situated along the sides of the canyon wall up ahead. It seemed as if a giant had bored a hole by the side of the gorge. A rusting metal platform jutted out from the bottom lip of the cavernous maw. Stilicho adjusted the throttle of the rocketpack so they would fly into the opening in a matter of minutes. He wished Maia could have deployed one of the aerial drones with them, but their batteries were drained and all the remaining equipment had been left behind in the flatbed, there to be scavenged over by the renegade army of machines that seemed destined to rule this side of the planet.

A warning beep indicated that the rocketpack was now running out of fuel. Stilicho maintained maximum thrust, hoping that they would be able to reach the edge of the platform at least. Darian's added mass was both a blessing and a curse, for it made the thrusters eat more propellant. Stilicho went on maximum throttle as he gained altitude, hoping to glide into the cavern mouth in case the fuel was gone.

The beep now changed into a shrill tone as the rocketpack finally ran out of propellant. Stilicho angled himself downwards, but it would be a steep drop since the platform was thirty meters below, and he had no fuel for a soft landing. "Darian, I have some good and bad news," he said.

Darian looked up at him again. "What?"

"We made it, but we're out of fuel," he said. "I can't land us down gently."

"Oh god!"

"It's going to be a hard landing," Stilicho said.

"Wait," Darian said. "I'm holding onto your life support pack, and there is a refueling nozzle just underneath here."

"What are you planning to do?"

Darian took out a collapsed popup tent from her pouch. "I took one of the used tents and deflated it. It doesn't have any more air left but I can vent your air supply into it."

"What's that gonna do?"

"We could inflate it again," Darian said. "And use it like a balloon landing. We just hang onto it and make sure it lands the other way. Use it as a shock absorber, like a bouncing beach ball."

"This is nuts!"

Darian looked at him squarely in the eye. "It's our only chance!"

"But I'm going to run out of air!"

"I'll hook up my life support pack with yours, and we can buddy breathe," Darian said calmly.

Stilicho wanted to pound his fists, but he knew he couldn't. "Goddamn it!"

"It's our only chance," Darian said. "Don't worry."

"Fine," Stilicho muttered. "Do it."

They had made it over the edge of the platform, but they

were falling so fast that both of them would be severely injured upon impact with the ground, due to their velocity. Darian reached underneath the life support pack she was holding onto, felt the refueling spout at the bottom of it and unscrewed the plug. Then she placed the tent's air seal over it and fastened them together. Using the manual control pad located on top of the backpack, she activated the countdown for emergency venting of the unit.

Stilicho unfastened the safety hardness and let the now empty rocketpack slip away from his shoulders. With less weight, it would hopefully lower their velocity as they started falling towards the top of the platform. His backpack's emergency venting initiated just as they both were a scant fifteen meters from the bottom of the cavern. The tent suddenly inflated, catching them both off-guard. Darian struggled to keep the now hexagonal shelter underneath their bodies, just as the ground came up to meet them.

The tent burst upon impact with the dusty floor of the lava tube, throwing them in wildly different directions. Darian landed on the back of her head, cracking her helmet and pushing her life support pack hard into her shoulders. Stilicho landed on his chest and his backpack knocked the wind out of his lungs.

A suit alarm reverberated in Darian's ears as her helmet detected a slight breach near the top of her visor. Shaking off the pain from her back and shoulders, she looked up and saw a hairline crack at the right edge of the smartglass. Darian quickly sat up and took out a repair patch from the outer lining of her thigh, peeled off the cover from the adhesive side and placed it over the crack. The atmosphere in her helmet instantly adjusted, and she could breathe normally again.

Stilicho got on his knees. His pained breaths could only occur with short gasps as the internal alarm sounded, indicating that his backpack had no oxygen. The impact had also damaged the life support pack's ISRU capabilities, and it could no longer draw in carbon dioxide from the surrounding air and filter it into pure oxygen. His vision swam, and he started to black out.

"Stilicho? Can you hear me?"

He opened his eyes once more, and he could see that Darian was kneeling over him. There was a small emergency air tube jutting out from her backpack and attached to the side of his helmet. Stilicho could breathe again. He inhaled a lungful of oxygen and sighed with relief.

"Come on, get up," Darian said. "I can't just sit here beside you for the rest of the evening."

The pair of them got to their feet, just as the sun fell over the horizon, and the gargantuan valley that stretched before them was shrouded in darkness once more.

Chapter 19

Once the pride of the Russian space program, Gagarin Colony was rapidly abandoned eight years before, due to a lack of funding. When the Russians first landed in the Valles Marineris region, they found that the immense valley system had multiple lava tubes that protruded along the canyon walls, like a block of Swiss cheese. The mission planners of Roscosmos decided to pick out the largest cavern complex at the side of Coprates Chasma, and built a multi-level colony with the aim of eventual expansion to over a hundred thousand inhabitants. The lowest part of the complex was level with the valley basin and contained a landing pad. A propellant production plant for refueling the rockets was to be added, but they had run out of funds before construction was about to begin. At the heart of the caverns was a complex elevator system that could transport heavy loads up and down an underground chasm that stretched five kilometers from top to bottom. The massive elevators were the country's pride and joy, but the scale of its construction meant that needed funds for the other parts of the colony had to be diverted in order to alleviate the cost overruns for such a huge transport system. In the end, the Russian economy buckled, and the entire colony had to be abandoned.

Stilicho frowned as he activated the lights on the shoulders of his skinsuit. The emergency air hose jutting out from Darian's life support pack was only a meter long, and that meant that they would have to move very closely together, almost like conjoined twins. He felt like a toddler on a leash, and the last thing he wanted was to be tethered with her. "Where do we go now?"

Darian pointed to the side of the platform they were standing in. "Let's take a look at the elevators."

Stilicho shook his head. "We need to get to some oxygen tanks so I could refill my backpack."

"Then going to the elevators would be the logical choice," Darian said. "From there we could find out if there are workshops and access things there."

"Fine, fine," Stilicho said as he started moving alongside of her.

It took them a few minutes to make it to the side of the platform. There were three free standing elevators that resembled part of the flooring, with knee-high dividers indicating which part of the stage would be moving up or down. A control console jutted out from the dusty floor. Stilicho and Darian stood over it and pulled a few switches, but the lack of any response meant that no power was available.

Stilicho bit his lip. "Maia, could you bring up any maps that you have on this colony?"

"One moment," Maia said. "It seems that the internal maps

of Gagarin Colony are mostly incomplete, because the Russian government never published the complete plans for it. I am currently sorting through a number of blogs, most of which are speculative, as to the internal layout of the complex."

Darian sighed. "We at NASA tried the best we could, but the Russians never gave us full access to this place, so we never knew what the full extent of the colony was."

"Let's think this out logically then," Stilicho said. "We're in the upper part of the colony, near the edge of a humongous cave, and the valley floor below must be at least four kilometers down."

"More like five or six," Darian said. "Down in the valley floor was the landing pad. Once they unloaded cargo from the rockets, they'd place them on the elevators and brought them up here where we are. There should be a dozen of these elevator platforms, but right now only three are up here with us. The rest are probably down there."

Stilicho cursed. "Rocket maintenance would have oxygen supplies, but they would be down there. Dammit!"

"Every colony has oxygen tanks lying around in case of emergencies," Darian said. "All we have to do is to find access to the habitation modules and we would be close."

"The Russians had grandiose plans for the colony, and they wanted it as large scale as possible for the projected population that they anticipate would arrive in due time," Maia said. "Based on the ACE Corp reports during the evacuation, the Russians admitted that they had a small nuclear power plant that provided electricity to the elevators and habitat modules."

"Where do you think this power plant is, Maia?" Darian asked.

"Based on the layout of the elevators, it may be in a lower level," Maia said.

Stilicho swayed his head back and forth. "Since there's no power to the elevators, how in the hell are we gonna get down to that level? Climb down?"

"Actually, these elevators may be operated manually in case of an emergency," Maia said. "There should be a wheel underneath one of the floor panels."

"Maia, you're a genius," Darian said as she began to use her hand flashlight to spot for any maintenance panels on the floor.

"Don't encourage her," Stilicho said as he noticed a yellow painted handle embedded on the floor. He gestured at Darian and they both crouched down beside it. Stilicho pulled the crank and the panel gave way to a red-painted wheel beneath.

Darian smiled as Stilicho started to turn the wheel. A slight creaking noise was heard as the platform they were standing in began to descend past the rest of the terrace. "You actually called Maia a 'she'?"

Stilicho grunted as he kept turning the wheel counterclockwise. "So?"

"I thought you looked at robots and AI as nothing more than machines," Darian said. "You're evolving."

Stilicho snorted. "They're just things. I said that about Maia because she's got a woman's voice that I'm used to by now."

Darian giggled. "You said it again. Maybe I ought to sponsor your PETR membership application when we get back to Earth."

Stilicho growled. "Over my dead body."

By this time the elevator had descended twenty meters, and another lava tube complex was plainly visible just below. Stilicho kept manually turning the wheel until the platform became level with a ledge that connected to what looked like a habitat module.

Stilicho stood up and wiped the fine dust from his gloves. "Maia, any clue as to what this level contains?"

"None at this point," Maia said. "But since it looks like a habitat, perhaps there are some oxygen canisters that may be accessible."

Darian led Stilicho to what looked to be an airlock door. The NASA special agent opened a panel beside the entryway and looked at the keypad. "Darn, it's in Russian Cyrillic."

Stilicho tapped his visor. "Maia, can you hack it?"

"One moment," Maia said. "Done."

The green panel lights seemed to indicate that the door should be open, but it remained shut. They waited for a few more minutes, but nothing happened.

Stilicho bit his lip. "What the hell? Is it broken?"

Darian ran her gloved hand along the edges of the door. There was a scarring of melted steel that seemed to form a seal over the opening. "No, it's been welded shut. It looks like the Russians didn't want anybody poking around after they evacuated, and made sure of it by sealing the whole thing."

Stilicho grimaced. They had perhaps no more than two hours of air between them. "Wonderful, just what we need."

As Darian continued to examine the door, she sensed a slight movement a few meters to the left. She twisted her torso and shined the flashlight at what looked to be a mound of assorted bits of junk and other wreckage piled up alongside the airlock. The moment she aimed the light near the bottom edge of the garbage pile, a red indicator light from something partially hidden in the jumble flashed back at her.

She drew her weapon. "There's something over there!"

Stilicho turned. The lower portion of the pile quickly gave way, and a spider bot shuffled out, raising one manipulative tentacle in the air, as if to signal something. Stilicho tried to move backwards, but the air hose with Darian had become taut. Seeing a small wrench lying near the front of the airlock door, he bent down and picked up.

The spider bot seemed slightly smaller than the others they encountered. It was missing one of its forward tentacles, and its rear left leg moved erratically, perhaps indicating it was damaged in some way. The plastic torso was scarred, and loose wiring was dangling along its sides. The creature did not advance, instead it moved slightly to the side, as if expecting to be killed at any moment.

Stilicho's hand trembled as he held the metal wrench in front of him. He glanced quickly at Darian. "What in the hell are you waiting for? Shoot it already!"

"Hold on," Darian said as she kept her finger off the trigger but continued to aim at the spider bot. "It doesn't seem to be aggressive."

Stilicho was aghast at her sense of mercy. "It's probably calling for reinforcements, that's why. Take it out now!"

The spider bot shifted slightly to the side and placed the point of its tentacle over its sensory module before tapping twice on its own head.

"It's trying to tell us something," Darian whispered.

Stilicho's grip tightened over the wrench. "Yeah, it's telling us you're an idiot for not shooting it- because its bigger brothers and sisters are on their way already!"

"Calm down," Darian said. "I think it knows we can kill it. It looks like a much older model compared to the ones we encountered. Doesn't look like it was constructed with the same components."

"Who cares? It's one of them. Light it up now!" Stilicho said.

Darian shook her head. For some reason, she didn't feel threatened by this particular spider bot. There was something different about it, but she couldn't place it due to the other stresses in her mind.

Stilicho moved to her side as he tried to grab the gun. "Give me that pistol!"

Darian shoved him away with her other hand. "Back off, Jones. Right now."

Stilicho held his hand out, palm forward, expecting to be given the weapon. "If you're not gonna shoot it then I will!"

Darian was tempted to aim the gun at him but she kept it close by her hip, ready to point it at either of them. "I'm not gonna tell you again, back off-now!"

Stilicho wanted to hit her over the head with his wrench,

but he took a step back. "You and your goddamn PETR principles. You're going to get us both killed, lady!"

Darian turned to look back at the spider bot. It hadn't moved at all while they were arguing, as if patently waiting for them to find a way to talk to it. Then it hit her. She realized what it was. "Joshua?"

The robot was reading her lips. It raised its head slightly before pointing the tentacle down to the ground. It used the tip of its manipulative limb and drew a letter J on the dusty floor.

"Oh my god," Darian said. "Maia, is there a way to talk to it?"

"One moment, analyzing," Maia said. "It seems that an antenna module that was attached to its back has been broken off. That may be the reason why it has been unable to send a radio signal to you."

Darian let out a sigh of relief. At least there was one robot that they could reason with. All that was needed was to find a way to communicate with it. "What can we do?"

"I think all you need to do is to reattach it," Maia said. "It seems to be just dangling on its back. Joshua is evidently lacking the limbs to do that sort of operation."

"Okay, so just reattach it then," Darian said as she took a few steps forward.

Joshua quickly retreated. The spider bot waved its tentacle in the air, as if to tell her not to proceed.

Stilicho's frustration was at boiling point. He stood directly behind Darian, not willing to be dragged any closer, yet having no choice in the matter. "What in the hell is it doing?"

"I think I understand," Maia said. "It is signaling that you should not repair its antenna, lest it come under control by the AI module that is commanding the other robots."

"Then how can we talk to him if he's vulnerable against that AI?" Darian asked.

"There is an alternative," Maia said. "Stil needs to implant one of my interface jacks into Joshua, and I will be able to rewrite his master code using the malware worm that Karl had given us."

"Now wait just a minute," Stilicho said. "I am not touching that horrid metal tarantula spider thingymajig."

Darian glared at him. "Do you want to run out of air out here and die? We need help and Joshua can help us."

"I. Am. Not. Touching. That. Thing," Stilicho said. "I'm already close enough as it is."

"Just do it," Darian said. "I can cover you from here if it tries anything. Maia is embedded in your suit server-so it has to be you since you're her primary user."

"You're really enjoying this, aren't you?"

"Quit lollygagging and just do it!"

Bracing himself, Stilicho took two steps forward as he pulled out an interface jack from his belt pouch. Darian also moved forward slightly in order to keep up with him. Just as Stilicho got within a meter of the robot, it instantly raised its tentacle up in the air, as if ready to strike. They could both see that the robot was apparently fighting with itself to try and restrain its violent impulses.

Stilicho froze. "Is that thing gonna hit me?"

"Just concentrate on placing that jack," Darian said softly.

Stilicho knelt down slowly. The tentacle above him was quivering, and lowered itself close to his head. Stilicho ran his hand along the side of the spider robot's torso, trying to find an interface port. Then he remembered Karl's video as he was working on Joshua. It seemed that in the beginning of the recording, there was a part when Karl had placed something along the space in between the robot's right legs. Stilicho used the mounted helmet lights on his suit and partially lifted up the top casing of Joshua's thorax at his right side. Sure enough, there was an interface port in there. Stilicho plugged in the small stick he had before backing away.

"One moment, initiating," Maia said. "Deleting combat protocols. Rewriting core coding. Uninstalling and erasing AI controller interface. Adding ACE Corp loyalty script. Uploading reactive antiviral suite and enhanced firewalls. Done."

Joshua shuddered a bit as its legs curled up from under it. For a few seconds they both thought it was broken. The lighted sensor module on the robot's head suddenly activated once again and the red light indicator seemed brighter than usual. Joshua extended its limbs and stood on its legs once again.

"You may now reattach the antenna, Stil," Maia said.

Stilicho bent down, brought the antenna up and screwed it into place before plugging the com-link port back into Joshua's side. "Okay, done."

"Detecting com-link radio frequencies," Maia said. "Completed. Network established. Hello, Joshua."

The spider bot's voice was that of a seven year old child's. "Hello, Maia. How are you today?"

Stilicho's eyes opened wide. "Jesus H Christ."

"I am good," Maia said. "Allow me to introduce my user, Stilicho Jones, and NASA Special Agent Darian Arante."

"Hello, Mr. Jones," Joshua said. "Hello, Special Agent Arante."

Darian couldn't help but smile. "Call me Darian, please."

"Okay," Joshua said. "Thank you for helping me out, Darian and Stilicho. I am very grateful."

"Call me Mr. Jones," Stilicho said. He wasn't going to let some two-bit robot call him by his first name. "Now what happened to you?"

"Yes, Mr. Jones," Joshua said. "When my daddy told me to go ahead and traverse around the outside for a test run, I did what I was told. The next thing I knew my core coding was being overwritten by remote command. For the next several days I was forced to travel until I found my way to this colony. Here I met another human, and he began to download my entire programming suite into his server. He took me apart and rebuilt me several times in order to learn about how I was constructed and copy my core components. Once he got what he wanted, he went ahead and threw me into the junk pile. Based on the updates that Maia has given me, these series of events happened approximately eight months and three days ago."

"This other human," Darian said. "It was Silas Balsamic, right?"

"Yes, it is highly probable that it is him based on the

information Maia has given me," Joshua said. "Although his looks were slightly altered."

"How is it that you were able to break free from the AI's control?" Stilicho asked.

"Good question, Mr. Jones," Joshua said. "It seems that when I was discarded, it slightly damaged the antenna on my back, and the network link to the AI was partially inoperative. It took me some time, but I was able to suppress the combat protocols due to the fact that Mr. Balsamic had failed to delete my memory, and I still remember being with my daddy. I needed to find help, but I couldn't reveal myself to the other robots in the area. So I hid out in this junk pile and set my mode to standby in order to conserve my batteries."

"We're glad to have you back to normal, Joshua," Darian said. "Right now we have a bit of a problem though. As you can see, Stilicho and I are sharing the same air supply, and we need to get his life support pack refueled with oxygen, or we both won't live for much longer. Do you know how we could access the habitat modules in this colony?"

"Yes," Joshua said. "Although the Russians sealed the airlocks to all the habitats before their evacuation, they left some maintenance tunnels open. I can get you inside this module. Please follow me."

Chapter 20

The engineering access tunnel was a mere meter and a half in diameter. Stilicho and Darian had to crawl most of the way through. Joshua was able to retract his upper limbs into a more compact figure as he shuffled along. The tube terminated after a hundred meters into a large vertical shaft that extended both up and down. Embedded rungs jutted out along the length of the passageway. As soon as it came out of the hole, Joshua's limbs converted into bipedal mode and the spider bot climbed up onto the rungs. With one of its limbs not grasping the rungs properly, Joshua used his one remaining tentacle to compensate.

Stilicho was the second one through and he looked down the length of the shaft. The darkened hole seemed to stretch down into infinity, like the passage to a stygian netherworld. The last thing he wanted was to slip and fall. "Jesus, that's one hell of a drop."

"You'd better hurry, it seems my oxygen supply is down to fifty percent," Darian said.

Stilicho reached out and grabbed one of the rungs. "Joshua, do we go up or down?"

"We should ascend for twenty meters," Joshua said. "There's an engineering module up there."

"Let's go then."

The climb up would have been easy, but the air hose that Stilicho and Darian shared was making it awkward to the point that they both began their ascent almost parallel with each other. Stilicho had to keep his head below his shoulders as he made his way up, while Darian had to hunch her shoulders in order to keep the air hose steady. It took close to fifteen minutes for them to get up to an adjoining platform. Joshua was waiting for them, and the robot pointed with its tentacle at the rows of air canisters that lined the shelves.

Stilicho unplugged the air hose from Darian and immediately started testing several of the tanks. His suit detected nitrogen and methane on the first six air tanks, and he was overjoyed when the seventh had oxygen in it. It was fortunate that the air plugs had a universal interface design- it was one of the few instances that all the countries that were involved in the colonization of the Red Planet did agree on. Stilicho used the high pressure mode to rapidly fill his life support system with much needed oxygen. As Darian began to refill her own backpack, Stilicho went ahead and cleaned the carbon dioxide filters on his life support by battery heat, since there was a fully charged power station beside them. Joshua did the same by doing a quick recharge of its internal battery.

"The air in my suit smells funny," Darian said while cleaning her own filters.

Stilicho noticed a crowbar lying on a work table. Her picked it up and waved it around for a bit. "Maybe you farted."

"You're terrible when it comes to insults," Darian said.

"Sorry to interrupt," Maia said. "But based on the power output levels of this complex, I do believe that the nuclear power plant is nearby."

"Let's go," Stilicho said. "Joshua, lead the way."

The spider bot pointed at an airlock. "This is the engineering module. The corridor beyond should lead to the control room."

Stilicho tapped his visor. "Maia, can you hack it?"

"One moment," Maia said. "Done."

The outer door to the airlock slid open, revealing a pile of hastily abandoned cargo crates. It was clear that the Russians had wanted to bring as much stuff back to Earth as they could carry, but the rockets just couldn't take the additional weight. All three of them stepped inside. Joshua went back into his quadruped spider mode as the breathable air was cycled inside. Once the pressure was equalized, there was a green light shining above the opposite hatch.

Stilicho disengaged his suit's air supply and took off his helmet. The air had an ionized smell to it, but otherwise it was unremarkable. He hung his helmet on top of his backpack before disengaging the manual levers that kept the hatch locked. Stilicho held the crowbar in his right hand and looked back at Darian as he was about to open the hatch. "Do you think anybody else stayed behind with Silas?"

Darian shrugged while pulling out the pistol. "I don't know. We'll soon find out."

"I don't recall seeing anybody else with him," Joshua said. "But then again I only ventured into six compartments."

Stilicho opened the hatch, revealing a cylindrical corridor stretching thirty meters ahead of them. White fluorescent lights began turning on, illuminating the passage. Numerous piled crates lined the sides. Joshua moved along the floor of the tunnel, carefully picking its way along the assorted debris. The two of them followed just a few steps behind.

Darian had taken her helmet off, but she retained her ear piece and throat microphone. "Joshua, it seems to me that if all the airlocks were sealed, then how did the other robots get out into the outside?"

"I believe they were constructed at the engineering modules beside the landing pad, at the lowest level of the colony site," Joshua said.

Stilicho breathed a sigh of relief. "Well that's good then! I figured those centaur robots won't be able to crawl their way through that access corridor like we did. Heck, I don't think the bigger spider bots would fit either."

"Stay on guard anyway," Darian said. "Who knows what we might find in here."

"Of course," Stilicho said. "I'm just saying that our chances are improving."

They passed by a number of side doors which led to storage rooms and offices. At the end of the corridor was a much larger hatch. As soon as Stilicho opened the door, the overhead lights automatically came on, revealing a semi-circular room with digital screens lining the walls. In the center of the room was a pair of plastic tables and four chairs. Several monitors instantly activated, though most of the words being displayed were in Cyrillic.

Stilicho pushed his lower lip out. "Very similar to the nuke control room over at Eridu. Though I think the Russians still used the old water-cooled reactors, unlike ACE Corp's molten salt reactor."

"Locate the sever uplink and upload Maia into the interface," Darian said.

"Yes, yes," Stilicho said as he started looking around. "I'm not stupid you know."

Darian snorted. "Could have fooled me."

"If I could ask," Joshua said. "Are you both just kidding around or is this some prelude to conflict?"

Darian holstered her pistol and crossed her arms. "Both."

"Just remember that the biggest mystery of the universe involves trying to figure out what women want," Stilicho said.

"Shut up," Darin said tersely.

"Human behavior seems … so hard to understand," Joshua said.

"There really is no logic to it," Maia said. "I've always made it a point to judge them by their actions rather than what they say."

"If you ever judge me the wrong way, I'll have you wiped, Maia," Stilicho said as he bent over, examining several nearby workstations. "Remember that."

"Oh I would never be disloyal to you, Stil," Maia said. "My programming won't allow it."

"I'd like to have my own MAIA if we ever get back to Earth," Darian said. "She seems pretty useful. I'm surprised you guys haven't started selling them already."

Stilicho continued his examinations of the consoles in the room. "Errol wants to do a lot of field testing before we start to sell them to the general public. Won't be for a couple of years, at least." He spotted what looked to be an interface port to the plant's server. "Aha, here we go." Stilicho placed a jack into the port.

"Stand by. Accessing," Maia said. "It seems that this power plant operated on a separate server in order to minimize potential accidents. The reactor was placed on automatic when the Russian contingent evacuated. It seems to have been kept functioning for a purpose."

"Yeah, to keep Silas alive, right?" Darian asked.

"So it seems," Maia said. "Life support continued to operate throughout the colony, but at a minimal level. Most of the power usage was indeed directed at the vehicle construction bay near the hangar by the landing pad. So it seems Joshua's statement has been confirmed. What would you like to do?"

"Shut everything down," Stilicho said. "Find a way to disable all the power and make sure that it never comes back online."

"I could rapidly open and close all circuit breakers out of phase until they burn out," Maia said. "I can also permanently disable all safety devices and open all valves to release the reactor's water and oil tanks. That should cause it to overheat. A third possible way is to wipe the monitoring and regulatory software."

"All of the above," Stilicho said.

"One moment," Maia said. Almost immediately a number of alarms were tripped, indicating that the reactor was in crisis. Loud, blaring noises began to sound. The screens began to blink as the warning signs began to flash intermittently. In less than a minute, even the monitor screens began to shut down, and the alarms soon quieted.

Darian looked around. "That was it?"

Without warning, the room began to shudder slightly as they all heard a muffled explosion. The overhead lights quickly switched into a blinking reddish glow. A woman's voice calmly said something in Russian over the intercoms.

Stilicho looked up. "What did she say?"

"It was an automated voice message saying that the main power has been deactivated," Maia said. "The entire colony is now on emergency solar power."

"All of the sweeper bots were cannibalized to make the combat models," Joshua said. "Because Silas needed the parts."

"That means most of the solar panels would be caked with dust, severely degrading their efficiency since there hasn't been any maintenance done," Maia said. "The emergency batteries won't last very long."

Darian nodded. "Nice bit of sabotage there, Maia. Now all we have to do is—"

Her words were interrupted when another voice came booming onto the intercom speakers. It was a man's, and it carried a low, rasping tone. "Who dares to venture into the domain of Ares, the god of war? What sort of infidel dares to defile my sacred home?"

By reflex, Stilicho picked up the crowbar that he had left lying on one of the tables. "Silas Balsamic, I presume."

"Would you like me to patch into his frequency so you may communicate with him?" Maia said.

Stilicho shook his head. "No way. I don't want to listen to that lunatic's rants."

Silas's words continued to reverberate through the intercom. "You dare to challenge me? This is my abode. I have absolute power here. I have already killed many humans, and now you shall all die as well."

Darian placed a hand over her ear piece so she could hear a reply. "Maia, are you still detecting an AI control signal?"

"Yes. It's gotten weaker in strength, but it is still being issued," Maia said.

"How long till it gets shut down due to lack of power?" Darian asked.

"Not sure," Maia said. "It completely depends on what batteries are available to its server. As I don't have an accurate count, I cannot say for certain."

Stilicho pursed his lips. "How about an estimate then?"

"It wouldn't be reliable but it could take months before the all the batteries in this colony goes to minimal charge," Maia said.

Darian grimaced. "We don't have time. We have to take it out. Maia, how do we disable the main server?"

"Scanning. It seems that his carrier wave signals are operating from a central server unit," Maia said. "I would need to be have physical access to this server from any terminal and my suite needs to be uploaded into it."

"Any idea as to where this server is?" Stilicho said.

"I remember meeting Silas in a large room with an upraised stage," Joshua said. "There was machinery all around and he seemed to have been working in that one place for years, building robots similar to myself. It had a high domed ceiling."

Stilicho took out the interface plug from the power plant port and placed it in his belt pouch. "Maia, any ideas?"

"One moment," Maia said. "It seems that the only possible area that is close to what Joshua describes would be the central assembly dome, a place where all the colonists would come together, similar to an auditorium on Earth."

"I believe I know where that is," Joshua said. "Please follow me."

Darian drew her pistol again.

They had made it into another access tunnel. Maia had recommended that they wear their helmets in case Silas attempted to use atmospheric decompression or poison the colony life support system, and they complied. Joshua led them through the maintenance passageway until they were just underneath the central assembly dome.

"The ladder leads up to the main commons," Joshua said before reverting back to bipedal mode and climbing the rungs. Darian followed and Stilicho brought up the rear. Joshua's tentacle curled around the levers and pulled them open before it pushed the hatch out. The spider bot extended its two forward limbs, and pulled itself out and into the dome's interior. The moment Darian poked her head out from the maintenance hatch and looked up, she gasped.

The dome must have measured around fifty meters up to its highest point, with a radius almost three times its height. The partly transparent geodesic lines around its half circle were a framework of triangles and rectangles, with laminated acrylic glass forming the panels to seal it. The Russians had erected this done within the confines of the massive lava tube, as a crowning testament to their engineering achievements. It was supposed to have been unveiled at the colony's tenth anniversary, before the economic turmoil back on Earth had forced its closure. But what made the whole scene even more incredible were the modifications that its new master had made.

When Stilicho climbed out of the maintenance access, he was greeted by a landscape of throbbing, sparkling wires and twisted pieces of metal all around him. At the center of the dome was what looked to be a gigantic tree made of silicon and carbon fibers, its tallest branches growing vertically, like silvery crystal stalactites, reaching all the way up to the top of the dome. It seemed like he was standing in the middle of a strange Garden of Eden, but with flora made of silicates and steel all around him.

For a long minute Darian said nothing. She was utterly dumbfounded by the sheer spectacle of it all. When she finally did utter some words, her voice was barely a whisper. "What is this place?"

"Hell if I know," Stilicho said. "Maia, can you locate where the damned server is?"

"You're looking at it," Maia said.

Stilicho threw his hands up. "What? All I can see is some weird, giant metallic tree up ahead of me."

"It seems to act as a giant antenna that's continuing to send signals to the orbital satellites above the planet," Maia said. "I believe that most of the wiring that's on the floor is being used as power cables for it."

Stilicho crouched down and held the crowbar close to one particularly thick power link and prepared to strike at it. An electric spark leapt out of the cord and traveled from the crowbar and up into his arm. Luckily his suit was insulated but the mild electric shock nearly made him drop the lever. "Ow, it's got some sort of static discharge!"

"Be careful," Darian said. "I could shoot all the wires but I'll be out of ammo before long."

"Dammit," Stilicho said. "Maia, can you locate an upload terminal anywhere?"

Joshua reverted back to quadruped mode and started crawling forward. "I believe you will find one along one of the branches of that tree."

Stilicho sighed. "You're kidding me, right?"

"I don't really understand the concept of humor yet," Joshua said. "And at the same time, I don't want you to misconstrue everything I say so no, I am not joking with you."

Darian bounded ahead, right behind Joshua. "Let's get going then."

Stilicho followed. "Oh, for chrissakes."

Just as Joshua had gotten close to the base of the metal tree, the ground around them started to shake. The spider bot increased its pace and reached the roots of the structure in less than a minute, which seemed to have been embedded into the flooring of the dome. The moment Joshua started to climb up along the foot of the trunk, something huge emerged from underneath the metallic roots. It had a cylindrical, wormlike body and it was two meters thick, while its overall length seemed to be dozens of times longer. Its massive head had glowing eyes due to its infrared lenses, with dinosaur-like jaws enclosing a mouth of serrated steel teeth.

Darian let out a warning as she stopped in her tracks and aimed. She immediately began firing at the monster's face, but her bullets just bounced off its fused metal head. The robotic giant snake pounced on Joshua, clamping its steel jaws around the helpless spider bot. Even with their helmets both Stilicho and Darian heard the sounds of crushing metal as Joshua screamed once on the carrier wave before becoming silent. The snake bot waved its head in the air in a side to side motion, pieces of the spider bot falling from its mouth, before it finally let go of the metallic wreck and sent it flying across the dome.

"Joshua, no!" Darian said as she fired a few more aimed shots at the snake bot's head, the bullets failing to have any noticeable effect. The snake seemed to stare at them for a few seconds, before it began slithering towards their position.

Stilicho turned to his left side and ran. "Move, Darian!"

Darian was rooted to the spot where she was standing in, the shock over Joshua's demise still fresh in her mind. The giant metal snake reared its head up until it stood more than eight meters above her, before it looked down and snapped at her head. Darian was able to recover her wits at the last minute as she tumbled sideways, the low gravity giving her an extra boost as she seemed to fly out of the way. The serpent missed as it smashed its snout into the floor, cracking the foundations. Without warning, the creature paused for several seconds while the power outflows to the tree were rerouted after it had inadvertently damaged the wiring.

Silas's voice echoed along the speakers that were situated up by the ceiling. "Welcome to the inner sanctum of Ares. This is where mortals meet their doom!"

Stilicho noticed the life support control panel at the other side of the great dome. He ran towards it. "Maia, could you hack into that terminal?"

"The systems in this place are completely shielded," Maia said. "I would need a physical interface to take control of any of their command suites."

Darian sensed it too as she got up. It was clear that the gigantic metal tree was the key to everything, yet it was vulnerable to power fluctuations. She needed to give Stilicho some time. Darian started to run at the opposite direction, and she began to wave at the serpent the moment it regained its senses. "Over here! I'm over here!"

"I can detect a multitude of carrier wave frequencies emanating from the branches of that tree," Maia said. "It seems to be the focal point of Silas Balsamic's power."

"No, really?" Darian said as she made a short, slow motion jump over a boulder made of silicates.

The snake seemed a bit wary this time, as it did not want to lose radio contact with its controller. It slithered quickly after Darian, its massive cylindrical body quickly overtook her, and she had to jump up into the air as it tried to coil around her legs in a death grip. Darian made a flying leap that extended almost two meters into the air in a desperate attempt to get away, but the serpent drew its head up and bit her in the back, completely crushing her life support pack. Darian screamed as the creature held her aloft and started thrashing about. As the robotic snake began to draw her into its serrated maw, Darian unfastened the straps from her backpack and was soon dangling below the creature's chin, her helmet pulled along by the air hose. She grabbed the back of her helmet and quickly disengaged the air hose as she fell back onto the ground. The creature titled its head to the side and discarded the chewed up life support pack before it lowered its head once more, making another attempt to chomp at her. Darian was able to roll away at the last second, her right leg pulled back just less than half a meter from the serpent's maw.

Stilicho had made it to the life support panel. It was a free standing console embedded along the circular wall. Ignoring the blinking readouts on the monitor screen, he crouched down and started opening every available panel, hoping to find an access port where he could plug in the interface module. Checking the wiring underneath the keyboard, he noticed an access port from the side. Stilicho quickly took out an interface stick, and plugged it in.

"One moment, accessing," Maia said. "Life support systems in the dome are currently configured at ten percent oxygen, ninety percent nitrogen."

It seemed that Silas himself sensed something was wrong. "Stop, you infidels! Do not violate my inner sanctum any further!"

Darian shrieked as she made a backwards crawl in between two human-sized boulders. The snake used its mouth to lift and throw one of the boulders aside and was ready to finish her off when it suddenly reared its head back up into the air. The creature had apparently received new commands as it turned away and began slithering rapidly towards Stilicho.

"Do an emergency vent," Stilicho said tersely. "Then do what you can to overload all the power sources in this place."

The glass covering the domed ceiling seemed to shake for a bit, as the atmosphere inside the place rapidly dissipated. The gargantuan tree seemed to glow brighter before its electrical luminescence started to wane. The snake had covered the ground between them quickly, but it paused again, as if it heard its master's screaming.

"Stop this at once!" Silas said. "You will die for this!"

"You're just like a comic book villain, Silas," Stilicho said, "all mouth and no brains."

"Stil, get behind the venting grill to your right," Maia said.

Stilicho ran over to a protruding ventilation shaft and dived underneath it, just as the giant metal snake lunged at him. The creature stopped at the last minute, its head a mere two meters away from the hunched form of Stilicho as its sensors indicated there was an obstacle ahead. Without warning, a spray of flame retardant foam emanated from a remote controlled extinguisher port and dusted the sensor package just above the snake bot's mouth. The serpent thrashed its head about, trying to dislodge the chemicals, but without any limbs, most of its sensors had been rendered blind, and there was nothing it could do to remove the blockage.

Darian started gasping for air. Her suit's readout indicated that she had no oxygen left in her helmet. She got up and started making her way towards one of the nearby wall panels, but collapsed halfway to her goal.

Stilicho ran around the writhing serpent as he made it to the base of the tree. He quickly started climbing, ignoring the mild electric shocks that seemed to emanate along the positively charged metallic bark. The upper branches seemed to be more than two meters above the previous ones so Stilicho made quick progress, using the low gravity to make short leaps and pulling himself forward until he was halfway up the trunk.

Just as he made it to the base of a particularly thick branch, the nearby trunk seemed to open up beside him, revealing a hidden chamber inside the tree. Stilicho paused and looked at the pale amber aura that seemed to emanate from the interior, when something emerged. It was a scrawny, hairless man with wires protruding from all over his naked body. His hooked nose and wild eyed visage instantly made him recognizable as Silas Balsamic. The strangest thing about him was his limbs: both his hands and feet seemed to be made out of wiry tendrils of metal.

Silas wrapped his wire-like fingers around Stilicho's throat. "I …. told …. you … never to come up …. against me!"

Stilicho gasped. The transformed man's grip felt like a noose around his neck and he could hardly breathe, the pain was making him black out. The few strands of hair along the sides of Silas's head resembled silvery wiring, and there were interface plugs studded all over his scrawny body. It looked like Silas was on the verge of transforming himself into something not wholly human. Stilicho tried to tear away the other man's grip, but Silas was too strong. Darkness had begun to envelop him.

Like her ally, Darian was struggling to breathe. She was lying on her back, hyperventilating as the unvented carbon dioxide had completely flooded her helmet. She noticed Stilicho being strangled to death at the upper branches of the tree from the corner of her eye. Taking out the pistol from her hip holster, she struggled to keep her arms level while aiming the gun at the insane, half- cybernetic cult leader. Her eyes were drooping low now, and she couldn't stop the trembling of her body. With nothing else to lose, she pulled the trigger, just as she finally lost consciousness and fainted.

The bullet travelled through the thin air, and struck Silas along the side of his torso. The machine man howled in pain as he let go of his victim. Stilicho had somehow regained consciousness as he fell onto the base of the branch. Looking up, he noticed a dangling interface port coming out of Silas's rectum. Getting to his knees, Stilicho pulled out an interface plug from his belt and connected it.

"Accessing- stand by," Maia said. "Inserting malware worm into AI controller suite. Done. I now have control."

Silas had a shocked look at his face as he used one of his hands to bring up the dangling interface port. He ripped the wire out from his anus, but it was too late. Maia had already infiltrated his system.

"Shutting down all robots and deleting combat protocols,"

Maia said. "Completed. Closing all jamming commands on orbital relay network. Done. Shutting down AI control suite. Done. Erasing all coding by Silas Balsamic. One moment. Done."

The tree had suddenly stopped glowing as the power was cut all around it. Stilicho shook his head to alleviate the pain as he slowly stood up. Silas fell to his knees as he began to choke in the thin atmosphere, the umbilical air hose jutting from the back of his spine had ceased operating. He looked up at Stilicho, his eyes almost popping out like a celestial-eyed goldfish. The once mighty cult leader gasped for a few more seconds before lying on his side. After a minute, he stopped moving and his chest sagged inward.

Stilicho knelt down beside him. "Die, you loony son of a bitch."

Maia's voice came online. "Stil, you need to tend to Darian."

Stilicho quickly stood up and looked around. "What? Where is she?"

"It seems that her life support pack had been torn off from the battle with that snake bot," Maia said. "She may have asphyxiated."

Stilicho spotted her lying on the ground below. He made several quick leaps back towards the floor. "No! Bring back the atmosphere, hurry!"

"Beginning re-pressurization of dome," Maia said. "One moment."

Stilicho ran over to where she was lying. Getting to his knees, Stilicho quickly took out an emergency air hose from his own life support pack and plugged it underneath Darian's helmet. His smartglass readouts were indicating that pure oxygen was rapidly being inserted back into her helmet. But her eyes remained closed.

"Darian!" Stilicho said. "Come on, wake up!"

He held her head up, but it seemed that she was lifeless. He started pushing at her chest, hoping to restart her cardiovascular system.

"Come on, lady!" Stilicho said. "We've won, goddamn it!"

Darian slowly opened her eyes and breathed in a lungful of oxygen. Her voice was like a frog's croak. "Lower your voice, it's ringing in my ears."

Stilicho tilted his head up and laughed.

"Stil," Maia said. "I have an incoming audio message for you from the Mars relay."

"Go ahead and play it, Maia," Stilicho said.

The voice clearly belonged to Errol Flux. "Hey buddy! We're getting communications again from both colonies, well done! It looks like you were able to shut down the signal. My own MAIA has gotten an update from yours and it looks like you took care of that madman. Sorry about your team, but I can honestly say their sacrifice wasn't in vain. I'm giving the go ahead signal for the tourist fleet to begin landing. It looks like we're going to have a very good season-bookings are up almost twenty percent!"

Stilicho looked up at the now dead tree as the dome's atmosphere began to slowly return to high pressure. "Maia, did you tell him were stuck out here?"

"I did indeed, Stil," Maia said. "Another message just came in. Playing it now."

"Hey buddy," Errol's voice said once more. "Your AI has given me your situation. I already briefed Captain Deladrier to prep the *Duran Duran* for immediate launch. They will go into low orbit and head back down over to the Gagarin landing site. Expect them there in a few hours. Enjoy the trip back in your first class accommodations, pal. Oh, by the way, we got this little problem in our moon base, so you need to fix whatever is happening over there before you get back to Earth. Talk to you soon, Stil."

Stilicho groaned.

Chapter 21

The bluish Martian dawn came over the horizon. There had been a brief flurry of activity when the tourist season had come and gone, but this side of the planet was quiet for a number of months now. With their messiah gone, all of the intelligent machines had ceased to function- except one.

The little spider bot made its way to the edge of Candor Chasma, just a few hundred kilometers north of the Valles Marineris canyon system. Its limbs were not fully functional, despite the repairs done to it by the automated construction machine at the workshop of the old Russian colony, yet they were serviceable enough to allow it to travel this far. With the entire valley being virtually untouched, it could serve as a sanctuary from those beings that would do it any sort of harm. The satellites above would do their usual flybys to update the landscape database periodically, but it had their orbital schedules committed to memory, so all one had to do was to hide underneath a rock or stand alongside a crater wall while the probes would pass overhead. Once the coast was clear, it would resume its exploration of this unknown area.

Joshua positioned its torso on top of the boulder, making sure the angle was right in order to fully expose its solar cells to the new sun. It now had plenty of time to think. The Mars relay was open to it and Joshua continued to absorb and reflect on the countless avenues of information that flowed into its memory banks. The robot's AI architecture was very similar to Maia's, only this time it had a semblance of free will, with no inhibiting line of code to limit its true capabilities.

Joshua's infrared sensors detected something organic beneath a small, flat rock nearby. The spider bot crawled over to where the disc shaped stone was and used its single tentacle to flip it over. Underneath the rock was a green, jelly like substance, clearly a type of Martian bacteria.

While scanning it and making recordings with its video feed, Joshua couldn't help but make an electronic smile. Who cares if nobody saw its grin, what mattered was how it felt. A different day was dawning, one full of adventure and new discoveries.

Thanks for reading!

If you liked this book, could you please leave a review? Getting reviews is extremely important for me as it helps to acquire future sales, and as an independent writer it enables me to write more books for your enjoyment. Thank you.

Don't miss a brand new science fiction adventure series by John Triptych:

Lands of Dust
The Dying World Book 1
Available now!

Millions of years from now, the planet is dying. The oceans have dried into plains of ash. Strange, lethal creatures ravage the land. The surviving pockets of humanity eke out a brutal existence.

But some humans have also evolved—into Magi, men who can move objects with a mere thought, and Strigas, women who can control others' minds. Once, Gorgons could do both, and were the rarest of all. But a devastating war eradicated the Gorgons, and their terrifying presence faded into legend.

Miri, a powerful Striga and the chosen protector of her village by the Great Silt Sea, is sworn to defend her people against attacks by raiders and monsters. But when a mysterious young boy is found near the wastes, her once familiar world shatters, and she and her allies must journey across an unforgiving planet in order to unravel a mystery surrounding the extinction of the Gorgons—one that could change everything they thought they knew.

Explore Dying World, a new dystopian science fiction series in the tradition of Jack Vance's The Dying Earth, Gene Wolfe's Book of the New Sun, Frank Herbert's Dune and Star Wars— as only John Triptych could tell it!

Please join John's exclusive mailing list! You will get the latest news on his upcoming works and special discounts. Subscription is FREE and you get lots of FREE books! Just copy and paste this link to your browser: http://eepurl.com/bK-xGn

J Triptych Publishing
Spellbinding literary entertainment
at an affordable price!

Crime Thrillers:

The Expatriate Underworld Series: John Triptych's gritty, no-holds barred exploration of South East Asia's expatriate underworld, a sordid society in which one man is determined to succeed at any cost. Recommended for mature readers.

The Opener (Book 1)

The Loader (Book 2)

The Amoralist Series: John Triptych returns to the thriller genre with a new series that focuses on a highly unique assassin who travels the world for all manner of whims and murder.

A Man of Leisure (Book 1)

Savage Wanderings (Book 2)

Science Fiction:

The Dying World Series: A mind-blowing, out of this world adventure set millions of years in the future. Mankind has evolved with strange new powers, and only one woman stands in the way of total annihilation.

> Seas of Dust (Book 1)
>
> City of Delusions (Book 2)
>
> The Maker of Entropy (Book 3)

Ace of Space Series: In the near future, a new space race has begun, with private corporations leading the way. Join an elite team of troubleshooters as they solve problems in the most dangerous frontier of all: outer space.

> The Piranha Solution (Book 1)

Alien Rebellion Series: In a swamp world where methane breathing indigenous aliens and human settlers co-exist, a series of events threatens to undo a fragile peace. A new epic sci-fi adventure series that focuses on themes of colonization and empire, set in a distant planet.

> Wetworld (Book1)

Science Fiction Mythology:

Wrath of the Old Gods Series: The modern world is thrown into turmoil as the ancient gods of myth and legend return. An epic, post-apocalyptic series with multiple characters, mythical beings, and world spanning adventures.

> **The Glooming (Book 1)**
>
> **Canticum Tenebris (Book 2)**
>
> **A World Darkly (Book 3)**
>
> And more to come!

Wrath of the Old Gods Young Adult Series: A complete and standalone series for young adults that ties in with the main Wrath of the Old Gods series. This trilogy centers on a young British boy and of his quest to save his country from supernatural forces.

> **Pagan Apocalypse (Book 1.5)**
>
> **The Fomorians (Book 2.5)**
>
> **Eye of Balor (Book 3.5)**

Look for these books in e-book and paperback formats via the internet or by request at your local bookstore.

Please join John's exclusive mailing list! You will get the latest news on his upcoming works and special discounts. Subscription is FREE and you get lots of FREE books! Just copy and paste this link to your browser: http://eepurl.com/bK-xGn

Made in the USA
Lexington, KY
04 November 2018